# Wait *for*
# *the* Rain

## ALSO BY MARIA MURNANE

*Perfect on Paper*

*It's a Waverly Life*

*Honey on Your Mind*

*Chocolate for Two*

*Cassidy Lane*

*Katwalk*

# maria murnane

# Wait for the Rain

LAKE UNION

PUBLISHING

Published by Lake Union Publishing, Seattle

www.apub.com

Amazon, the Amazon logo, and Lake Union Publishing are trademarks of Amazon.com, Inc., or its affiliates.

ISBN-13: 9781477827413
ISBN-10: 1477827412

Cover design by Mumtaz Mustafa

Library of Congress Control Number: 2014951898

Printed in the United States of America

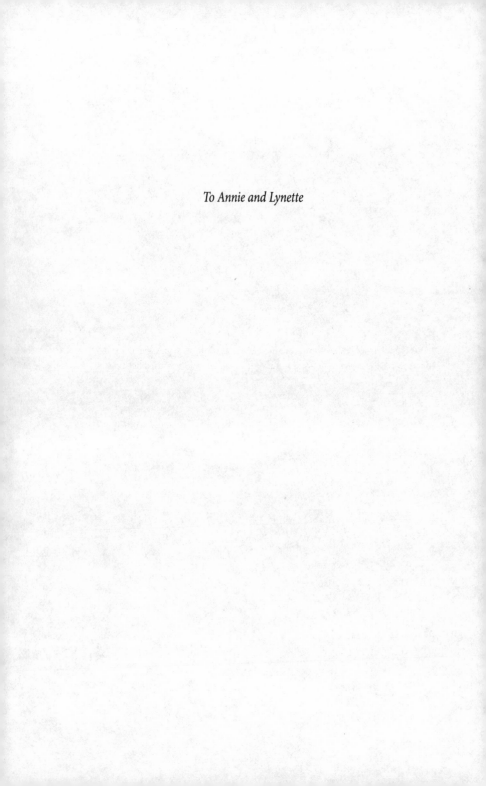

*To Annie and Lynette*

# Chapter One

"You awake yet, hon?" Carol asked in her perpetually cheerful voice.

Daphne yawned into the phone. "Barely, but yes."

"Barely's good enough for me, and it's certainly good enough for the airline. Are you all packed?"

Daphne glanced at her bulging suitcase in the hall. "*Over*packed. It's the curse of motherhood."

"But Emma isn't going with you, right?"

"No, she's off to Utah with her dad. But I still packed way too much. I had to stop myself from tossing an iron in there. What is wrong with me?"

Carol chuckled. "Well, I guess it's better to be overprepared than the alternative, right? I'll be over in just a few minutes to grab you."

Daphne glanced out the window into the pitch-black Columbus winter and wondered how anyone could be so peppy at such an ungodly early hour. "Okay, thanks, Carol. See you soon." She hung up the phone and set it on the kitchen counter, then with another sleepy yawn opened the overhead cabinet. She reached for her favorite mug, the pink ceramic one Emma had made years earlier that said "I love you, MOMMY!" in wobbly blue lettering. It had been a Mother's Day gift back when Emma was in third grade. The pink was a bit faded now, and the handle had a small chip that seemed to be growing, but Daphne treasured it like gold. Despite her daughter's occasional groans of protest, especially those weekend mornings when she had a friend or two over—*Mom, that's so embarrassing!*—Daphne still used it nearly every day. If and when it became necessary, she would fix the crack with superglue. Retiring the mug to the back of the cabinet, much less to a dusty box in the garage with other mementos from Emma's early years, was simply not an option, at least for now. Daphne had never been one to hold on to possessions that had outlived their use, but when it came to her little girl's things, that was a different story. Going on sixteen now, Emma was growing up so fast, and Daphne was determined to cling to what little remained of her childhood for as long as she could. She couldn't yet bring herself to think about what her life was going to be about once Emma left for college. Just the idea of it was almost unbearable.

Her eyes still not entirely open, Daphne poured herself a cup of steaming black French roast, extra strong, and glanced at the time on the coffeemaker: 5:17 a.m.

She yawned again. It was much too early to be out of bed, much less on a day when she didn't have to rouse a slumbering teenager before school. She stirred cream and sugar into the mug and wondered how cold it was outside. It was certainly dark out there, and they'd been saying it would probably snow again today, or maybe there'd be freezing rain, which in her opinion was the worst weather of all. As she sipped her coffee, her mind traveled back to the period of her life when rising before the sun was the norm, not the exception, back when feeding Emma in the early morning hours was as much a part of her day as packing Brian a sandwich to take to the office.

Back when the house was rarely this quiet.

Or still.

Or . . . empty.

It was all of those things now, at least when Emma was at Brian's place. Or, as of last weekend, Brian and Alyssa's place.

Daphne stiffened at the thought. *I can't believe he's really getting remarried.*

She looked around the tidy kitchen and dining area, a bit too orderly for a house with a teenager living in it, even though Emma was only there half the time. She closed her eyes. *I can't believe this is my life now.*

She felt a pang deep inside as a vision flashed before her, one of Emma decorating her spacious new bedroom at the house in tony Westerville that belonged to the woman who would soon be her stepmother. It was a spectacular, magazine-worthy structure, one of several high-end properties Alyssa's family owned in the Columbus area. Daphne imagined her daughter giggling and gossiping with Alyssa as she unpacked, sharing her secrets and stories and crushes—things she never seemed to tell Daphne anymore. Daphne pictured the two of them chattering like classmates as they strolled arm in arm down the driveway of Emma's new home. Of Brian's new home. Of *their* new home.

Daphne closed her eyes and willed her mind to erase the painful visual. She took a deep breath. *Don't torture yourself like this. You know you're better off without him.*

She set down her coffee and glanced at Emma's monthly calendar on the refrigerator, secured front and center with an OSU magnet. As usual, her daughter's schedule was packed with volleyball practices and games, piano lessons, chorus rehearsals, study groups, and a smattering of birthday parties. Recent additions to the list were driver's training and an SAT prep course. Daphne had not only typed up and color coded the schedule but memorized it, and she took great pride in making sure Emma never missed an activity or appointment.

Daphne picked up the mug and made one last trip into her bedroom to confirm that she hadn't forgotten anything essential, although given that she'd triple-checked everything on her list after packing her enormous suitcase last night, she knew the chances were slim if not zero. Then she stopped by Emma's room to have a quick peek inside, something she often did when Emma was staying with Brian. She never *entered* the room, determined to give her daughter the privacy her own mother had never afforded her as a teenager, but she found it comforting to see Emma's things there, even if she was currently elsewhere. As usual the room was relatively clean, the bed made, the pink-and-white-checkered comforter smoothed evenly over the twin bed. The white walls were sprinkled with posters of pop stars and award ribbons from various events and competitions. A cork bulletin board above her white wood desk was covered with smiling photos of her and her girlfriends, the matching white chair tucked neatly underneath. A thick blue binder lay atop the desk next to a small stack of textbooks. Her daughter had inherited Daphne's knack for keeping things organized, something Daphne loved given how messy Brian was. It had been a daily battle just to get him to put his dirty clothes in the hamper, a battle Daphne had given up fighting years ago but had never been able to understand. How hard is it to toss clothes into a hamper or hang up a wet towel? Besides, they'd had bigger problems in their marriage than laundry.

On her way back into the kitchen she looked over at the empty oak table in the quiet dining room. Her imagination suddenly flashed to an image of breakfast time at Alyssa's place, where she pictured Emma, Brian, and Alyssa conversing energetically over pancakes about their upcoming adventure. It was Emma's spring break, and the three of them were headed to Park City to spend the week skiing, snowboarding, snowshoeing, sledding, and whatever else outdoorsy people do in the Utah mountains. Despite Emma's grumbling about a week away from her friends, not to mention her electronic devices, Daphne knew she was looking forward to the trip. No doubt she, Brian, and Alyssa would have a fabulous time together.

*Just like a real family.*

Daphne flinched at the thought.

In a few months it would be official. Alyssa would become the new Mrs. Brian White, assuming the title of Emma's stepmother.

Daphne felt another stab at the thought of Alyssa playing such a formal—and important—role in her daughter's life, one Daphne had wanted so desperately to keep all to herself. She glanced at the clock again, then peered through the white plantation shutters. A moment later she spotted Carol, the unofficial matron of their tidy block, emerging from the two-story Colonial-style house across the street. Bundled up in a massive red ski jacket and shiny black rain boots over what looked like a white flannel nightgown, she carefully navigated her way through the swirling snow flurries.

Daphne picked up the coffee and closed her eyes, again willing her anxiety to pass.

*Be happy for Brian.*

*He's not a bad person.*

*Things will get better for you.*

*Things have to get better.*

The divorce was now final, so it wasn't like she could expect him to stay single forever, even though part of her secretly wanted him to. He'd been dating Alyssa for more than a year, but for Emma's sake he had waited to move in with her until they were officially engaged, and Daphne had to give him credit for that. He was clearly trying hard to be an involved father now—much more than he had when Emma was younger. If he and Daphne didn't share a daughter, she'd be free to cut ties with him, but unfortunately that wasn't an option, emotionally or logistically. While no longer her husband, for better or for worse he was in her life for good.

*This is how things are now.*

She squeezed the pink mug tight, desperate to escape from the suffocating disappointment that her life wasn't what she thought it would be at this age.

She just wished she knew how to do that.

How to be alone after being part of a couple for so many years.

How to find herself again.

How to start over.

*I could have had a career. Now I have just the shattered pieces of a family.*

She blinked a few times to shake the visions from her head. It was time to focus on the reason why she was up so early this dark winter morning.

*The birthday trip. I can't believe I'm really going.*

Carol's knock on the door jarred her from her thoughts. She rinsed out the mug and carefully placed it in the drying rack, then hurried to open the front door.

# Chapter Two

"A week in St. Mirika sounds just heavenly, especially given how darned cold it is here right now," Carol said as she carefully merged her SUV onto the freeway. It was snowing harder now.

Daphne was having difficulty wrapping her head around the fact that she was actually doing this. In just a few hours she'd be setting foot on one of the most coveted island destinations in the Caribbean. Home to soaring palm trees, a sparkling green ocean, and sandy white beaches, St. Mirika truly resembled paradise—or so it appeared in the photos she'd seen. For months her travel companions and longtime friends KC and Skylar had been sending around links to websites showcasing the dazzling beauty of the island.

She pressed a fist against her chin.

*What will it be like to see them again?*

They'd called themselves the Three Musketeers back in college, but it had been ages since the three of them had gotten together.

Daphne had changed a lot since those days.

*I wonder what they're going to think of me now.*

Carol didn't seem to notice Daphne's apprehension. "I've never been to the Caribbean, but I've heard it's just stunning. Norman's not much of a tropical vacation kind of guy. In fact, if it doesn't involve attending an OSU football game, he's not that interested in traveling." She shook her head with a sigh. "I adore the man to the moon and back, but I will never understand his obsession with that football team."

Daphne smiled to herself at the thought of Carol's equally good-natured husband, whose favorite activity in the world was lounging in his sacred leather recliner and watching his cherished Buckeyes take the field on his big-screen TV—if he wasn't attending the actual game, of course. And Norman was hardly alone in his passion. After all these years Daphne was still amazed at the affection the Columbus area had for the Buckeyes of *the* Ohio State University, as the school was officially called. Sometimes she felt like the only person in town who hadn't gone to school there. She saw Northwestern, her alma mater, as a university that had a football team. From what she could tell, OSU was *a football team that had a university*. On game days she still felt conspicuously out of place if she wasn't dressed in red, even if all she was doing was buying groceries.

"Where are you staying down there?" Carol asked.

Daphne glanced out the window toward the horizon, which was still dark. The first glow of the sun wouldn't appear for at least another hour. "I'm not exactly sure. Skylar's in charge, and she said my only job is to get myself on a plane and meet her and KC at the airport bar."

"Sounds like the perfect vacation for you at the perfect time." Carol knew about Brian's recent engagement. "You do so much organizing for Emma as it is. It will be good for you to sit in the backseat and take it easy for a few days."

Daphne nodded softly. "I can't remember the last time I wasn't in charge, not to mention the last time I went to a bar, so it should be an interesting few days, that's for sure." Despite Daphne's nervousness about the trip—her first as an unmarried woman in more than . . . fifteen years?—she was looking forward to seeing her old friends again. It had been so long since the three of them had gone on vacation together.

Too long.

Ten years in fact, when they'd spent a couple days in Chicago to "mourn" turning the Big Three O. They wore black all weekend and made silly jokes about being over the hill—while knowing very well their best years were ahead of them.

And now, here they were once again, reuniting to celebrate their fortieth birthdays.

Daphne tried to wrap her head around the vivid yet distant memory of the Chicago trip juxtaposed with the immediacy of the one she was about to embark on.

*Am I really about to turn forty years old? How did that happen?*

"Your friend Skylar sounds like she's on top of things," Carol said. "It's nice having people in your life like that: go-getters who can take charge once in a while, so it's not all on you."

Daphne nodded. "She's a redhead, and she basically meets every stereotype that goes with it. Strong willed, intelligent, no-nonsense, testy if provoked, and fiercely loyal. You don't want to mess with Skylar, but you *definitely* want to be friends with her." Daphne paused. *That's how Skylar used to be, at least. Will she have changed as much as I have?*

Carol smiled. "She sounds like quite the firecracker. Where does she live?"

Daphne frowned in thought. "She's in New York now, although I'm not sure how much time she actually spends there. She's in sales and has a lot of people working for her, so she's constantly on the road. It's been a while since I've seen her in person." *How have so many years slipped by? I used to see Skylar every day. Every single day.*

Carol patted the steering wheel. "Sounds like an exciting life she has. I've barely been out of Ohio, although when I was in my early twenties, I did spend a glorious week frolicking around Miami with a handsome—and much older—Italian man."

Daphne quickly turned her head. "You did what?"

Carol laughed. "It was *years* ago. Before I met Norman."

"How much older was he?"

Carol pursed her lips. "I never asked, but let's just say he was old enough to be my father. I knew it wouldn't last, but everyone needs a bit of adventure now and then, right?"

Daphne smiled wistfully and looked out the window again. "I guess so," she said, while thinking, *I used to be adventurous.*

Her mind began to wander again, traveling backward until it hovered over the last time she'd lived with Skylar. After graduation they'd both begun full-time jobs in Chicago, Skylar having landed a coveted spot in an executive training program at a software company, and Daphne working as an admin at a small travel magazine. Their entry-level positions were barely a notch above internships, but both young women excelled and were soon promoted—Skylar to sales associate, Daphne to fact checker. Thrilled with having taken their first official step on the corporate ladder, they'd celebrated by ditching their dingy futon and buying a real couch for the small yet cozy two-bedroom apartment they shared in Lincoln Park. In the following weeks they'd spent many nights sipping inexpensive wine on that purple velvet couch, laughing and dreaming about the spectacular careers they were about to embark upon.

Both of them were young, eager, and intelligent. Their energy and optimism was palpable. The road ahead was boundless, and they couldn't wait to make some footprints.

Then one snowy evening in January, Daphne and Skylar were tucked in a corner of their favorite wine bar a few blocks from their apartment, enjoying a quiet conversation. Daphne heard the chime of the bell and looked up to see Brian walk through the door with two coworkers, the three of them in town from Columbus for a conference. Brian and Daphne only briefly made eye contact, but a few minutes later he walked over to her, introduced himself, and said, "I'm going to kiss you tonight."

She and Skylar had laughed at his audacity, but there was something in his self-assuredness that appealed to Daphne, a little voice that whispered that if such a dashingly handsome man was so taken by her, it had to be for a very good reason. Brian just *knew* they were meant to be together, and that made her think he had to be right, because no man had ever looked at her that way before.

The introduction led to a drink, which indeed led to the predicted kiss, which led to a long-distance romance Daphne hadn't expected—but which she couldn't resist. She was completely swept off her feet by Brian's conviction that she was the One, and before she knew it, she'd quit her hard-earned magazine job and moved to Columbus to be with him.

Less than a year later they were married.

Once the wedding and surrounding hoopla was over, Brian's parents bestowed upon the happy couple a charming three-bedroom house in Grandview, which Daphne dutifully decorated with all the wedding presents and gift checks they'd received. It was fun playing house while she was still dizzy with the spell of newlywed bliss, still awed that a smart, handsome, successful man like Brian had chosen *her*, but once that domestic project was done, she had planned to find a new job in journalism and get the professional side of her life back on track. She'd worked hard at Northwestern and at her first venture into the working world, and she wasn't about to throw away a promising career just because she now wore a diamond on her left ring finger.

Nature, however, had other ideas.

Little Emma joined the family soon thereafter, and in what seemed like a blink, it was official: Daphne was now a housewife in suburban Ohio—with a newborn to look after. Almost overnight, her world became a blur of marriage, homeownership, and motherhood. She was woefully unprepared for all of it. However, despite her tender age, she did her best, and as the months went by, she became less overwhelmed and more comfortable in the role, although at times she still felt like a child herself.

Brian, who was five years older than Daphne, reveled in playing the part of provider to his young family, but early on it became clear that he had a very traditional vision of what that meant. While he was happy to *care for* Emma, he wasn't interested in *taking care of* her. He loved his daughter, but he loved her changed, fed, and ready for bed. Getting her that way was, in his opinion, Daphne's job. It wasn't what Daphne had envisioned, but he was paying the bills, so who was she to argue? If he wanted to relax with a drink at the end of a long day at the office, who was she to hand him a crying baby? She didn't mind, or she told herself she *shouldn't* mind. This was her life now, and it was okay, because that's what she'd signed up for, right?

She'd focus on the journalism thing once Emma was a little older. There was plenty of time. Eventually she'd go back to work, maybe get her master's, reboot her career, and everything would fall into place. Not quite in the order she'd pictured for herself, but it would fall into place nonetheless.

At least that's what she told herself.

Then came the miscarriages, four in total. The doctors had no explanation, but as it became more and more apparent that Daphne wasn't going to be able to carry another baby to term, she secretly feared she was being punished for not being a good parent, that her inability to bear another child was a direct result of a deep-seated remorse that she'd become a mother too soon. It was a shame laced with guilt that weighed heavily on her.

Not that she didn't love Emma. Of course she did. She adored her daughter and would do anything for her. After the miscarriages, however, she rededicated herself to motherhood, to doing everything in her power to ensure that her miracle baby had the storybook childhood she deserved.

Meanwhile, Skylar stayed at the software company, paid her dues, and slowly but surely proved her mettle. Now she was leading a global sales team and traveled the world, while Daphne had lived on the same block in Grandview for nearly seventeen years. And had never written a single article.

"Daphne, sweetheart, you there?" Carol waved a hand near Daphne's face.

Daphne blinked. "I'm sorry, I was daydreaming for a minute. What did you say?"

"I said you must be excited to see your friends."

"I am. I can't believe how long it's been." Daphne lightly touched her cheeks and wondered how much different she looked from when she was thirty. She'd seen the tiny crinkles that had begun to appear in the corner of her eyes when she smiled. Skylar and KC were sure to notice them too. She'd even bought some eye cream recently, although she hadn't forced herself to use it yet. It was still sitting unopened on her bathroom counter, almost smugly, as if daring Daphne to admit defeat.

"Why so long?" Carol asked.

Daphne shifted in her seat. "After the last trip there was talk here and there about planning another one, but nothing ever seemed to get off the ground. Then KC moved to California, and with her and Skylar on opposite coasts and me in the middle, geography got in the way. Plus Emma's activities take up most of my free time, which makes it hard for me to plan, so the years sort of flew by . . ."

She knew she was making excuses.

She'd been the one to resist getting together again.

Since she and Brian had split up, Daphne had been particularly remiss in communicating with her friends. Outside of Carol, she hadn't really spoken to anyone about the divorce, and what she'd shared had been limited at best. Talking about it only seemed to make her feel worse, so instead of working through her emotions, she'd stuffed them deep inside and focused on Emma, on her part-time job at the flower shop, on staying in shape, on cleaning the house.

On anything other than how much energy she'd poured into building a life that in the end didn't make her—or Brian—happy.

On anything other than the implosion of the illusion she'd been projecting to the world—and to herself—for years.

On anything other than coming to terms with reality.

Carol made a swirly motion with her right index finger. "I know what you mean about the years just zipping by. I'm still wondering where my fifties went. But given the way you talk about these gals, I hope it's not another ten years before you three get together again. Close friendships are like plants. They need tending to now and again, or they might dry up and blow away."

Daphne smiled at Carol, who at times felt like a mother figure to her—and nothing like her own mother. Daphne's mother, without ever engaging her daughter in meaningful conversation about *why* her marriage had broken up, had made it clear that she felt Daphne should have done more to save it, that she should have fought more for Brian. She'd also had the sinking feeling that her mother didn't think she was good enough for Brian. She'd never told anyone either of those things, and she wasn't sure which one hurt more.

When they reached the airport exit, Carol turned on her blinker and carefully navigated off the freeway, then slowed to a stop in front of departures. Before Daphne even unbuckled her seat belt, Carol jumped outside and popped the back hatch of the SUV, then pulled out Daphne's suitcase. "Sweet bejesus, you weren't kidding about overpacking," Carol said with an exaggerated groan. "This thing weighs a ton! Did you pack Emma in here?"

Daphne laughed. "Get back in the car. It's *freezing* out here. And you're wearing a nightgown!"

Carol waved a dismissive hand in front of her, batting away a few snowflakes in the process. "Nonsense. I may not be the most stylish cow in the barn, but I know a thing or two about good old-fashioned manners. Now give me a hug good-bye before I have icicles hanging off my nose. If I skedaddle, I can make it home in time to take a hot shower *and* walk the pooch before *Good Morning America* comes on. See how exciting my suburban life is?"

Daphne gave her neighbor a squeeze. "Your suburban life is wonderful. Thank you so much for the ride."

"When you get back, I'll take you to Jeni's for a double scoop of salty caramel, and you can fill me in on the details. It will be your belated birthday celebration."

Daphne winced. "Ugh, don't remind me about my birthday."

Carol wiggled her index finger. "Darlin', if I were turning forty again, I'd be jumping for joy. Now scat." She shooed Daphne away, then climbed back into the cabin of the SUV and tucked her nightgown inside before shutting the door.

Daphne waved good-bye as Carol drove away, then turned on her heel and headed into the airport, the heated air quickly enveloping her like a bear hug. She removed her wool coat and knitted hat, tucked the hat into her oversized tote bag, then rolled her suitcase toward the check-in counter. As she waited in line, she felt a stirring of gratitude for having a woman like Carol as a neighbor, especially since she and Brian had split up. Carol had been very good to her, always there to listen, never to prod or judge, unlike the chilly vibe she'd felt from several of the mothers at Emma's school, a standoff-ishness that subtly suggested that being a single parent was somehow an assault on the cherished institution of the suburban nuclear family.

She thought about Carol's question, about why so much time had passed since she and Skylar and KC had gotten together. Daphne crinkled her nose. When was the last time she'd seen them? Had it really been the Chicago weekend ten years ago? It couldn't be, could it? Skylar had extended several invitations over the years, but Daphne had always found a reason to refuse them.

Not that she didn't want to see her friends.

Of course she did, right?

She knew Skylar and KC were just as busy as she was, or at least she figured they were. That's what she told herself. They were all so busy, their lives so different. She still considered them to be her best friends, but the truth was, she rarely talked to them anymore. Outside of Emma's universe, for years now Daphne had barely talked much to anyone. With all the carpooling back and forth for all the activities, not to mention all the bake sales, fund-raisers, and PTA meetings over the years, there never seemed to be enough time to keep in touch with the outside world.

She sighed. *I'm still making excuses.*

It hadn't happened overnight, but Daphne had gradually brought that isolation upon herself, reasoning that being a good mother meant putting her own interests aside and focusing on what Emma needed, even though that chapter of her life would eventually end.

She looked up at the departures display and had an unsettling thought.

*Where am I going?*

# Chapter Three

"Hey, hot stuff! Glad to see you made it in one piece." Skylar set her drink down and adjusted the designer sunglasses perched on top of her head, then stood up and held her arms open wide. "Now get over here and embrace me."

Her nerves fluttering even more than she expected them to, Daphne let go of her suitcase and hugged her friend, suddenly feeling like she might cry. She hadn't realized until right then how much she'd missed having Skylar in her daily life, how much she missed being able to share her deepest secrets—no matter how silly or foolish—with a friend who never made her feel silly or foolish.

*Please still like me,* she thought.

Not appearing to notice the conflicting emotions coursing through Daphne's psyche, Skylar returned her hug with affection and topped it off with a kiss on the cheek.

"It's really good to see you," Skylar said as they released each other. "I can't believe it's been ten years. We have so much to catch up on, I don't know how we're going to fit it all into just a few days."

"I know. It's hard to believe Chicago was that long ago already," Daphne said. She felt her heart beating faster than it should be and willed it to slow down. *Relax. You can do this. She's your friend.*

"Can you believe we're forty?" Skylar said, her green eyes expertly framed by black mascara. "I'd like to think we haven't aged a day since our last trip together, but we both know I'd be lying."

Daphne smiled, grateful to see that Skylar's straightforwardness hadn't diminished. For an instant she thought about mentioning the eye cream on her bathroom counter but decided not to. Skylar looked older than when Daphne had last seen her, but she wasn't any less pretty, at least in Daphne's opinion. She did, however, look more confident. It was clear she was a woman who knew what she wanted—and usually got it. *Why can't I be like that? I used to be like that.*

Daphne clenched her hands into fists. *Stop it. You're here to have fun, don't ruin this for yourself.*

She looked at Skylar's head. "I've never seen your hair so straight and shiny. It's like a shampoo commercial." Daphne knew the comment was a bit shallow for the circumstances, but she couldn't help herself. She didn't want Skylar to know she was mentally walking on eggshells, so she overcompensated.

Skylar smoothed a hand over her auburn locks. "That's because I ironed it this morning. Just watch, in this humidity it'll be a jungle in no time. I've decided that my new goal in life is to make enough money to have a stylist travel with me to blow out my hair every day."

Daphne laughed. "*That's* your life goal?"

Skylar shrugged. "Among others. I like to keep things interesting. How was your flight?"

"Uneventful, which is just the way you want a flight to be, I suppose. I slept most of the first leg. How about yours?"

Skylar rolled her eyes. "Ugh, a nightmare. I was in London last week and was supposed to fly here directly from there, but then at the last minute I had to go to Paris for a conference, then back to

New York for another two days of meetings. I'm exhausted. You have no idea how much I need this vacation."

Daphne remembered that Carol had made a similar comment on the ride to the airport, how in her eyes *Daphne's* life was hectic. What would she think of Skylar's schedule? Ferrying around a teenager and working a few hours a week at a flower store seemed utterly mundane in comparison to the professional canvas Skylar was painting.

Skylar resumed her seat on the barstool and patted the empty one next to her. "So enough chitchat. How are you doing? I haven't seen you in the flesh since you and Brian split up."

Daphne sat down too. "I'm doing great, just really busy. You know how it is, there never seems to be enough hours in the day to fit everything in." She spoke faster than she normally did, but in spite of that she was surprised at how nonchalant she sounded. When she and Skylar had been roommates, she'd never been able to hide her true feelings like this.

Skylar sipped her drink. "I'm glad to hear it. I'm still getting used to the fact that things didn't work out between you two. The way he approached you at that wine bar that first night . . . I guess . . . I really thought it was going to stick."

Daphne felt a stabbing sensation in her chest at the still-vivid memory of that first encounter with Brian, at what it represented, and suddenly she felt like she might cry. She wasn't prepared to deal with her emotions right now.

*Please don't cry. Don't let her see what a mess you are.*

She forced a smile that she hoped seemed genuine. "I'm doing fine, really."

"How long has it been since you called it quits?" Skylar asked.

"A little more than two years. The divorce took a while to get sorted out, but that's final now."

"So you just . . . grew apart?" The look in Skylar's eyes suggested she wanted to deepen the conversation. Both Skylar and KC had reached out by phone multiple times over the years, but Daphne almost always replied by e-mail, unwilling—or unable—to open up to her friends about her crumbling marriage, about the effect it was having on her. When she'd broken the news that she and Brian were parting ways, she'd made it clear that infidelity hadn't played a role, but she hadn't shared much more than that, not wanting to confess that they'd been unhappy for years.

Now Skylar was knocking on the door once again, but Daphne couldn't bring herself to open it. She was too afraid her stylish, successful friend would feel sorry for her, and she felt sorry enough for herself.

"Pretty much," she said with a shrug. That's all she'd really told anyone about the reason for the split. And it was true . . . in a sense. What Daphne hadn't been able to articulate—or admit—was that the main reason she and Brian had drifted apart was because neither of them was ever going to be the person the other needed for the marriage to work.

Brian was meant to be with a woman who was perfectly content being a wife and stay-at-home mom, one who dreamed about nothing beyond the white picket fence, one who didn't need anything else to be completely fulfilled. While Daphne loved being a mother and *did* want the white picket fence, she also wanted more than that. She needed a partner who wanted to share the caregiver role with her, one who supported her ambitious side, one who encouraged her to pursue the budding career she'd put on hold to have Emma.

It was a mismatch from the beginning, but at the time Daphne was too young, too naïve, too blind, to see it.

And now it was too late.

How had she wasted all those years, given up so much?

For what?

Her mind turned back to the cold, rainy Friday night when she and Brian had finally decided to pull the plug. Emma was sleeping over at a friend's house, so Daphne had made a reservation for two at their favorite restaurant, hoping an evening out together might rekindle the spark between them, might help them rediscover the connection that had been gone for so long that she could no longer remember what it felt like. Not that she and Brian ever fought that much. They bickered on occasion as every couple does, but for the most part they got along fairly well. The fundamental difference between them was deeper than either of them wanted to admit, so almost without realizing what they were doing, they centered their relationship around the one thing they both cherished: their child. They continued to communicate about the day-to-day logistics of running the household, an approach that let them keep their family intact without acknowledging that something between *them* was dying.

Until that rainy night.

Midway through dinner, after yet another conversation focused nearly entirely on Emma, Brian had looked up from his pasta, a weariness in his eyes, and said, "What are we doing, Daph?"

She had no response, because she didn't know either. She'd just stared blankly back at him, wondering how they'd gotten to this place, wondering what had happened to them, wondering how she could be *married* to this man . . . yet feel so completely alone.

That night he'd packed a suitcase.

"Daphne?"

The sound of Skylar's voice yanked Daphne back to the present. She blinked and looked at her friend.

"I just want you to know that I'm really sorry it didn't work out," Skylar said.

Daphne kept the smile on her face. "Thanks, but that's all in the past now. I'm doing great, *really* great actually. Life goes on, right?" *Where is my life going? Please don't cry.*

"How's Emma?"

"She's doing wonderfully. She's almost as tall as I am now, can you believe it?" Daphne felt a surge of emotion at the thought of her daughter, a mixture of love and heartache as she realized Emma, Brian, and Alyssa would be well on their way to Utah now. She briefly looked over Skylar's shoulder, unable to maintain extended eye contact, but her smile remained frozen. "She's got a lot on her plate, juggling school and friends and all her extracurricular activities; you know how teenagers are. She's spending this week at a resort in Park City with Brian." *And his fiancée. Why can't you say it? Brian is getting remarried. Just say it! Just tell her!*

"How old is she now?" Skylar asked.

"Who?"

Skylar looked confused. "Emma."

Daphne swallowed. "Yes, of course, I'm sorry. She's fifteen."

Skylar slightly narrowed her eyes. "Daphne, are you okay?"

Daphne nodded. "Yep, I'm good, just a little tired from getting up at the crack of dawn." Knowing she wouldn't be able to fight off the tears much longer if she didn't change the topic of conversation, she cleared her throat and pointed to a suitcase propped against the bar. The bright green bag had a sticker across it that said, "Running Is Cheaper Than Therapy." "I'm guessing that's KC's?"

Skylar laughed. "You think it's *mine*? My therapist would love that."

"Where is she?"

"I'm right here, sweet cheeks." Daphne felt a tap on her shoulder. She swung around to see her much shorter friend, smiling and freckled and looking as tan as if she'd already been on the island for a week. She was wearing a light blue baseball hat that read "USA

Volleyball," her sandy-blonde hair pulled back into a ponytail. Like Skylar, she looked older than the last time Daphne had seen her, with noticeable crinkles around her eyes when she smiled.

Before Daphne could speak, KC practically hurled herself forward and wrapped her tiny arms around Daphne's torso. "I'm just thrilled that we're all together again. Thrilled! Poor Max has had to listen to me babble on and on about this trip for months. I think he's as happy as I am that it's finally here just so he can get some peace and quiet with the babies. He practically pushed me out of the car at the airport this morning."

"The babies?" Daphne asked.

"Martha and Oreo, our kitties." KC gestured to her purse. "Want to see a video? Cutest things you've ever seen."

Skylar sipped her drink. "We'll take your word for it."

Daphne smiled at KC. "I've missed your random chatter. It makes me think of all those late nights we had in the dorms, talking about everything under the sun."

"And sometimes until the sun came up." KC pointed to the ceiling. "Think how many pizzas we must have eaten."

The memory of those long-ago marathon conversations, which bounced effortlessly from topic to topic, from romance and religion to politics and pop culture, stirred up more internal angst for Daphne. *Why don't I engage with people like that anymore? What happened to me?*

"Where have you been?" Skylar asked KC. "Were you doing laps waiting for Daphne's flight to get in? Or maybe some sit-ups?"

KC smiled and put her hands on her hips. "You mock me now, but we'll see who's laughing when I make you two do my beach workout with me."

Daphne adjusted her tote bag over her shoulder. "Beach workout? I don't think I like the sound of that." She looked at Skylar. "Do you like the sound of that?"

Skylar set down her glass and put her hands behind her ears. "I'm sorry, what was that? My only form of exercise these days is exercising selective hearing." She stood up and clapped her hands together, then gestured to the bartender for the bill. "Okay, ladies, let's get this party started. I'm *so* excited to be the hell out of Manhattan. It's absolutely arctic there right now."

Daphne held up the black coat she'd been carrying in the crook of her arm. "Same goes for Columbus. What am I going to do with this thing all week?"

KC grinned. "It was eighty-two when Max chucked me out of the car on his way to go surfing."

"Are you teaching fitness classes at the beach now?" Daphne asked.

KC nodded. "I'm still mostly at the gym, but now I also run an outdoor boot camp on Tuesday and Thursday mornings. The sand is great because it's low impact but high resistance."

"I'm highly resistant to this conversation," Skylar said. "If you seriously plan to do some crazy-ass workout while we're here, I may have to lay my towel out on the other side of the island from you. I haven't been to the gym in ages." She pointed to her rear end. "If you want proof, feel free to have a squeeze."

KC's eyes lit up, and she looked from Skylar to Daphne. "I was kidding before, but maybe I *could* lead you both in a beach class while we're here! That would be so fun."

"My selective hearing is acting up again," Skylar said as she reached for her phone. "Sorry, just have to quickly check my e-mail."

"I'm in okay shape, but I definitely couldn't keep up with you," Daphne said.

KC patted her on the shoulder. "Sure you could! Many of my students are divorced women in their thirties and forties, so you're right in my demographic."

Daphne felt another twinge deep inside. *I'm a demographic now. I'm a cliché.*

"That's not a criticism, not at all," KC quickly added when she saw the look on Daphne's face. Skylar, who was now typing furiously into her phone, didn't seem to notice. KC kept her hand on Daphne's shoulder and gave it a squeeze. "My divorced clients are usually in fantastic shape, or well on their way there. Most of them are back in the dating scene—or easing their way there—so they want to look and feel their best. I think that's a positive thing. Not that you need help in any of those departments." She removed her hand and placed it on her own cheek. "Am I talking too much? I feel like I'm talking too much. I hope I'm not putting my foot in my mouth here."

"Don't worry, I get what you're saying," Daphne said. *I hardly look or feel my best lately. For a long time, actually.*

"Are you seeing anyone? They must be lining up for you," KC said.

Daphne cleared her throat and tried to sound casual as she answered, "Not right now." The truth was, she hadn't gone on a single date since she and Brian had split up.

She knew she needed to put herself out there. *Doing so* was a different story. Columbus was hardly a hotbed of single men her age, and it wasn't as if people were clamoring to set her up with eligible candidates. She was too shy to attend singles' mixers alone, and she didn't have any single female friends to drag along—or to drag *her* along. She knew of a handful of divorced fathers through Emma's school circuit, but that road seemed laced with too many gossipy thorns. More than once (usually after a couple glasses of wine) she'd started filling out an online profile, carefully uploading the most flattering photos on her laptop, but when it came to describing herself to the world, she was embarrassed at how little she had to say. Hobbies? Career highlights? Notable accomplishments or adventures? She couldn't think of a single thing to write that didn't revolve around Emma, so inevitably she ended up pressing "Delete."

She wanted to believe in herself, to trust that her limited résumé "outside the home," as it were, was no reflection on her value as a person.

But the truth was, she didn't.

Deep down, she felt it wasn't enough. She *wanted* to expand her life, to climb her way out of the structured world she'd built for herself, but she was paralyzed by fear of what that represented: that she'd somehow failed.

Her marriage had been far from perfect, but that didn't mean she hadn't put a lot of work into it, and its dissolution had been crushing. She didn't know if she could take another blow like that. The idea of starting all over was daunting. *I'm almost forty years old. How do I begin dating again?*

Skylar, who was still focused on her phone, typed furiously for a moment longer, then tossed the device into her purse. "Okay, ladies, let's make some noise. We're here, we're forty, and it's time to stir up a little trouble in St. Mirika." She polished off her drink and signed the bill. "I know that didn't rhyme, but I don't really care. Now let's get out of here."

As they followed Skylar toward the taxi stand, once again Daphne felt her heart begin to beat a little faster, knowing that stirring up a little trouble was exactly what she needed, yet still a bit anxious at what that might entail. "I'm not sure I'm ready for this," she whispered to KC.

"Ditto," KC whispered back.

"I heard you both," Skylar called over her shoulder. "Selective hearing goes both ways."

# Chapter Four

"Wow, Skylar, this place is *gorgeous*." Daphne let go of her suitcase and took in the spectacular scene around her.

"Well done." KC craned her head back to marvel at the high ceilings.

The three of them were standing in the foyer of the sprawling beachfront property, which led into a spacious living room lined with floor-to-ceiling glass windows that opened to a large wooden deck overlooking the beach. The tile floors were a soft tan color, the walls a crisp white. The structure of the house was slightly curved like a half moon, with rounded hallways on either side. A number of seashell-themed prints dotted the walls, the watercolor hues a mixture of blue, green, and yellow that blended seamlessly with the bright sky and sparkling ocean outside.

Skylar studied a note on her phone, then pointed left and right without looking up from the screen. "Parker's secretary says there are three bedrooms down each hall. All of them face the ocean and have their own bathroom and entrance to the deck."

"Who is Parker?" Daphne turned and looked at her. She knew Skylar had arranged a beach house, but she'd assumed it was a rental. This place looked too nice to be a rental. Then again, Skylar didn't fly coach.

Skylar tossed her phone into her purse. "Our CEO. This is one of his vacation homes. He told me we're welcome to it as long as we don't trash the place."

KC laughed. "*Trash the place?* You sound like we're still in college."

Skylar held up a finger. "I'm aware of my tendency to regress verbally, but I promise it's only in social situations. I sound like the consummate professional whenever necessary. Now, who wants a margarita before dinner? Parker's secretary said she'd make sure the bar was stocked for us."

KC adjusted her baseball hat. "I'm digging Parker's secretary."

"She dresses like she's stuck in the eighties, but she's efficient; I'll give her that." Skylar headed toward the large island in the center of the enormous—and pristine—kitchen. "So who wants that margarita?" Just then her phone beeped. She pulled it out of her purse and glanced at the display, then made an annoyed face. "Oh sugar, I have to take this. Just a sec." She answered briskly. "Hi, Geoffrey, did you track down those figures on the Halston account? Yes . . . I heard about that . . . okay . . . yes . . . Hold on a minute, I just landed, let me open my laptop." She covered the phone with her hand and whispered, "I'm sorry, ladies, can you get the drinks on your own? I need to deal with something first."

KC pointed toward the beach. "No worries, I think I'm going to go for a quick run anyway. I also need to call Max to let him know I made it here in one piece."

"I should check in on Emma too," Daphne said, although Brian was pretty sure they wouldn't have much reception in the mountains. "Where should we put our things?" She peered in both directions.

Skylar pointed down the hall to the left, then to the one on the right and continued to whisper, "Choose any bedroom you like, except for the one on the end that way. That one's mine, *suckahs*. Parker said it has a steam shower."

Daphne looked at KC. "I could get used to this lifestyle."

KC put her hands on her hips and nodded. "I know I live on the beach, so shouldn't complain, but this place puts my little cottage to shame."

The two of them wheeled their suitcases into bedrooms down the hallway to the right. Daphne carefully unpacked her things into a large white dresser and matching armoire, then turned on her phone and watched the screen flicker to life.

No messages.

She dialed Emma's number, but it went straight to voice mail. With a start she wondered if she'd be able to connect with her daughter at all this week; she felt unsure how well she'd handle such a lapse of communication. Not that Emma communicated all that much lately, even those precious days when they were under the same roof. Once a cuddly chatter bug who couldn't get enough of Mommy, Emma was now a typical overscheduled teenager who spent most of her limited free time in her room, studying, playing with her phone, or hanging out with friends—oftentimes simultaneously. Girl talk with *Mom* wasn't high on her priority list, which left *Mom* alone most of the time. In her head she knew Emma was only doing exactly what teenagers do, that in fact her behavior was perfectly normal and indicative of a healthy, supportive upbringing, but that didn't make it any easier to experience.

Maybe the adjustment to the changing relationship with her daughter wouldn't be so difficult for Daphne if she weren't a single parent now.

If she had a husband to hold her hand as together they watched their baby girl prepare to leave the nest.

If together they took another figurative step toward the rocking chair on the front porch, one imperfectly perfect day at a time.

If she didn't feel so alone.

She pressed a palm against her forehead. *Stop it! Stop being so negative! Stop dwelling on the past!*

She felt a few tears welling up in her eyes, then glanced at the closed door of her bedroom, not wanting Skylar or KC to see how fragile she was, desperate to keep up the illusion of the person they thought she still was, of the person she wished she still were. If her old friends saw her the way she used to be, maybe Daphne could see herself that way too, if only for a few days.

*Try to have fun,* she told herself. *These women care about you.*

She stepped into the immaculate bathroom to inspect her face in the mirror for evidence of tears. She heard a noise and glanced out the window. KC was standing on the main deck, dressed in gray running shorts and a pink sports top with the same baseball cap she'd worn on the plane. She carefully pulled one foot up behind her to stretch her quadriceps, then the other. She followed that with a stretch for her calves and hamstrings, then adjusted her hat, walked down the steps onto the beach, and took off running, a tiny cloud of sand swirling around her sneakers.

Daphne felt a sense of admiration at the familiar sight of her old friend's ponytail flapping out of the back of her trademark baseball cap. KC was now a grown woman and the proud stepmother of two young men about to embark on their own journey through adulthood (not to mention the mother of two cats, apparently), but she clearly still embraced life like the bubbly teenager she was when Daphne had first met her, back when Daphne had the good fortune of being paired up as her roommate in the freshman dorm.

Daphne looked at herself in the mirror. In college she had been bubbly too. And relatively sporty—not in KC's league by any stretch of the imagination, but she'd played on various intramural teams, taken dance electives here and there, and generally enjoyed staying in decent shape. Eager to experience everything the venerable institution had to offer, she'd also popped in and out of multiple clubs on campus, dabbling in art, drama, photography, and even debate before setting her focus on writing for the school newspaper. She'd excelled in her classes, joined a sorority (Skylar was in her pledge class), made lots of friends, and over four years of coed life in Evanston, gradually checked off the standard rites of passage of the typical college experience. She was walking the colorful, exciting, interesting path she'd always imagined for herself. Following in the footsteps of many a Northwestern University graduate, she would have a successful career in journalism, where she'd crisscross the globe as a freelance travel writer to discover exotic, far-flung destinations, or maybe patrol the sidelines at major sporting events for *Sports Illustrated*, or perhaps even win a Pulitzer as a rookie beat reporter at the *New York Times* for uncovering local election fraud. At some point down the road, marriage would be the next box to check off on the list, followed eventually by homeownership and children, everything tracking according to plan.

Then Brian came along, and the distant future of that picture suddenly became the present, propelling her ahead of schedule on the itinerary. Now, as she studied her aging reflection and thought about what had happened since that fateful night she'd met him, she felt . . . defeated. What did she have to show for all those years of hard work, of everything she'd invested in their family, of the budding career she'd sacrificed?

She had a wonderful daughter; there was no denying that. Emma was bright and friendly and growing into a delightful young woman. Daphne adored her, and she was proud of the way she was raising her.

But she also had a broken marriage.

31

And a broken spirit, if no longer a broken heart. She'd given up on salvaging the connection that had once existed between her and Brian, but that didn't make it any easier to face a future that looked nothing like the one she'd envisioned for herself.

She used to be full of joy and optimism like KC, at least most of the time. That was one of the reasons the two of them had always gotten along so well. Where had that side of her gone? When had she stopped seeing promise in the inkblot and started seeing . . . spilled ink?

She lightly slapped her cheeks. *Stop feeling sorry for yourself. Look where you are right now. You're going to be fine!*

If only she believed that.

She looked outside again and watched KC disappear down the shore, then decided to change and go for a walk on the beach herself. It would be fun to explore her new surroundings, and she could use some fresh air. Plus, she had no idea how long Skylar would be on that call.

Back in her bedroom Daphne changed into a pair of white shorts and a fitted purple Northwestern tank top, slathered sunscreen over her fair skin, then reached for her straw hat and headed back toward the kitchen. Skylar was in full work mode at a desk in the living room, staring intently at her laptop, and talking with Geoffrey. She wore a wireless headset and pecked feverishly on the keyboard.

"Uh huh . . . uh huh . . . and did the German office confirm when they'd get us that report? Uh huh . . . got it . . . and what about France? We need them both by Wednesday or Parker's going to have my head. Okay . . . yep . . . got it. And yours too. I really need yours." She glanced up at Daphne and mouthed the words "I'm sorry."

Daphne smiled as she put on her hat, then pointed to the beach and mouthed "Going for a walk." She wondered how many people were on the other end of that phone call, and if any of them knew where Skylar was at the moment. Her friend played down her professional success, but Daphne knew how hard she'd worked to achieve it. Skylar had been like that in college too. A social butterfly who was frequently the first girl in line at the keg on the weekends, she was just as frequently the last girl to leave the library during the week. Not too many people back then seemed to know that Skylar had a stealthy studious side, which was just the way she liked it. But Daphne had been her roommate in their sorority house and had seen the more ambitious aspect of Skylar's personality firsthand. While KC spent much of her nonclassroom time on the soccer field, Daphne and Skylar spent a good chunk of theirs studying, and that shared work ethic—or was it fear of falling behind in a sea of over-achievers?—had firmly cemented their friendship.

As she watched Skylar in action on the conference call, Daphne's mind drifted from their college days to her suburban life in Grandview, where she often felt a similar, if less overt, sense of competition within the stay-at-home-mom community. The pressure to excel, even in something as innocuous as a bake sale, was often palpable. She knew it was absurd, but that didn't make it any less real. She'd seen the raised eyebrows for the store-bought goodies on those fold-out card tables. How much could be said without a single word being uttered.

Skylar half nodded to acknowledge Daphne's gesture, then flickered her eyes across her laptop and resumed typing. "Got it. And what did Melissa have to say about the delay in the China roll-out? That market's not going to wait. If we don't move soon, next quarter's going to be a steep climb. Okay, let's see what data Thomas has. Can you get him on the call?" Her fingers flew effortlessly across the keys, as if they belonged to a piano and not a computer.

Daphne tiptoed toward the glass door and quietly exited the house. Once outside, she crossed the deck and climbed down the short flight of stairs to the beach, where she saw the footsteps KC had left in the soft white sand. She decided to go in the same direction, figuring they'd run into each other on KC's way back. She kicked off her flip-flops and held them in one hand, then trotted toward the water to let the tiny waves wash over her bare feet as she strolled along the shore. The sea was a bit warm yet refreshing, the color a spectacular shade of green. She'd never been in an ocean this warm—or seen one this beautiful. It was a far cry from Lake Erie, that was for sure.

She walked for about a hundred yards, passing two additional houses as she went. Both were larger than the one she and her friends were staying in but similar in design, each with floor-to-ceiling windows opening to a sprawling deck facing the ocean. She saw no sign of life inside either place and wondered if they were vacant.

*Are all the homes here used only a couple weeks a year?*

She couldn't imagine that kind of wealth. She and Brian had always lived comfortably by most standards, especially in the Midwest. His parents' generosity in buying them a house, and his partnership at the firm had made Brian's expectation that she be a stay-at-home mom hard to overcome, although a few months ago she'd taken the part-time job at the flower shop just to keep herself busy on the days when Emma was at Brian's house. Before Daphne and Brian had split up, every summer their family of three had taken an annual trip, usually to Hilton Head or Naples. They'd always stayed in relatively fancy hotels, but owning deluxe beachfront property on a tropical island was in a completely different league.

She looked down and kicked up a wedge of powdery sand.

*I wonder if Alyssa's family owns a beach house somewhere?* It was certainly within the realm of possibility. Alyssa's family was one of the most prominent in Columbus.

Daphne pressed her palms against her eyes and willed herself to think about something else. She wasn't jealous of Alyssa because she was with Brian, but she *was* jealous of the life they were now leading. That was all Daphne had ever wanted for herself and for Brian—to be happy together.

She turned her gaze back to the ocean, mesmerized by the green hue of the water as she walked. Out in the distance she spotted a catamaran cruising by. She stopped to pick up a shell, then waded out a few feet into the gentle waves, the water not yet reaching her knees. She studied the shell in her hand for a few moments, then lifted it to her ear and wondered where it had come from. She stroked it with her fingers, then reached her arm back and flung it awkwardly into the air. She watched it wobble in a high arc, then plop harmlessly into the water maybe twenty feet in front of her.

"Nice throw," she heard a voice shout behind her. "Go, Cats!"

She turned around and saw a man standing on the deck of yet another spectacular oceanfront property, his hands spread along the railing. He held up a beer bottle in a toasting gesture and appeared to be smiling at her, although it was hard to tell given the distance.

"You've got quite an arm there. Did you play softball at Northwestern?" he yelled.

She put her hands on her hips and squinted. She couldn't see him very well, but she could tell he was tall. He was wearing a straw fedora and green swim trunks, no shirt. She guessed he was probably in his early thirties. He also appeared to be in very good shape, at least physically.

Before she knew what she was doing, she cocked her head to one side and yelled back at him. "Are you making fun of me?"

He chuckled. "Guilty as charged. Are you a Northwestern grad?"

She nodded, then felt her cheeks flush as something dawned on her. *Oh my gosh, I think he's flirting with me. And I'm flirting right back.*

The unfamiliarity of engaging in playful conversation with an attractive stranger, not to mention one who wasn't wearing a shirt at the moment, was unnerving.

And, Daphne realized, kind of fun. *Keep talking to him! You can do it!*

She started walking toward the house. "Did you go to Northwestern too?" She immediately regretted asking him, afraid that he would answer yes and follow up by asking her when she graduated. Her momentary surge of courage began to wilt, replaced by a fear of appearing foolish—and forty. *Please don't ask me when I graduated.*

She slowed her pace. Maybe if she didn't get too much closer, he wouldn't notice the fine lines around her eyes. Just in case, she decided to keep her sunglasses on. *I should have opened that jar of wrinkle cream.*

"What did you study there?" he asked.

She swallowed. "Journalism." *Please don't ask me what I did with the degree.*

He took a sip of his beer. "I wanted to go to Northwestern, but unfortunately the powers that be in the admissions department didn't share that sentiment, so I ended up at Michigan. Not as expensive, just as cold. Much better football team, however."

Daphne smiled. "Touché. I live in Columbus now and have learned a thing or two about college football." Now that she was closer to him, she could see he was undeniably handsome, with tanned skin, broad shoulders, thick and wavy brown hair that looked like it could use a trim, and light green eyes. He was good-looking, but his smile seemed genuine, which eased her nerves a bit and helped quash her inner monologue, at least temporarily.

He gave her a knowing look. "Oh yes, Buckeye Nation is a force to be reckoned with, especially in the Midwest. Anyhow, while I'm a Wolverine and not a Wildcat, I *do* like purple." He pointed to her tank top with his left hand, and when he did so, she caught herself glancing at his ring finger. It was empty.

She felt her face flush and hoped he hadn't noticed where her eyes had just been. She stiffened. *Why did I just do that?*

She couldn't remember ever checking the ring finger of a man who was clearly so much younger than she. *Thirty-two, maybe?*

He bent down and reached into a large cooler on the deck, then fished out a bottle and held it up. "Can I offer you a frosty cold beer? I can't drink these all by myself."

She shook her head. "I'm fine, thanks."

"Are you sure? It could be my way of making up for heckling you about that tragic throw, although truth be told, that tragic throw needed to be heckled."

She smirked. "Thanks, but my tragic arm and I are good. I'm guessing you're not alone?" She gestured to the cooler. "That's a lot of beer for one person."

He pointed a thumb behind him. "Bachelor party."

"Is that so?" She hadn't attended a bachelorette party in . . . how long had it been? KC hadn't had a bachelorette party. Before that . . . her mind drew a blank. She reached into the far corners of her memory and tried to clear away the cobwebs.

He removed the bottle cap. "This is my *seventh* in the past year."

Daphne felt her eyes open wide. "Seventh? You must be quite popular."

"I wouldn't say that. Then again . . . maybe I would." He gave her a wry smile.

She put her hands on her hips, then realized it was the second time she'd done so. She quickly removed them. "Are you holding down the fort all by yourself?"

He took another sip of his beer. "It's a hard job, but someone has to do it. I only get rattled when a pretty woman walks by."

She immediately looked at the ground, secretly thrilled by his comment but at a complete loss as to how to respond. So she said nothing. Instead, she just stared at the sand, stunned that such a handsome man had recognized her not as a mom or a new divorcée, but as a woman.

She'd forgotten what that felt like. *He's really flirting with me!*

She still didn't speak, however, and the seconds began to tick away.

Just before the pause in conversation became awkward, he cleared his throat. "*Anyhow*, to be honest, I'm not sure why all my friends decided to get married at the same time, but I'm going broke with all the festivities. Last month it was Florida, now here, and next month a bunch of us are going down to Patagonia to go ice climbing."

Finally she looked up and regained eye contact, albeit through her sunglasses. "Are you here with a big group?"

"Thirteen, plus the groom."

"Wow. That's quite a turnout for such a far-off destination. I don't think I've ever had thirteen friends who would travel so far, no matter what the occasion. The groom must be a great guy."

He held up one finger, then two, then a third. "Beach, beer, golf. Yes, he's a great guy, but men, especially this crew of clowns, will travel far and wide for those three little words."

She smiled. "I suspect you're omitting a select word or two for my benefit. That sounds pretty PG for a bachelor party."

He laughed and tipped his beer at her. "Nothing wrong with being a gentleman."

She pushed her sunglasses on top of her head and peered over his shoulder at the house. "Are all of you staying here?"

He pointed toward the deck floor, then down the beach. "There are nine of us here, and five more in a smaller place a couple houses that way. I kind of feel like I'm in a fraternity again, although this place is a hell of a lot nicer than the rat hole I used to live in." He gestured over his shoulder toward the glass doors. "I've been waiting for my turn in the shower for a while now. I've long given up any expectation of hot water. I'm just hoping to get in the shower before I turn thirty."

She stiffened as the comment yanked her back to reality. *He's not even thirty?*

Suddenly feeling foolish for flirting, however awkwardly, with him—not to mention for thinking he'd been flirting with *her*— she quickly put her sunglasses back on. He was clearly just being friendly, and she was too out of practice to know the difference. Her internal monologue returned with a vengeance. *What were you thinking? Why would a man like that flirt with you? He's in his twenties and gorgeous, and you have a teenage daughter and newly signed divorce papers in your desk drawer at home.*

"I'm Clay, by the way. Clay Hanson," he said.

She glanced down the beach, mentally plotting how to exit the conversation without appearing rude. "It's nice to meet you, Clay."

"Do *you* have a name?" He looked amused. Could he tell how flustered she was?

She clenched her hands into fists and forced herself to look at him. *Stop being so awkward!* "Oh gosh, I'm sorry. I'm Daphne."

He raised an eyebrow. "Daphne? That's not a name you hear every day. I like it."

She smiled slightly but didn't reply. Instead, she looked down at the ground and wondered why it was so hard for her to accept a compliment.

"What's your last name?" he asked.

She looked back up at him and responded, "White." She didn't feel the need to mention that White was her married name and that she wasn't married anymore but that she'd kept it because she wanted to have the same last name as her daughter. What was the point?

He nodded slowly. "*Daphne White.* I like that, sounds like the name of a movie star."

She scratched her cheek. "You think? I've always felt it has the ring of a Disney character."

He chuckled. "It's a pleasure to meet you, Daphne White. When did you get to St. Mirika?"

"About an hour ago." She moved her fingers to the tip of her nose and wondered if she was already getting sunburned in spite of her hat. She'd never been one to tan, somehow always going straight from pale to pink. "What about you? How long have you been on the island?"

"This is our third day. I think I'm still a bit hungover from the first afternoon. I'm afraid to know what I'm going to feel like by the end of the week." He pressed a palm against his forehead.

"I've heard how those bachelor parties can go." *My ex-husband's was more than fifteen years ago, but I'm not going to mention that.* She gestured toward the ocean. "I can't believe how beautiful it is here. The water is so clear and *green*. It's mesmerizing."

He turned and pointed behind the house. "If you think this is pretty, you should go explore the cliffs on the other side of the island. The rock formations are off the hook."

She caught her breath at the thought. Daphne was terrified of heights.

Clay kept talking. "They also have a cool bridge up there you can walk over. It's a bit steep getting there, but definitely worth it for the view. I've also heard the monkey forest here is pretty cool, but I don't know if we're going to make it there."

"Thanks, maybe we'll check them both out. My friend Skylar's sort of in charge of our schedule this week, so I'm not really sure what we have planned."

"What brings you here? Bachelorette trip?"

She flinched. "Not quite, more like a reunion."

"Oh yeah? What kind of reunion?"

She hesitated. *Should I tell him the truth? That I'm here to celebrate my fortieth birthday? Do I have to tell him?*

"Daphne White, earth to Daphne White," he said.

She blinked and touched her nose again, even though it wasn't itching. *Stop overthinking this!* "Oh, I'm sorry. What did you say?"

"I asked what kind of reunion are you having?"

"Oh, um . . ." She turned her head to the left and was relieved to see KC a hundred yards or so down the beach, doing jumping jacks. Daphne waved, but KC didn't appear to see her, and Daphne couldn't help but smile at the sight. *Who does jumping jacks at all, much less on the beach?* She loved how KC simply didn't care what anyone thought of her.

"Just with some girlfriends from college. I haven't seen them in a while." She pointed in KC's direction. "I just spotted one of them, actually. I should probably go catch up with her."

Clay finished his beer and stood up straight. "I should probably get a move on too, or I'll never get that shower. I may have to break down a door soon. This really is like living in the Sigma Chi house all over again, minus the beer-soaked floors."

Daphne laughed and waved as she turned to go. "It was nice meeting you, Clay. Good luck salvaging that hot water."

He tipped his head slightly before stepping toward the glass door. "Have fun with your girlfriends. Don't get into *too* much trouble, but speaking of my shower situation, be sure to dip your toe in the figurative hot water, at least a little bit. How often are you on a tropical vacation?"

She smiled. "I'll try my best."

As she walked away, she felt the smile remain on her face. She knew he was just shooting the breeze, but she was proud of herself for having flirted at all, even if it was just for fun. It was a tiny step, but for her it was an important one in the right direction: forward. *That wasn't so bad, was it?*

On her way toward KC, Daphne was visited by memories of her own housing experience in college. Her first year in the dorms, she and KC had shared a room with two other girls, the four of them essentially existing in Habitrail-like conditions, yet not once had any of them batted an eyelash. Everyone did it, no one thought twice about it, and that was that. It was college! Looking back *now*, however, she had no idea how she'd managed in such a cramped space. She and Brian had shared a bathroom, but she had her own sink. She'd also had her own closet.

She looked at KC, who was no longer doing jumping jacks. Now she was chatting energetically with an older couple, all three of them gesturing up at the sky. Daphne's eyes followed. A cluster of dark clouds had appeared over the mountains from the east, heading their way.

As Daphne walked up to the threesome, KC held out an arm game-show style. "Here's one of my pals right now. Daphne, we were just talking about you. I was telling these nice folks about how you and Skylar and I have reunited to *ring in our forties*." She made a swirly motion with her finger in the air, then wiggled her hips.

Daphne smiled. "It's nice to meet you."

"I'm Harry Lewis, and this is my wife, Eleanor. Welcome to the best years of your life . . . so far," the man said with a knowing wink. His hair was silver white, as was his wife's. "We're from Connecticut and are here celebrating forty years as well, but of *marriage*, if you can believe it."

KC put a hand on Daphne's shoulder. "Isn't that awesome? It's so inspiring."

"Forty years is impressive, that's for sure," Daphne said. "What's your secret?"

"Are you married, dear?" Eleanor asked.

Daphne shook her head. "I'm divorced." She didn't elaborate, suddenly dreading that the conversation might pull her backward again, the tiny swell of optimism she'd felt after her conversation with Clay evaporating before her eyes.

"What's the secret to a long and happy union?" KC asked. "I'm happily married, but it's only been five years. I'd love any tips on how to make it to the Big Four O."

Eleanor interlaced her arm around Harry's. "For *me* . . . it's a romp in the sack with the pool boy every Tuesday afternoon while Harry plays golf. Keeps me feeling playful."

Daphne and KC both stared at her, wide-eyed.

"I'm kidding, kidding!" Eleanor let out a hearty laugh that belied her petite frame, then looked up at her much taller husband. "Look at their faces, Harry. I told you, *it's funny.*"

"She's used that line before," Harry said with a mock eye roll. "Gets people every time."

KC put a hand on her heart. "You got me, that's for sure. Nice one."

Daphne was struck by their energy, their vitality, and the obvious joy they gave to each other just by being together. She could never imagine her mother interacting with her father like that. Her parents' relationship, as Daphne had always perceived it as a child, was much more distant. They got along fine and rarely argued, but she'd never seen them laugh or express sincere *affection* toward each other. A peck on the cheek was the extent of what she'd witnessed, and Daphne could probably count those instances on two hands. Much like the way her own marriage had been toward the end, to

Daphne her parents' union at times appeared to be more of a business arrangement than a relationship founded on romantic love. But they were still married, and Daphne wasn't, so who was she to judge what worked for them?

Standing at that moment before Harry and Eleanor, whose marriage was so unlike her parents', so unlike her *own*, Daphne felt an unexpected—and welcome—flicker of inspiration. *Maybe happily ever after does exist? With the right person?*

"So what *is* the magic recipe for making it work?" KC asked. "Or is there one? I grew up thinking I'd never get married, and because of that I'm secretly afraid that I'm going to mess it all up." KC's parents had divorced when she was five.

Daphne quickly turned her head. She'd assumed KC's skepticism about the viability of "until death do us part" had disappeared after she'd met Max.

*Maybe I'm not the only one wondering if I'm . . . the only one?*

"I believe laughter is the secret to the success of our relationship," Eleanor said as she looked at Harry. "For forty years this man has been making me laugh, and when you're laughing, you're being *yourself*. If you're not being yourself, you're not in a good marriage. Plus, a man might be quite dashing in his younger years and get away with a less than pleasant personality, but what woman wants to spend her golden years with a saggy, old coot who doesn't have a sense of humor? Not me, that's for sure!" She let out a little cackle and patted Harry's arm.

Harry shrugged. "I just stick around because Eleanor's easy on the eyes."

Eleanor touched his nose with her fingertip. "You're not so bad yourself. Then again, my eyes aren't what they used to be."

"I *love* you two." KC interlaced her hands in front of her. "Will you adopt me?"

Daphne sighed. "Will you adopt me too?"

Harry chuckled. "Our four children might object to that. They're grown and have kids of their own now, but they still want their share of the Christmas loot."

Just then a deep rumbling sound interrupted the conversation.

"Was that thunder?" Daphne asked. Where had that sound come from?

"Check it out." KC pointed to the sky, which was now quickly filling with dark clouds that just moments before had seemed so far away. "We're about to get drenched!"

Daphne watched in wonder as the clouds moved with a ferocity she'd never seen. Before anyone could speak, the sky erupted above them. As the heavy drops came pouring down, Daphne turned to run for shelter, but KC grabbed her arm. "Where are you going?" she asked her.

Daphne looked from KC to Harry and Eleanor, neither of whom had moved an inch.

Eleanor tilted her head back and opened her arms. "Isn't this just fabulous? I told you!"

"You weren't kidding: it's *amazing!*" KC raised her voice so that they could hear her over the din of the rain. "This happens every day here?"

Harry nodded. "Just about. It's one of the reasons we love St. Mirika so much."

Eleanor twirled around in a circle, her arms out like a cross. "It's my favorite time of day here. So magical and pure."

"How long does it usually last?" KC asked through the din.

"Just a few minutes, sometimes a bit longer," Eleanor said. "Sometimes I wish it would go on forever. There's something about a burst of rain that makes everything fresh and new, don't you think? It's as if Mother Nature is giving us another chance."

Daphne wiped a few drops from her forehead. "I guess I never thought about it that way." She looked up at the ominous sky, intrigued by the unfamiliar sensation of warm rain running over her skin. It felt refreshing . . . soothing . . . *healing.*

She made eye contact with Eleanor as the significance of what was happening to her began to take shape, an invisible beauty that made sense only to her. Or maybe to all of them. "I think you're right," she said with a tiny smile.

"That's the magic of this seaside oasis, my dear." Eleanor gave her a knowing smile in return. "It makes you see things in ways that never occur to you in the real world."

．　　．　　．

"*There* you two are. The margaritas are ready, they are de-li-cious, and they aren't going to drink themselves." Wearing an oversized yet stylish straw hat and a white linen tank dress, Skylar was standing on the deck as Daphne and KC approached the house. The rain had stopped and the skies had quickly cleared, allowing the hot sun to resume its beating down on them—nearly drying their clothes and hair on the walk home. Save for a few drops lingering on the railing of the deck, there was scant evidence that just a few minutes earlier their stretch of beach had been smack in the path of a tropical thunderstorm. It was like magic.

Skylar held up her glass, then pointed to the kitchen. "There's a pitcher in the fridge. I tried to wait for you, but I couldn't hold out any longer. After that call from hell, I needed to self-medicate."

"No need to apologize," KC said as she trotted up the stairs. "I'd love a margarita, but I need to hydrate before I partake in any self-medication. Otherwise, I might not make it to dinner."

Skylar scoffed. "Please. As if *self-medicating* is even in your vocabulary. When's the last time you had more than one drink?"

KC pointed to Daphne. "If you have a vocabulary question, she's the queen."

"I wasn't asking a *vocabulary question*. I was asking a question about *your vocabulary*," Skylar said.

"Who's on first?" KC asked with a grin.

Daphne held up her palms. "I'm not getting involved in this conversation."

Skylar gestured inside. "Fine, fine, I concede defeat. Filtered water's in the fridge. How was your run?"

"Beautiful," KC said. "Although I got a little overheated toward the end. I did a bunch of jumping jacks when I was done, and at one point I was tempted to run right into the ocean to cool off."

Skylar looked at Daphne. "Did she just say *jumping jacks*?"

Daphne smiled. "Right on the beach. It was quite a sight to behold."

KC tapped her chest. "Hey now, there's nothing wrong with the good old-fashioned jumping jack. It gets the heart rate up, that's for sure." She patted Skylar on the shoulder on her way into the house.

"I prefer sex for that," Skylar called after her.

KC disappeared behind the glass door, and Daphne looked up at the sky. "Did you see that crazy rain?" she asked Skylar.

Skylar nodded. "I heard it from my desk, then came out here after my call and caught the tail end of the downpour. Amazing how quickly it came and went, isn't it?"

"It was incredible," Daphne said softly. Eleanor's words were still bouncing around in her brain. *There's something about a burst of rain that makes everything fresh and new. It's as if Mother Nature is giving us another chance.*

*I want that chance,* she thought.

Skylar took a seat in a reclining patio chair and reached for her margarita. "We're bound to get soaked a few times this week, although that's not too unusual for this part of the world."

"Yet another reason to love it. I'm so glad you brought us here," Daphne said. For a moment she considered sharing what Eleanor had said, but something held her back, as if she needed to keep it to herself for now. Instead, she stretched out in a lounge chair and inhaled deeply. The fresh, salty air stung her nostrils a little bit, but she didn't mind.

She didn't mind at all.

KC reappeared holding a large glass of water, then pointed down the beach. "I saw a neat little spot we should check out at some point. It was a thatched hut with a big banana on the roof and a good-sized line in front of it, so they must be selling something yummy in there."

Skylar sat up and removed her designer sunglasses, then squinted down the beach. "Ah, the hut with the banana. Parker mentioned that place. I think he said it's called Banana Banana. Or maybe it was Bananarama? It was definitely Banana something or other. Regardless, he said they make really good smoothies. We should definitely go there."

Daphne looked at her. "If it's really called *Bananarama*, I want to go there just because of that name."

"Me too." KC took a seat on a bench. "I loved that band. And I *love* tasty smoothies. You think they have kale?"

"Kale in a smoothie? That's disgusting," Skylar said.

"Says you." KC rubbed a hand over her abdomen. "Leafy greens are good for the digestion."

Skylar put her sunglasses back on. "Leaves belong on trees, so if you think I'm getting them in a freaking *smoothie*, you need to up your medication."

"I'm not on any medication," KC said.

"Well, maybe you should be," Skylar said. "The pharmaceutical industry is what keeps our economy running, you know. It's practically your civic duty to take *something*."

Daphne laughed. "You're both nuts."

KC grinned. "Nuts are good in smoothies too."

"Will you shut up already?" Skylar said. "I'm losing my appetite."

"Fine, fine. Maybe we could go tomorrow after our beach workout?" KC said.

Skylar sipped her margarita. "Do as you will, but I'd literally rather be sitting on a conference call than sweating my ass off while on vacation. Ergo, while I'm game for a leaf-free smoothie, I won't be joining you in any self-inflicted torture."

"I love sweating while on vacation," KC said. "It's the best."

"Sometimes I wonder how we're even friends," Skylar said.

KC pumped her fist. "Too late! I'm grandfathered in. You're never getting rid of me."

"Lucky me," Skylar said with a mock sigh.

"Speaking of conference calls, did yours turn out okay?" Daphne asked Skylar.

Skylar shrugged. "Okay enough. Unfortunately, I have a feeling I'm going to be on the phone a lot this week. It's just impossible to disconnect entirely."

"It's a cruel . . . cruel summer . . ." KC sang as she skipped into the house to refill her water glass.

"Will you grab me some water too?" Daphne called after her.

"I'm on it," KC yelled over her shoulder.

Skylar took another sip of her margarita and looked at Daphne. "So how was your walk?"

Daphne felt a rush of energy at the question, an unexpected reaction that secretly thrilled her. "Beautiful! I still can't get over how white the sand is, and the water is so *green*. Everything is so calm and serene here."

"That's island living for you. It's like going back in time, before iPhones and Facebook took over the world."

Daphne looked out at the beach. "I take a lot of walks at home, and I can't remember the last time I didn't pass at least a handful of people on their phones. Counting KC I saw exactly four people during my walk here, and definitely no phones."

Skylar leaned back in the patio chair. "That's what I love about tropical vacations: the relaxed, low-key energy that seems to permeate the air. When I'm not on a soul-killing conference call, that is."

"You work so hard, it's really impressive," Daphne said. "You've *always* worked so hard. I think that's one of the reasons I did too, when we lived together. I had to keep up with you."

Skylar shook her head. "I highly doubt that. You were pretty driven, even more so after we graduated. I had no doubt you were going places."

An awkward silence followed.

"If you *wanted* to, I mean. I hope you know what I mean," Skylar added. "You know how smart and capable I think you are, right?"

Daphne smiled and hoped it looked convincing. "I do, and thank you. You deserve to take a break for a few days. That's all I'm saying."

Skylar glanced at her watch. "Easier said than done. I still have to check on one more thing before dinner."

Daphne gestured toward the shoreline. "KC and I met a sweet older couple when we were walking on the beach. I think they said they're from Connecticut."

KC emerged, carefully carrying three glasses of water. "Did I hear my name?"

Daphne reached for a glass. "I was just about to tell Skylar about Harry and Eleanor." She turned toward Skylar. "They're here to celebrate their *fortieth* anniversary."

KC handed Skylar a glass, then took a seat on the bench. "Pretty cool, huh? They seem really happy together."

Skylar nodded. "Forty years is quite a milestone in and of itself, but forty years and *happy* is almost unheard of. Good for them."

KC took a sip of water. "They told us laughter is the key to a successful union, because when you're laughing, you're being yourself, and if you're not being yourself, what's the point? I liked that."

"I liked that too," Daphne said softly. She tried to pinpoint when she'd stopped being herself with Brian. *Too long ago.*

"Funny how hard it is to be yourself sometimes, isn't it?" Skylar said. "Doesn't make a lot of sense when you think about it."

Daphne felt her neck get hot and hoped the conversation wasn't leading in a direction she didn't want to go. She cleared her throat. "Anyhow, it was wonderful to see them happy together after so many years."

"My parents were never happy," KC said. "If my mom hadn't gotten pregnant, I doubt they would have married."

Skylar looked at Daphne. "Your parents are still together, right?"

Daphne nodded, grateful for the shift in course, however slight. "They're hanging in there, for better or for worse, although the way my mom loves to complain about everything, I suspect that for my dad it's mostly worse. What about yours?"

Skylar held up her glass as if in a toast. "They hit fifty years last summer."

Daphne tried to wrap her head around the idea of being married for that long. "Wow. I think my parents are at forty-two."

"Max and I are heading on six," KC said. Then, as if reading Daphne's mind, she leaned over and squeezed Daphne's knee. "For what it's worth, my parents didn't even make it to five." Daphne gave her a grateful smile in return, but she didn't say anything.

Skylar sipped her drink. "Half a century. Insane, right? I don't know how they do it. They seem pretty content too. I mean they bicker here and there, but for the most part they genuinely enjoy each other's company. If I were married to the same man for that long, I think I'd kill the poor guy. I can't even imagine being married for *one* year, much less fifty." Marriage and children had never been in Skylar's plans.

"Did they have a big party to celebrate?" KC asked.

Skylar nodded. "We all went to Hawaii."

Daphne turned her head. "You mean *all of you*, including your million nieces and nephews?" Skylar had three sisters and two brothers who were all married with multiple kids.

Skylar took another sip of her margarita, then set it on the bench next to her chair. "The whole burrito. It was a zoo. Total chaos. I swear to God we took up half the hotel. It was fun, but also exhausting. I spent nearly every night at the bar trying to de-stress."

"More self-medicating?"

"*Exactly*. Perfect use case." She glanced at the dwindling liquid in her margarita glass. "Speaking of which, I might be in need of a refill soon."

Daphne closed her eyes and leaned back in her chair. "I can't imagine having a family that big. When I was a kid, by default our family vacations were always so tame." Daphne was an only child.

An only child with an only child.

She'd never been on a vacation with her own parents as an adult, although she and Brian had once gone on a cruise with his parents when she was pregnant with Emma. The elder Mr. and Mrs. White weren't unkind people, but they were so formal and reserved that for the entire week Daphne felt like she was still auditioning for the role of daughter-in-law—even though she was already married to their son.

Throughout the duration of their union that feeling had never gone away. *Will they like Alyssa better?*

She tried to push the negative thoughts aside as she heard KC asking Skylar a question. "Did everyone get along okay on the trip?"

"Pretty well, or well enough. There were at least two tantrums a day, but usually only one was by an adult."

Daphne blinked. "What?"

Skylar pushed her arm. "I'm joking."

"Oh, got it." Daphne was still only half paying attention, still thinking about how Brian's parents had never quite warmed to her. In the early part of her marriage, she'd tried so hard to get them to like her, and while they'd defrosted slightly over the years, she'd grown to accept that they were never going to embrace her with open arms, figuratively or literally. They just weren't that type of people. But it still stung that they had never seemed all that interested in the person she was, treating her instead as their son's wife, now ex-wife, or as their granddaughter's mother. Never as Daphne. *And I let it happen.*

Skylar gave her a strange look. "Daphne, are you okay?"

Daphne forced a smile, but she knew it was a bit stiff. "Yes, sorry, I'm just a little scattered right now." *I'm a mess. Can't you two see that?*

"You clearly need to get used to hanging out with me again. You're way out of practice," Skylar said.

"Agreed. We need to break you in," KC said.

Daphne stared out at the water, unable to look her friends in the eye. "I'll take that." It pained her that she couldn't open up to the people she'd once shared everything with. She wanted to, but she just couldn't do it. She felt pitiful for her inability to break free from her stagnation, to make changes she knew she needed to move herself forward.

After a few moments of silence, Skylar sat up in her chair and stretched her arms over her head. "So *anyhow*, the big Aloha Family Adventure went well, and no one ended up in the hospital, although one of my sisters nearly lost it when my nephew sailed out of one of the swinging hammocks at the hotel and landed right on some tiny old Japanese lady."

KC covered her mouth with her hand. "Oh my gosh! Was he hurt? Was *she* hurt?"

Skylar shook her head. "Luckily no, but when he landed on the lady, it startled her so much that she farted, like *really loud*. She didn't speak a lick of English, but apparently flatulence is a universal language."

Daphne laughed, and KC let out a little shriek. "That's hilarious!"

"My nephew thought so too. We all did, but my sister was mortified. She's a bit uptight if you ask me, although I'm not one to judge anyone's parenting style. I don't even have a cat."

"Parenting is tricky, that's for sure," Daphne said. "It's not like anyone gives you an instruction manual, you know? So you end up feeling your way through, learning as you go."

"Same goes for being a stepmother," KC said. "I pretty much walked in blind and still have no idea if I'm doing it right. But neither one of them is in jail, so that's a good sign."

Daphne smiled at KC, wishing she could be as forthright with her lack of confidence. *I'm still hoping I'll figure it out too.* Why couldn't she just admit that?

Skylar stood up and stretched her arms over her head again. "I honestly don't know how people do it. I have no problem running a global sales operation, but for the life of me I couldn't handle raising kids." She pointed at Daphne. "I'm so impressed that you have a *teenager* and still look so good. I think being a mom would age me rapidly."

"I bet you'd make a great mom," Daphne said. She meant it. Skylar was perhaps the most competent person she knew.

Skylar turned toward the house. "I guess I could do it if I had to, but to be honest I don't think I was born with that gene. I'm more than happy being the cool aunt who lives in New York City."

KC pumped a fist in the air. "That's the spirit! Who wouldn't want a cool auntie who lives in New York City?"

Skylar tipped her glass at her. "Exactly. Now come on, ladies, let's get you each a margarita."

• • •

Twenty minutes later, Daphne leaned over the granite island in the kitchen and looked at KC, who was stretching on the floor next to the barstools. A sea of gleaming copper pots and pans hung overhead on an oval rack. Daphne wondered if they'd ever been touched. "You're really still playing soccer?" she asked. KC had just shared her plans to participate in an adult tournament the following weekend.

KC moved her legs into a straddle position, then leaned to the right to grab her toes. "Why wouldn't I still play? I love it."

"I think it's fantastic that you're still playing," Skylar said. "I bet you run those young whippersnappers into the ground."

KC looked up at her with a grin. "I don't know about running anyone into the ground, but I do a pretty good job of holding my own out there."

"Are you the oldest one?" Daphne asked KC.

KC shook her head. "Not by a long shot. Tons of older people play soccer. In fact, the tournament next weekend is over-forty."

"A whole tournament for people over forty?" Daphne raised her eyebrows. "I've been to a few volleyball tournaments with Emma, and they're pretty intense even for the kids. Seems like a soccer tournament would be really hard on your body."

KC sat up and stretched her hands over her head. "It's a lot of running, but it's not that bad if you have subs. I've been playing in tournaments for years, but this is the first time I'm old enough to play in the over-forty division, so I can't wait."

Skylar gave her a strange look as she reached for the pitcher of margaritas. "Do you realize how weird that sounds?"

KC laughed. "They have over-thirty, over-forty, over-fifty, even over-sixty. That way you can always play against people your own age, so it's competitive. I'm really looking forward to it. After all these years of chasing around youngsters in the over-thirty division, in the over-forty I'll get to be the fastest one again."

"Only you could make turning forty sound like something to aspire to," Skylar said. "You should work in advertising. You could probably package up sand and sell it at the beach on spring break."

"Wouldn't it be nice to be on spring break again?" Daphne said with a wistful smile. "To be that young again?"

KC switched her stretch to the other leg. "Guys, we *are* young."

"We're not *that* young," Skylar said.

KC nodded. "Well sure, we're not twenty anymore, but who cares? We're not *old*, just older than we used to be."

Skylar pointed at her. "Seriously, you should join an advertising agency. You could make millions."

"I feel old," Daphne said softly, surprised at her candor. She thought of her conversation with Clay, how she'd been too embarrassed to tell him the reason behind her reunion with her friends.

KC looked up at her. "Well, you shouldn't. Didn't you hear what Harry and Eleanor said to us? To them, *we're* the youngsters. Just because I can't run as fast as I did when I was in college doesn't mean I'm *old*. It doesn't mean I can't still play soccer and have fun."

"Harry and Eleanor seem to have made quite an impression on you," Skylar said.

KC nodded. "They seem like good people."

Daphne nodded too. "Supersweet. A little, um, *feistier* than I expected for people their age, but they have a warm aura about them."

"Oh, now I want to meet them," Skylar said. "I like me some feisty."

KC pulled one foot behind her and moved into the hurdler's stretch. "Trust me, you guys, as a woman who is married to an older man, I know from personal experience that age is just a number. It means nothing unless you *let* it mean something. It's all in how you think."

"You should say that in a Yoda voice," Daphne said. She remembered how Clay said he wasn't even thirty yet. What would he think of this conversation? Was KC just kidding herself into believing forty wasn't over the hill? Then again, KC had never looked healthier, or *happier*, than she did right now. Maybe she was onto something. Daphne leaned over again and gently nudged KC with her foot. "Speaking of age, are your stepsons in their twenties now?"

KC lifted her head and smiled. "One is! Isn't that nuts? Josh is nineteen and a sophomore at UCLA, and Jared is twenty-two and living with his girlfriend in a cute little bungalow in Santa Monica. Can you believe I have a stepson old enough to be living with his girlfriend in a cute little bungalow in Santa Monica?"

Skylar held up a hand. "Please change the subject immediately. This conversation is too horrifying to continue without more alcohol in my system."

KC grinned, then stretched both legs in front of her and leaned forward to grab her toes. "Okay, fine, we'll go back to soccer. It's a fantastic workout, but it's also supersocial, especially the coed leagues. Going out for beers after the game is practically mandatory. Max and I love it."

"I love going out for beers," Skylar said. "Maybe I should find a league that just does that. No actual exercise, just socializing and drinking."

Finally done with her stretching, KC jumped up and put a hand on Skylar's shoulder. "I think they call that *going to a bar*."

"Semantics," Skylar said. "But a league like that would be a better investment than my gym membership, which I barely use."

"You and Max met through a soccer league, right?" Daphne asked KC.

KC nodded. "Another perk of the coed system. I found myself a husband, and I wasn't even looking for one."

"I wish I were athletic," Skylar said.

Daphne looked at Skylar. "You mean so you could meet your husband that way too? I thought you didn't want to get married."

"I don't. But what's not to like about coed recreation? Sweaty, athletic men in shorts? Count me in."

"I can't imagine playing soccer with men," Daphne said. "Do people get hurt a lot?"

KC opened the refrigerator and pulled out a pitcher of water. "The men in our league are pretty chill. Once in a while some Rambo type will go in crazy hard for a tackle, but those types don't usually stick around too long because they get the evil eye from everyone. Most of the people I play with go out of their way *not* to hurt anyone. Everyone knows we all have to go to work the next day."

"Well, it sure keeps you looking great, that's for sure." Skylar looked at her own upper arm, then gave it a squeeze. "I keep telling myself I need to work out more, but the truth is I hate exercising too much to do anything about it. After a long day at the office, if I'm actually home and not on an airplane or at a work dinner or a client event or on a date, I'm like, why go to the gym when I can stay right here on my supercomfy couch and drink wine?"

KC laughed. "You *sure* you don't want to try my beach class tomorrow morning? I've already got Daphne signed up."

Daphne coughed. "You have? I uh . . . I thought that was just a suggestion."

KC removed her baseball hat and pointed it in the direction of her bedroom. "It was a suggestion that we will be converting into a reality. Okay, ladies, I'm off to take a shower. What's next on the itinerary?"

Skylar held up her nearly empty margarita glass. "I need to shower too, but first I'm going to finish this delicious beverage. Then, unfortunately, I have to make another work call, but I promise it won't take long. I was thinking we could have dinner at a place not too far from here called Captain's Grill. It's right on the beach, and apparently the food there is amazing."

"Sounds perfect," KC said. "How dressy is it?"

Skylar gave her a look of mock surprise. "You brought a dress?"

KC grinned. "I brought *one* dress. So let me know which night I should wear it."

"I can't imagine you in a dress," Daphne said. "Did you even wear one to your wedding?" Max and KC had gotten married at City Hall in a family-only ceremony.

"I wore a white tank dress from J.Crew," she said. "Does that count?"

Skylar rolled her eyes. "For *you*, that counts. And to answer your question, Pippi Longstocking, tonight is casual. We'll do the dressy dinner thing for Daphne's birthday. But I have a proposition for you. If Daphne and I do your beach workout, you have to go shopping with us for girly stuff, deal?" She turned and looked at Daphne. "That's a fair deal, right?"

Daphne nodded. "Sounds equitable to me."

KC hesitated for a moment, then shook Skylar's hand. "Okay, I can live with that. Deal."

Skylar smiled. "Nice. I heard there are some cute stores in the main downtown area. Maybe we'll head over there tomorrow and gussy you up."

KC trotted toward her bedroom. "Do what you must. I'm not wearing makeup, though!" she called over her shoulder.

"Once a tomboy, always a tomboy," Skylar said as KC shut her door. "God help her."

Daphne lifted her margarita for a toast. "And here's hoping she never changes."

Skylar clinked her glass against Daphne's. "I'll drink to that."

# Chapter Five

Captain's Grill wasn't technically *on* the beach, but without burrowing the table legs and chairs into the sand, the outdoor seating area of the charmingly rustic restaurant was about as close to the shore as it could be. The tables were spread over a raised wooden deck, each one flanked by a large white umbrella ready to be opened for protection from the sun, or perhaps the sudden onslaught of a rainstorm, which, as Daphne now knew, was not an uncommon occurrence on St. Mirika. A string of white lanterns dotted a high fence lining the three edges of the deck not facing the water, which secluded the deck and created a protective illusion that it was the lone dining spot on the beach.

"Wow, that's tasty," KC said as she sipped her mango sangria.

"Isn't it?" Skylar said. "St. Mirika is famous for it. I don't know why it hasn't taken off in the States. Maybe I should quit selling software and start selling mango sangrias instead."

"Maybe I'd come work for you," KC said. "You said I'm good at selling things, right?"

Skylar nodded. "With your charisma and my connections, we'd make a fortune."

Daphne gazed out at the ocean, utterly mesmerized by the view. The sun was just beginning to set, casting a soft orange glow across the sky and spreading over the water, which gently rolled up against the shore.

"You okay there, sweets?" Skylar asked her. "You look a little dazed."

Daphne nodded slowly and kept staring at the horizon. "I feel like we're on a movie set. I've never seen anything like this."

"It really is paradise," KC said. "I love living in Hermosa Beach, but this takes the word *beautiful* to another level." She cocked her head at Daphne. "What's a word for more beautiful than beautiful?"

Before Daphne could respond, Skylar held up her glass. "Sangria."

Daphne laughed. "Well done."

Skylar took a sip of her drink. "Thank you. I'm no Daphne White, but I do have a pretty extensive vocabulary when it comes to cocktails. And this sangria is spectacular."

Daphne glanced out at the ocean. "I think St. Mirika is the most, um, *sangria*, place I've ever been."

"Me too," KC said. "Max and I went to Maui for our honeymoon, but this blows that out of the water."

Daphne put a hand on KC's arm. "Speaking of the water, have you ever seen water so *green*? It's like toothpaste, don't you think?"

Skylar made a sour face. "What kind of toothpaste do people use in Ohio? That sounds disgusting."

"This place really is out of a movie set," Daphne said. "Not that I have anything to compare it to, but high rolling with Skylar kind of *feels* like hanging out with a celebrity, so it's almost like we're in a movie right now."

KC turned her head as if on a swivel. "So is this the scene where the handsome stranger sends over a bottle of champagne? Skylar, does that sort of thing happen to you?"

Skylar smirked and picked up the menu. "Shush, both of you. My job is light years from Hollywood, and you both know it. Now, let's order." She reached into her purse and removed a pair of designer reading glasses from a sleek black case.

KC laughed and pulled out her own glasses case, although decidedly less fancy. She waggled it in the air. "You too?"

Skylar nodded and frowned. "Horrifying, isn't it? I was in denial for months, but I finally caved over Christmas after my nieces and nephews made fun of me for holding the presents away from my eyes so I could read who they were from."

KC laughed. "I was in denial until Max threw his pair across the breakfast table and told me to put them on. He said for weeks he'd been watching me do the same thing with the newspaper and he couldn't take it anymore."

Skylar looked at Daphne. "What about you? Have your eyes betrayed you yet?"

Daphne shook her head. "Not yet. But then again, as we know, I'm still in my thirties."

"Touché," Skylar said with a dry smile. "What about your hair? Have you yanked out any wiry grays yet?"

Daphne immediately touched the sides of her head. *Do I need to be pulling hairs out?* She'd noticed a stray gray here and there but hadn't done anything about it. Were they obvious? She was too afraid to ask. "Not yet," she said.

Skylar tapped her left temple. "I call the worst offenders *angry hairs*, you know, the ones that grow in every direction besides *down*? I hate those little buggers. I started yanking after my little niece asked me if I had tinsel in my hair. That was quite a rude awakening, to say the least."

KC laughed. "That's hilarious. In my book, gray hair is a badge of honor, like you've earned it!" She tapped her heart.

"I have zero interest in reading that book," Skylar said. "My hairdresser says I'm not ready to color it yet, but when the day comes, I'm heading straight to the salon to take the plunge."

"I'm going natural all the way," KC said. "Like a cotton ball."

"I bet even with a head of white fluff, you won't seem old," Daphne said. "You're too much like a little kid."

"I wear compression socks when I run sometimes," KC said. "Does that count for something?"

Skylar laughed. "I don't even know how to respond to that."

As they perused the menu, Daphne stole a glance at Skylar, who, even with reading glasses perched on the bridge of her nose, looked put together *and* on top of things, as if she knew something no one else in the room did. She looked confident. Successful. Classy. An impeccable package she'd created all on her own.

When was the last time Daphne had felt any of those things about herself? Where had her self-confidence gone? Where had *she* gone?

"Daphne, hon, you there?" Skylar said.

Daphne looked up from her menu to see KC, Skylar, and the waiter all staring at her. She felt her cheeks flush.

"Are you okay, Daphne?" KC looked concerned. "You disappeared for a moment there."

Daphne nodded. "Yep, totally fine, just taking everything in."

"Are you ready to order?" Skylar gestured to the waiter.

Daphne looked up at him. "Oh yes, of course. Sorry. I'll . . . I'll have the mixed green salad and the glazed salmon, thank you." She closed her menu and handed it to him.

Once he was gone, Skylar tapped her fork against her glass a couple times, then lifted it up. "I'd like to make a toast to *us*: the Three Musketeers together again, at last."

"Aw, I love you guys," KC said.

"You love everything," Skylar said. "But seriously, can you believe we met when we were eighteen years old, and now we're forty? That means we've been friends for more than half our lives."

"Wow," Daphne said under her breath. "That's cool but kind of scary too."

"Totally," KC whispered back.

Skylar kept talking. "Yes, my dears, we've been friends for more than twenty years now. It seems like just yesterday the three of us were wearing scrunchies and drinking wine coolers from a straw in the dorms. Thank God the digital age wasn't around when we were in college. If any of those photos got out, my meticulously constructed image as a serious businesswoman would be in serious jeopardy."

Daphne sipped her drink. "That's for sure. Remember that time you made out with Jason Green in the study lounge with the glass windows and didn't know there were like ten of us watching?"

KC raised her hand as if in a classroom. "I remember! That was awesome. People were taking bets on when you two would come up for air."

Skylar closed her eyes and took a deep breath. "Apparently I had blocked that incident from my memory, but thank you both for reminding me. Now I get to relive it in all its classy glory."

Daphne smiled. "You're very welcome. And for the record, you were very classy. It was quite PG-13, from what I remember."

KC held up a finger. "Also for the record, I never wore a scrunchie because they fall out too easily when I run. *My* go-to look was the reverse french braid, if you remember. I rocked that thing."

Daphne held up a finger too. "*Also* for the record, while I admit to the scrunchie thing, I'm not forty yet. I still have two more days in my thirties, so don't drag me down with you just yet."

Skylar sighed dramatically. "Jeez, Louise, I'm trying to give a *toast* here. Will you two please shut down the peanut gallery and let me finish?"

"Of course, I'm sorry. We didn't mean to cause a kerfuffle." Daphne reached for her sangria.

KC giggled. "You and your SAT vocabulary. Who uses the word *kerfuffle*?"

Skylar snapped her fingers twice. "Focus, ladies, focus. It's clear you're not used to drinking sangria."

Daphne and KC both sat at attention and looked at her as she stood ceremoniously.

"Okay then," Skylar said with a nod, then cleared her throat. "*Anyhow*, I'd officially like to thank both of you for joining me in what I'm sure will be a trip I will remember forever. Despite our earlier conversation about age, turning forty is a big deal, and I can't think of two women I'd rather celebrate the occasion with than you, two of the smartest, kindest, most interesting people I've had the pleasure of meeting in my life. And believe me, I've met a *lot* of people. I know I don't see either of you very often, but I *think* of you often, and I want you to know that I love you both very much. So here's to the Three Musketeers, together forever." She sat down and clinked her glass against KC's, then Daphne's.

KC reached over and put a hand on Skylar's shoulder. "That was a beautiful toast. You're going to make me cry."

"No I won't." Skylar immediately shook her head. "You never cry. You're always too freaking *happy* to cry. Of all those people I just said I've met in my life, *none* of them has ever been as happy as you."

"I could cry tears of joy?" KC said, a hopeful expression on her face.

Skylar rolled her eyes. "I'll believe that when I see it."

KC grinned at her. "Okay, you're probably right."

Skylar set down her glass and reached for her purse. "To commemorate the occasion that has brought us here, I thought you both might like to see something. Do you ladies remember this?" She removed a small pink notebook.

Daphne caught her breath at the sight of the leather binding. "Is that . . . Daisy the diary?"

Skylar held the book against her chest. "The one and only."

"I can't believe you still have her," Daphne said. "Do you still make entries?"

Skylar laughed. "Oh God no. I haven't touched the thing since college. I can't believe I found her, to be honest. But I'm so glad I did. I thought you two might want to read what you wrote in good ol' Daisy at the end of our senior year. Do you remember when we each predicted what our lives would be like twenty years after graduation?"

"No way! I forgot all about that!" KC said.

Skylar smiled. "I know it hasn't been quite twenty years, but close enough. Should we see what we each wrote? I haven't read it yet because I thought it would be fun to wait until tonight. I have absolutely no memory of what I predicted."

KC wiggled her fingers at the diary. "I wanna see! Gimme."

"Only if you read what you wrote out loud," Skylar said. "I'll go first." She opened the diary to a bookmarked page in the back and began to speak. *"In twenty years I will be CEO of a large company, probably in New York or London."* She shrugged, then handed the book to KC. "Getting there, I guess."

"You're *more* than getting there," KC said. "You're a rock star." She began to skim the page. "Okay, what did I write . . . Here it is! *In twenty years I will be leading a Peace Corps unit in South America or Africa.*" She laughed and handed the diary to Daphne. "Hey, that's not bad! I'm hardly leading a unit, but I did join the Peace Corps for a couple years."

"Well done," Skylar said. "Your turn, Daphne."

Daphne scanned to her section of the page, then quietly began to read. *"In twenty years I will be an award-winning journalist."*

A brief yet undeniably awkward silence followed, none of them sure what to say. Skylar looked like she was about to speak, but then the waiter returned with their entrées, followed by a busboy who refilled their water glasses. Once they were gone, Skylar quietly tucked the diary back into her purse and pressed her palms together. "Alright then, my official work at this dinner is done. Enough of the speeches and emotional mumbo jumbo, blah blah blah. Let's get to the good stuff."

"Good stuff?" KC raised her eyebrows. "You mean as in dessert?"

Skylar sighed. "I mean as in *girl talk*, Einstein. We're forty. We're not dead."

Daphne lifted a forkful of salmon and willed herself to smile at Skylar. "I think I'd pay to watch you in a meeting with your staff. I bet it's pretty entertaining." *I was going to be an award-winning journalist.*

"Oh yes, I run a tight ship," Skylar said, then tilted her glass toward KC. "So tell us, what's it like being married to a man in his fifties? I've never dated anyone that old, I mean that much *older*. You know what I mean."

KC cut into her mahimahi. "It's pretty great. He's emotionally mature, a fantastic life partner, my best friend and confidant: everything I could ask for, to be honest."

Skylar narrowed her eyes. "Really?"

KC swatted Skylar's arm. "Yes, *really*. Why are you so surprised?"

"I guess I'm just cynical that you can find all that in one person."

"Then I guess I'm just lucky," KC said with a grin.

"*He's* lucky," Daphne said to her.

KC put a hand over her heart. "Aw, thanks, Daphne."

Daphne took a big sip of her sangria. *I used to think I'd found all that in Brian. I couldn't see that it was an illusion of my own making. I was too young.*

Skylar looked at KC. "How old exactly is Max?"

"He'll be fifty-three in August," KC said.

Skylar leaned back in her chair. "No wonder you're not fazed by the idea of turning forty. You're always going to feel young in Max's circle. Maybe I should start dating older men too, then I won't have to worry about my wrinkles when I smile."

Daphne pictured the wrinkle cream in her bathroom.

"I'm thinking about trying Botox," Skylar added. "It might be time."

Daphne turned her head. "You are?" She'd never heard anyone outright mention Botox before, although she suspected a good chunk of the women in Columbus had done it. Daphne was one of the youngest mothers at Emma's school, but many of the others appeared to defy their age in ways that seemed less than natural. Then again, she'd bought wrinkle cream, so who was she to judge? They were all fighting the same war, just with different weapons.

Skylar nodded. "I figure if it makes me feel better about my appearance, what's the harm? When I feel good about my appearance, I feel good about myself."

KC smiled at her. "I've always loved that about you. You do what makes *you* happy, period. Screw what anyone else thinks."

Skylar tipped her head. "Why, thank you."

"You have that quality too," Daphne said to KC. "I've always admired that."

"We *all* have it. That's why we gravitate toward each other," Skylar said. "The cream rises to the top for a reason."

Daphne wished she were half as secure as her friends. For better or for worse, they knew who they were inside, and they were at peace with it. She struggled to stay focused on the conversation, trying to dissolve the images floating around in her head. Of her empty house in Ohio. Of the family photos now boxed up in the garage. *Stop it! You weren't happy in that life! It's time to move on!* This time she dug a fingernail into her palm to snap herself out of the trance. KC and Skylar had moved on to another topic of conversation.

"So how was your fortieth anyway?" Skylar crossed her knife and fork on her plate to indicate that she was done with her entrée.

"It was fun," KC said. "Nothing crazy."

"What did you do to celebrate?" Daphne asked, grateful that they hadn't noticed her drifting off . . . again. Or if they had, that they hadn't pointed it out.

KC's eyes got a little brighter. "*Well,* in the morning Max and I went for a long run on the beach."

Skylar pretended to shoot herself in the head. "Of course you did. I'd rather wax my lady bits than go for a long run on any morning, much less my *birthday*. But go on."

KC looked from Skylar to Daphne. "After our run Max showered and went to the office, and then a couple of my girlfriends took me to a yummy lunch at my favorite Mexican restaurant. Then that night Max put together a little dinner party at the house. Nothing crazy, just three couples, including us."

"He cooked for you?" Daphne asked. Brian had never cooked for her. Actually, that wasn't true. Before they were married, he'd made her a handful of candlelit dinners, but that stopped after Emma was born. So much had stopped after Emma was born, and then the miscarriages happened. *I was going to write for the* New York Times.

KC nodded. "Max loves to cook. I think that night he made shrimp scampi. That man has many talents, I tell you. Then after dinner we all walked downtown to play Bingo."

Skylar coughed. "Please tell me I heard that wrong."

KC grinned. "I can't say that you did."

Daphne cocked her head to one side. "You really played *Bingo*?"

"You bet we did," KC said. "And we rocked it."

Skylar groaned and set her drink on the table. "You realize that you turned *forty*, not *eighty* right? Good lord."

"Trust me, it's not as bad as it sounds," KC said. "This time of year they have Bingo every Friday at this bar called Watermans, which is on the main drag off Hermosa Beach that runs right up to the shoreline. It's all for charity, and it's packed with people of all ages. Trust me, we weren't the youngest people there, and we weren't the oldest either; kind of a rowdy crowd, but all in good fun. It's a blast, and they have some cool prizes too. Max won a pair of really nice snowboarding goggles."

Daphne flinched at the word *snowboarding*, her mind suddenly yanked to Park City. Her imagination began to torment her again, pinching her insides with a vision of a smiling Emma, Brian, and Alyssa perched on top of a snowcapped mountain, posing for a new family photo.

Grieving for the future she thought would be hers, for the family unit she'd spent years trying to keep intact, Daphne took a sip of water and balled her free hand into a fist under the table. *Please stop torturing yourself. You don't deserve this. Let it go.*

"So what's going on with your love life? Who's your latest boyfriend?" KC was asking Skylar.

Skylar took a sip of sangria. "Currently it's an Italian named Antonio, although his turn in the rotation is just about up."

The comment jolted Daphne back into the present, and she looked at Skylar. "You're still doing the rotation system?" she asked.

"I am. It's not necessarily what I envisioned for myself at this age, but it works for me, and if I've learned anything in my life, it's that you have to go with what works for you."

"Amen to that. How many are in the rotation right now?" KC asked.

Skylar closed her eyes and counted on her fingers. "These days it's Antonio, Michael, and Trevor. Oh! And Kristoff. Yikes, almost forgot Kristoff. He's new."

KC laughed. "I've never been able to keep track of all your men. You're amazing."

"It really is impressive," Daphne said. "When we were roommates, our answering machine was always on overdrive. Remember that time when you were dating two guys named Ben at the same time? I have no idea how you pulled that one off."

Skylar shrugged. "I like men, what can I say? Plus, my system keeps life interesting."

"So how does the rotation work exactly?" KC asked.

"There's no formal structure to it. They just kind of come and go in waves, and some of them circle back around after a while. Some never cycle back in, however. It really depends on a lot of factors. Some move away or get married. Or it just fizzles. I hang out with each guy for a month or two, and then before we get a chance to start bickering or anything, I move on to the next one. I have enough drama to deal with at work; I don't need it in my personal life too. With the rotation, I'm able to keep things light and playful, which is all I really want from a relationship. I have my sisters and girlfriends for the deeper stuff."

"You don't ever wish you could settle down with just one man?" Daphne asked. It was all *she'd* ever wanted.

Skylar frowned. "I don't know. Maybe if I met one who made me want to, but that hasn't happened yet. When I was younger, yes, I figured I'd get married someday down the road, but then I got so focused on my career and my priorities kind of changed. I'm not sure if that's because I haven't met the right person or because I'm just wired differently from other women. You know I have issues with commitment. I can't even decide which city I want to live in. Okay, I'm officially rambling. Damn, this sangria is good."

KC laughed and kissed her glass. "I'm kind of in love with it."

"How do you meet most of the men you go out with?" Daphne asked Skylar.

"It depends. Some through work, others through friends. Once in a while I do the online thing. There's no real formula," she said.

"Seems like a lot of couples meet online these days," KC said. "It's amazing how much the world has changed. Remember the days when a guy would actually call you on the phone to ask you on a date?"

Skylar gestured for the waiter to bring another pitcher of sangria. "Trust me, that doesn't happen anymore. It's all done over e-mail and text now. And while online dating is an easy way to meet a lot of men, it's not an easy way to meet the *right* men."

"Why is that?" KC asked. "Can't you just weed out the bad ones before ever meeting them? I would think that would make it a lot easier."

Skylar held up a finger. "*Theoretically*, yes. But in my experience, what you see in the profile and what you get in real life are usually quite different, and not in a good way." She looked at Daphne. "You know what I mean, right?"

Daphne bit her lip and shook her head. "I haven't tried the online thing."

Skylar looked surprised. "Really? Is it that easy to meet men in Columbus?"

Daphne didn't know what to say, so she took a big sip of her sangria and didn't say anything.

KC jumped in with another question for Skylar. "So how are the guys different from their profiles? You mean their photos are really old?"

Skylar nodded. "That happens sometimes, a lot, actually, especially with men in their forties. Another thing I've learned is that if a guy's photos are all faraway, it's probably because he doesn't look good up close, and by that I mean he's ugly. Same goes for if he's wearing sunglasses. Sunglasses usually equals ugly."

KC laughed. "You don't mince words, do you?"

Skylar shrugged. "I'm just being honest." Then she tapped her head. "I've also learned that if a guy is wearing a visor or a hat in his pictures, it's because he doesn't have much hair, if he has any at all. And most men claim they are at least an inch, if not *two*, taller than they really are, which for the life of me I don't understand, just like the hair or sunglasses thing. Do they really think I'm not going to notice they're short or balding or ugly the very moment we meet, like *immediately*?"

"Maybe they plan to be sitting down the whole date?" Daphne said with a hopeful look. "And wearing a hat and sunglasses?"

Skylar pointed at Daphne. "That happened to me once, not joking. The guy was sitting on the barstool when I arrived, and when he stood up like a half hour later, I thought he was still sitting down. That's how short he was. Lesson learned. Now if they don't list their height on their profile, I ask."

KC tapped her own head. "I'm shrimpy, so I've never really cared about the height thing."

Skylar gestured to herself. "Try being five nine. Trust me, you would care."

KC frowned. "You're right. Online dating sounds less awesome than I thought."

Skylar shook her head. "It's not *all* bad. I know a lot of people who have met some great people through it. You just have to know what to watch out for so you don't waste your time. And it's not just men who embellish their profiles. Women do too."

"How so?" Daphne asked.

Skylar framed her face with her hands. "For example, my male friends tell me they won't go out with a woman if her profile only includes photos that are up close."

Daphne touched her own cheek. "Why not?"

"Because that usually means she's overweight."

"Oh." Daphne sucked in her breath. "I never thought of that, but I guess it makes sense."

KC made a sad face. "That sounds mean."

Skylar shrugged. "It's reality. And those are just the superficial things. I think the biggest problem with dating sites, at least at our age, is that they're so female heavy that the most appealing men get bombarded with messages, and they just can't keep up. I know some quality guys from work who have profiles up, and they're so overwhelmed that they barely have enough time to weed through everything coming in, much less proactively search for women to contact."

"Women are really that aggressive?" KC asked.

"Yep. Apparently some women offer sex for money too."

"What?" Daphne's jaw dropped open.

Skylar rubbed her fingertips together. "I went on a date with a guy who told me a woman once cut to the chase after a few messages. She made it pretty clear that if he was willing to pay, she was willing to give."

Daphne's mouth was still open. "Wow."

"I don't think I could contact a man on a dating site. I'd be too chicken," KC said.

Daphne nodded. "So would I." *I'm too chicken even to post a profile.*

"It's not really my style, but women today are assertive, so if I see a guy I want to meet, I'll reach out," Skylar said. "But I don't expect to hear back because I'm not sure if they'll ever even read the note. My friend Jay says he gets *hundreds* of messages a month, and he's not even that attractive, although if you ever meet him, please keep that information to yourself. I've also learned that the men in their late thirties or forties are usually looking for younger women, so even if they *are* proactive in their searches, I don't even show up in the results—unless I were to lie about my age, which apparently a lot of women do for that exact reason. So the men who contact me are usually way older or way younger. It's rare that I hear from someone who is remotely attractive *and* relatively age appropriate."

Daphne frowned and took another sip of sangria. "This conversation is getting depressing."

"Totally," KC said. "It's depressing *me*, and I'm not even single."

Skylar shrugged. "It is what it is. Another fundamental flaw in the system is that the profiles have to be written, and not everyone is a good writer." She gestured to Daphne. "I know I don't have Daphne's gift for words, but at least I can put together a freaking sentence. If a guy doesn't know the difference between *you're* and *your*, it makes him look dumb, no matter how many advanced degrees he may have. Am I right?"

KC winced. "I have terrible grammar. You'd hate me online."

Skylar winked at KC. "*You*, I could never hate. But that's the problem with online dating. It forces you to notice things you wouldn't if you met someone organically, but when all you have to go on is the profile, it's tough. That virtual first impression sticks."

KC frowned. "This is not what I thought online dating was like *at all*. They make it look so fun in the commercials."

Skylar laughed. "Everything looks fun in commercials, Little Miss Sunshine. Buying Cialis looks like a trip to Disneyland in the commercials." She pretended to use a megaphone. "*Hey, everybody! I have erectile dysfunction! Isn't that fantastic?*"

Daphne laughed, grateful to be doing so in the midst of such a disheartening conversation. "What kind of men do you, um, *search* for?" she asked Skylar. The process sounded so clinical to her. "For example, what do you consider age appropriate?"

"I'll go older or younger by a decade or so, but I won't do married," Skylar said.

KC's eyes got big. "*Married?* Married people do online dating?"

Skylar nodded. "I hate to break it to you, Little Bo Peep, but married men do a lot of things."

KC covered her ears with her hands. "I don't know if I want to hear this."

Skylar reached over and removed one of KC's hands. "Please. I'm sure Max is as loyal as a German shepherd. I've just met a lot of married men over the years who don't seem to be all that concerned with the fact that, you know, their *wife* is at home waiting for them." She turned to Daphne. "I'm sure you've been hit on by married guys, right?"

Daphne shook her head. "Not that I'm aware of."

Skylar gave her a look. "I find that hard to believe."

Daphne stared at her lap. She'd been in such a fog for so long that she'd almost stopped paying attention to men entirely.

"How do you know they're married?" KC asked.

Skylar took a sip of her drink. "You mean online or in person?"

"Both."

"*Online*, sometimes they say it outright. But when I've met them in other situations, like at a trade show, for example, it depends. Sometimes they're wearing a wedding ring, but not always."

Daphne looked back up. "If they don't have a ring on, how do you know?" For the first time, she wondered if Brian had ever cheated on her. She certainly hadn't strayed, even when things between them were beyond repair.

Skylar set her glass on the table. "Sometimes the tan line gives it away."

KC laughed. "That's so sad, it's funny. Men think they can get away with that?"

Skylar reached for the sangria pitcher and refilled all their glasses. "Yes, some men are that stupid. A few weeks ago, after work, I met a man at a bar who told me he was in Manhattan for a few days for business. Very handsome, charming, the whole deal. And no ring, no *tan line* either. He bought me a couple drinks, then asked if he could take me to dinner the following night before heading home over the weekend."

Daphne and KC both leaned in closer.

"And?" KC said.

"And I said sure. Why wouldn't I?"

KC grinned. "Your life seems so fun. Most weeknights I go to bed at nine thirty."

Skylar continued. "So he pulled out his phone to get my number, and I noticed that his wallpaper backdrop was a picture of a little boy. I asked if it was his son, and he said yes. He didn't immediately follow that up by explaining that he was divorced, so I asked if he was married."

"And?" Daphne asked.

"And he hesitated for a moment before responding that yes, he was married, but that I should give him credit for being honest."

KC laughed. "Wow, that guy had some balls."

Skylar sipped her drink. "Oh, it gets better."

"What happened?" Daphne asked.

"He told me I should sleep with him because married men never have sex, meaning he'd put a lot of effort into it."

"That's not true!" KC shouted, then immediately covered her mouth with her hand. "Oops, sorry I got a little fired up there."

Daphne looked down. In the last years of their marriage, she and Brian rarely had sex. Early on they were intimate nearly every day, but after Emma was born that tapered off. Not overnight, but gradually, so gradually that it wasn't noticeable—until one day when it was.

"What did you say to the guy?" KC asked Skylar.

Skylar held up her index finger. "Before I could respond to his comment, he told me that I should *also* have sex with him because—and I swear I'm not making this up—because he has a big dick. Those were his exact words. 'I have a big dick.'"

"No way!" KC yelled, then covered her mouth with her hand again. "I'm sorry, I'm not used to drinking sangria. Or to hearing awesome stories like this."

Skylar laughed. "It's okay. You're funny when you drink."

"He really said that with a straight face?" Daphne asked.

Skylar crossed her heart. "You know I would never lie to you two."

"What did you say back to him?" Daphne asked. "I'd be speechless."

"I think I would have up and left." KC pounded her fist on the table.

Skylar gave them a sly smile. "I did leave, but first I came up with something pretty good. I stood up and casually reached for my purse, and then I smiled and told him *he* was a big dick. Then I calmly strolled out of the bar."

KC pumped her fist. "That's my girl!"

Daphne clapped her hands. "Well done. I'd probably still be sitting there with my mouth open."

Skylar bowed her head. "Thank you, thank you."

"I'm so fired up right now," KC said. "Can't no man be messing with my Skylar!"

"I love it when you drink," Skylar said to her. "Anyhow, the online thing isn't all bad. It just depends on what you're looking for, and when getting married and having kids isn't priority number one, you can have a little more fun with it. I have some girlfriends in New York who are hell-bent on finding a husband, so they treat online dating like a full-time job. They're basically managing a spreadsheet, trying to keep track of everyone."

"Sounds exhausting," Daphne said.

"I agree, but sometimes it's a necessary evil if you don't want to sleep alone, or if you want to procreate. So enough about *my* love life. What about you? What's the story in Columbus? If you're not online, how do you meet most of the men you go out with?" Skylar asked.

Daphne felt her neck get warm. She took a sip of water, then pretended to be looking at something on the beach.

Skylar and KC both turned their heads to follow her gaze.

"What are you staring at?" KC asked.

Daphne awkwardly pointed toward the ocean, which was barely visible in the moonlight. "Oh, I, um, I thought I saw a dolphin jumping."

"For real?" Skylar squinted. "Your eyes really *are* good."

"That's an understatement," KC said. "I can't see anything out there."

Daphne swallowed and looked at Skylar. "So getting back to the men in your rotation. What do they do for a living?"

Skylar set her glass down. "Kristoff's a banker, Michael's in pharmaceutical sales, Trevor's an attorney . . . and Antonio's a bartender. I've learned that bartenders are usually a lot of fun to date because they have hilarious stories. Drunk people do funny things."

"What are all their ages?" KC asked.

Skylar closed her eyes again to think. "Give me a minute . . . okay . . . Antonio's twenty-seven, Michael's thirty-three, Trevor's thirty-nine, and Kristoff is forty-two." She opened her eyes. "I think that's right."

KC whistled. "*Twenty-seven?* Wowsa. That's twenty-five years younger than my husband. A quarter century!"

Skylar shrugged. "What can I say? I don't discriminate. Plus, you're the one who said age is just a number, right?"

"I did say that," KC said. "I guess I never really thought about it backward like that."

The waiter returned to clear their plates, and after he was gone, KC picked up her drink and looked at Skylar. "The rotation thing sounds fun, but complicated. And maybe a little draining," she said.

"All of those adjectives are accurate, but enough about *me*." Skylar looked at KC. "I want to talk about you and Max again. How's the sex? Do men get better at it in their fifties? Or does it, you know, start to wilt a little bit?"

Daphne felt her cheeks flush. "Don't you think that's a little personal?"

"No," Skylar said without looking at her. "We're in the inner circle here, no subject is off-limits. So how is it? Is he paying close attention to the aforementioned Cialis commercials?"

KC laughed. "*No.* I have zero complaints in that department. Max is in great shape all the way around."

"He must be to keep up with you," Daphne said. "Although I don't know if anyone could keep up with you."

"How's his business going?" Skylar asked.

"Fantastic! Commercial real estate is booming in LA right now, so they're growing like gangbusters on the construction side. Jared's been there since graduation, which Max is thrilled about. He doesn't want to push, but it's sort of his dream to groom his firstborn to take over the business when he retires."

"What does Josh think about that? Is there any competition there?" Daphne asked. As an only child she'd always been curious about the sibling dynamic. Why were some adult siblings such close friends, while others rarely spoke to each other?

KC reached for her napkin. "Trust me, there's no rivalry there, at least where the family business is concerned. Josh would *never* want to work for his dad, much less have an office job of any kind."

"Not his vibe?" Skylar asked.

KC shook her head. "Far from it. He's only a sophomore, so we'll see how it pans out, but as of now he's planning to do Teach for America for a couple years. And after that, who knows? But I doubt commercial real estate is in his future. He's too much of a free spirit for an office job. I love that about him. Personally, I think he'd make a great elementary schoolteacher because he has such a gentle way about him."

"I could say the same about you," Daphne said to her.

KC smiled at Daphne and used her fingers to make a heart.

"I would be a horrible teacher," Skylar said. "I don't have the patience for it."

"Your dream of making enough money to hire a traveling hairstylist would be out the window on a teacher's salary, that's for sure," Daphne said.

Skylar held her glass in the air. "An excellent point. Yet *another* reason why I could never be a teacher."

"So to finish up on your original question: Max is great, Josh and Jared are thriving, there are no complaints, all is good on the home front." KC clinked her glass against Skylar's.

"You really love those boys, don't you," Daphne said to KC. It wasn't a question. The glow she saw in KC's eyes when she talked about her stepsons was how Daphne felt when she thought about Emma. A love so unconditional and pure, it was overwhelming at times. Emma was nearly old enough to drive now, but sometimes when Daphne looked at her, she still saw the miracle baby she'd carried home so gingerly from the hospital, and in those moments it took every ounce of Daphne's willpower not to smother her daughter with kisses, be it in the middle of a piano recital or volleyball match—or God forbid in front of other kids at school. She'd learned her lesson about that.

KC's face lit up. "You have no idea. Biggest surprise of my life."

"I'm glad you found Max," Skylar said. "I remember you used to say you would never get married and have a family, but I always felt that you would make a great mom. You're such a positive role model."

"I certainly didn't expect to become a stepmom of two teenage boys at age thirty-five, but it turned out to be one of the best things I ever did. Life can really sneak up on you, you know?"

Daphne felt a pang in her gut. *It sure can.*

"So speaking of kids, tell us about how Emma's doing," KC said to Daphne. "Is she in high school now?"

Daphne nodded. "She's a sophomore, which I still can't believe. She's getting her driver's license soon."

"Wow, I remember during our last birthday trip, you were telling us how you'd cried when you'd dropped her off at kindergarten," KC said. "Soon you'll be dropping her off at college."

"Oh gosh, don't remind me."

"Is she dating?" Skylar asked.

Daphne shook her head. "Not yet. Not ever, I hope." *Not that I know of. I bet Alyssa knows. Stop thinking about Alyssa!*

"Do you have a recent picture?" KC asked.

Daphne reached for her purse. "I have millions." She pulled out her phone and scrolled through the photos, then handed the phone to KC. "Here's one from her volleyball tournament last month."

KC smiled at the phone, then handed it to Skylar. "Look at that adorable face. Where did all those freckles come from? She looks more like my daughter than yours."

Daphne touched her own cheeks, then looked at her arms. "Brian and I have no idea. I have like ten freckles on my entire body, and he has even less."

Skylar studied the photo, then handed the phone back to Daphne. "She's still in that awkward gangly stage, but it's pretty clear she's going to be a swan once she emerges on the other side. Prepare yourself."

Daphne held the phone against her heart. "The thought of her going on a date makes me feel a little sick."

"So speaking of dating, what about *you*?" Skylar asked Daphne. "Are you dating anyone worth mentioning?"

Daphne felt her cheeks flush, and then she reached for her water glass. "No, not really." *Not at all.*

"Are you dating anyone *not* worth mentioning?" Skylar asked. "Those guys make better stories anyway."

KC grinned. "I agree. Any exciting flings? My divorcées are always regaling the class with tales of their romantic adventures, most of which don't really qualify as *dating* but sound pretty entertaining."

Daphne shook her head slightly, her nose still in her water glass.

Skylar raised an eyebrow. "A smart, attractive, single woman like you, and no stories to share? That doesn't add up."

Daphne suddenly felt a familiar sensation in the back of her head, and she knew that within seconds, her eyes were going to well up with tears. She noticed the waiter approaching them with dessert menus and was grateful for the forced break in conversation.

Skylar put her reading glasses back on and studied the list. "Do either of you want anything? I'm too stuffed for anything big, but I could be convinced to share something."

Daphne stood up. "I'm pretty full as well. I think I'll pass. Will you excuse me for a minute? I'm just going to run to the ladies' room." She tucked her chair close to the table and struggled to keep the tears at bay before her friends could see them. *Don't cry. Don't cry.*

KC held up her purse. "I have dark chocolate squares if you want one."

Skylar's eyes lit up. "Ooh, perfect. You still carry dark chocolate with you everywhere you go?"

"Always."

Skylar waved her fingers at the purse. "Gimme."

Daphne forced a smile. "Save me a square, okay? I'll be right back." *Please start talking about something else while I'm gone.*

She hurried inside toward the restroom, her eyes fixated on the wood floor. She didn't feel any tears yet, but she could feel her cheeks getting hot. The restaurant was filled with strangers she would most likely never see again in her lifetime, but she still hoped none of them would notice how upset she was. How embarrassed she was for losing her composure, *again*. How frustrated she was for still feeling like this: socially paralyzed, afraid to start dating, afraid of everything it represented. *Let the past go!*

Once safely ensconced in the empty restroom, whose bright white walls were adorned with nautical-themed paintings, she dotted a few tears away with a Kleenex. A small smudge of mascara under her left eye was the only evidence that she'd been on the verge of crying. She wiped it away and took a deep breath, then took a step back and looked at herself in the mirror, grateful to finally be alone. *What happened to you?*

The face looking back at her was the same that Skylar and KC remembered, but the person behind it wasn't. Where was the wide-eyed optimist who loved to laugh, who loved to try new things, who never backed down from a challenge, and who was excited about her future? *Where did you go?*

She splashed cold water on her face, then patted her cheeks with a paper towel—hard. *Get it together. You're stronger than this!* She dug around in her purse for some lipstick and blush, then did her best to conceal the fact that she'd been inches away from dissolving into tears. *You're going to be fine.*

Less than satisfied with the results but knowing she couldn't spend the evening hiding inside the restroom, she forced a less than convincing smile into the mirror, patted her cheeks one more time, and then made her way back outside.

.　　.　　.

"I still vote for the Monkees," Skylar said as Daphne returned to the table. "Davy Jones was dreamy."

KC shook her head. "No way. *Definitely* NSYNC. Justin Timberlake all the way, baby."

"JT is hot, I agree. But *DJ* was timeless. You'll see."

"What are you two talking about?" Daphne took a seat, relieved that the conversation had turned away from her dating life.

"We're debating who was the best boy band ever," Skylar said. "Super Jockette here is overlooking the obvious choice."

"What about the Beatles?" Daphne said.

"I don't think the Beatles count as a boy band," KC said. "They're so famous that they're like a regular band."

"Agreed," Skylar said.

"Emma likes One Direction," Daphne said.

Skylar shook her head. "History will prove me right. You just watch, my friends." She tapped her palms against the table. "So speaking of bands, who's up for a nightcap? I heard there's a great spot just down the beach that has live music."

KC began to speak, but Skylar put a hand in the air. "Wait. That wasn't a question, so allow me to rephrase. *Time for* a nightcap. There's a great spot just down the beach that has live music."

Daphne made a sheepish face. "Can we take a rain check? I woke up at five this morning."

KC followed suit. "I was up at three thirty. And you guys know I need my sleep."

Skylar gestured for the bill. "You can sleep when you're dead. Chop chop."

"What time is it?" KC asked.

Daphne looked at her watch. "Nine thirty."

KC yawned. "I may have to take back what I said about not being old. I'm kind of exhausted."

"Me too," Daphne said. "I can barely keep my eyes open. I'm sorry, Skylar."

Skylar signed the credit card receipt and stood up. "You're *really* too tired to go?"

KC and Daphne nodded in unison.

"Even for one drink?" Skylar looked incredulous.

They nodded again.

Daphne looked at her hands. "I'm sorry. Can we go there tomorrow night?"

"The bed in my room looked so comfortable," KC said in a tiny voice. "And that sangria made me so sleepy."

Skylar sighed. "You two are somewhat pathetic. If you were this lame in college, I don't know if we would have been friends."

"We know," KC and Daphne said in unison, although now they were kind of laughing.

Skylar held up a finger. "Okay, fine, I'll give you *one night* to get acclimatized, but only one. Our time together on this fabulous island is limited, so I want to make sure we get the most out of it."

"I promise I'll be more fun tomorrow," KC said.

"I don't know how fun I'll be, but at least I'll be awake," Daphne said.

KC poked her in the rib. "Stop it, you're always fun."

"Thanks, KC." Daphne gave her a weak smile. *I wish I felt that way.*

"Let's walk home," Skylar said. "I need to work off that amazing meal I just inhaled. Unless you wimps are too *tired* to walk?"

"I'm up for that," KC said.

The three of them descended the back steps of the restaurant, then removed their shoes and began strolling along the sand. They had taken a cab to the restaurant, which had wound through the quaint streets leading into the center of town, but in a straight line their house was barely a mile down the beach. It was dark out now, but the gentle air was still warm, the sand soft and squishy between their toes. The beach was dotted with couples and small groups meandering about. An older man sat alone on a large towel, staring out at the water. Daphne wondered what he was thinking. *Is he happy? Or is he hurting inside? Does he feel all alone?*

"I love the sound of the ocean," KC said. "There's something about it that's so soothing."

"I feel that way about a nice glass of wine . . . or three," Skylar said.

KC and Skylar kept walking, but Daphne didn't move or respond to Skylar's joke. Instead, she stood still and kept her eyes on the dark water.

"You okay, Daphne?" KC returned and put a hand on her arm.

"You left us again," Skylar said.

"I'm fine, just . . . tired." Daphne kept gazing out toward the sea.

"You sure?" Skylar didn't sound convinced.

Daphne nodded and forced yet another smile. The act was beginning to wear on her.

Skylar put an arm around Daphne and pulled her along the beach. "Hey, I just realized that you skipped to the restroom right when we were about to delve into your love life."

KC clapped her hands and did a little skip. "Ooh yes, let's hear about that."

Daphne wiggled out of Skylar's embrace and kept looking out at the water, afraid to make eye contact, afraid she would start crying if she did. "There's not much to tell."

Skylar waved a dismissive hand. "Nonsense. There's always something to tell. The magic is in *how* you tell it. So you're not dating anyone seriously, no big deal. Tell us about the last guy you smooched."

Daphne felt the tears coming back. *Please don't make me do this.* She began walking a little faster.

"Hello?" Skylar said.

Daphne didn't reply.

"I can't imagine dating again," Daphne heard KC say behind her. "I wasn't very good at it when I was single. I'd definitely be worse at it now."

Then Skylar spoke. "What are you talking about? I hope you'd be bad at dating, given that you're *married*."

Daphne glanced behind her and saw KC give Skylar's midsection a squeeze. "You know what I mean," KC said to Skylar.

Skylar and KC quickened their pace and caught up to Daphne.

"So spill and tell us something juicy," Skylar said. "And for the love of God, will you stop walking so fast? I'm going to get a cramp here."

Daphne slowed down—but just barely. She studied the sand in front of her, her toes sinking into it with each step.

"What is going on with you, Daphne?" Skylar said. "You're acting really weird."

Daphne suddenly stopped in her tracks. She took a deep breath, then finally let her eyes flicker toward Skylar. "I'm not ready to date yet, okay?"

Skylar glanced at KC, then back to Daphne. "Wait a minute. Are you saying you haven't dated since you and Brian split up?"

Daphne nodded.

"At all? In two-and-a-half years?" Skylar said.

Daphne began walking again. Fast. Then the tears arrived. This time for real. *Is it too late for me? Am I capable of having a healthy relationship? Do I even know what that means?*

She wiped the tears away with the back of her hand and kept moving, as if by staying in motion she could somehow escape the embarrassment of what she'd just shared. Skylar and KC were her best friends, but she didn't want them to see her this way. She didn't want them to know how much she was hurting inside, how empty she'd become. She kept walking as fast as she could, the tears now streaming down her face.

"Daphne, hon, please stop," Skylar called from behind.

KC trotted to catch up to her, a concerned look on her face.

Daphne tried to will the tears away, but it didn't work this time. She began crying harder, then coughing in a futile effort to make herself stop. Finally, she gave up walking and stood there, her shoulders slumping.

KC put a hand on her arm and squeezed. "Are you okay?"

Skylar joined them and caught her breath when she saw Daphne's face. "Oh, hon, what's wrong?"

Daphne didn't respond. Instead, the three of them stood there on the beach, Daphne now sobbing uncontrollably.

KC began to pet Daphne's hair. "Whatever it is, it's going to be fine."

After a few moments in which no one spoke, Daphne finally choked out the words. "Brian's . . . getting remarried."

Skylar sighed. "Damn it."

"Oh sweetie, I'm so sorry," KC said. She kept petting Daphne's hair.

Daphne coughed again and wiped the tears away from her eyes. "I haven't been on a single date since we split up, and now he's marrying *Alyssa*. Beautiful, perfect, thirty-three-year-old *Alyssa*."

"She sounds like a bitch," Skylar said.

Daphne let out a weak laugh, then dropped her flip-flops and crumpled downward to sit on the beach. She pulled her knees up to her chest, the tears still streaming down her cheeks, although with less intensity now.

Skylar and KC sat down next to her.

"I'm sorry," KC said. "I know that must sting."

"I'm forty years old and have to start all over. I'm a failure," Daphne whispered into her knees.

But Skylar and KC heard her.

KC began to rub Daphne's back. "Oh sweetie, that's not true, that's not true at all."

"Don't think like that, Daphne," Skylar said. "You're a *mother*, for crying out loud. How can you feel like a failure when you've raised a sweet girl like Emma, when you've done so much for her?"

Daphne rested her forehead on her knees. "Emma doesn't need me anymore."

KC began petting her hair again. "That's not true. Girls *always* need their mothers. I still talk to mine all the time."

Daphne kept her forehead pressed against her knees. "I know it's just a phase she's going through, but it hurts that she doesn't talk to me like she used to. Some days she barely talks to me at all."

"She's fifteen," Skylar said. "Who talks to their mom at fifteen? I think I went my entire junior year in high school without talking to mine. I was too busy obsessing over which pair of acid-wash jeans to wear with my Reebok high-tops."

Daphne coughed out a laugh. "I remember those high-tops."

"Me too. You rocked those kicks," KC said.

"My sisters have gone through this exact same thing," Skylar said to Daphne. "You can't take it personally."

"Rationally I know that, but I just miss her," Daphne said.

"I think it's good for teenagers to pull away from their parents a little bit. It means they're experimenting with the idea of becoming adults one day by testing the boundaries a little bit, which is an important step for them," KC said.

Skylar pushed KC's shoulder. "Look who's playing the role of the wise old lady."

KC laughed. "Josh and Jared each went through a bit of a phase, not exactly rebellious, but definitely a period where Max and I were hardly topping the list of people they wanted to spend time with. Yes, it takes some getting used to, but you'll adjust. In the meantime, try not to let it eat at you."

"But you and Max had each other to turn to during that phase," Daphne said, finally lifting her head. Then she looked at Skylar, her eyes watery. "And your sisters have their husbands. I have . . . just myself." She began to cry again, her shoulders slumping.

"Hey now, you have us," Skylar said. "We're not going anywhere."

Daphne wiped more tears from her cheeks. "I just feel so guilty . . . and sad . . . that I couldn't give her the family that I wanted for her." *That I wanted for myself.*

"Don't do that to yourself," Skylar said. "Lots of kids have divorced parents."

"I can't help it. I'm trying to keep it together in front of her, but I'm terrified she's going to see that I don't know what I'm doing with my life anymore, and that it's going to mess her up somehow."

"My sisters all tell me that kids come with their bags packed anyway," Skylar said. "You can do your best, but at the end of the day they are who they are."

"I agree," KC said. "Divorce doesn't mess children up. Living with unhappily married parents does."

"Besides, married or divorced, no family is perfect," Skylar said.

More tears streamed down Daphne's cheeks. "I'm so embarrassed," she sniffled.

KC gave her a strange look. "Embarrassed? Why in the world would you be embarrassed?"

"Because it's been more than two years, and I can't get over it."

"Over Brian? Or over the end of the marriage?" Skylar asked.

Daphne sighed and stared out at the ocean. "I'm not sure anymore."

"There's a big difference there," Skylar said.

"Do you still love him?" KC asked.

Daphne took a deep breath. "I think . . . I think part of me will always love him; I mean he's the father of my child . . . but no, I'm not *in love* with him anymore." The truth was, she hadn't been in love with him for a long time, and he certainly hadn't been in love with her. Was that what hurt so much? That they'd both wasted so many years on a marriage that wasn't working? Going through the motions just to keep up outward appearances?

"Then that's a *good* thing," KC said. "It's okay to mourn the demise of the relationship. You were together for a long time."

"I think it's more than that," Daphne whispered.

Skylar and KC exchanged a glance, then remained silent, giving Daphne time to elaborate.

Finally, Daphne spoke the truth. The complete truth. She told them the entire story, unvarnished.

When she was done, she stared at the sand. "I think . . . I think I feel like a failure for entering into a marriage that was probably doomed from the start," she said quietly.

"Don't say that," Skylar said. "You and he were madly in love. How were you supposed to know it wouldn't work out?"

Daphne pushed a strand of hair out of her eyes. "I just wish . . . I just wish I could go back and tell myself to wait until I knew him better, to focus on *myself* before molding my entire life around someone else's. All those places I was going to go, all those stories

I was going to write . . . I never did any of it." *I was going to win a Pulitzer.*

"I'm sorry for bringing the diary," Skylar said. "That was a boneheaded move. I didn't think it through."

"It's okay," Daphne said. "I know you didn't mean anything by it."

Skylar and KC kept watching her, KC still lightly stroking her hair. A few moments passed before Daphne spoke again. "I was too young to get married," she whispered. "I gave up too much."

"I know you were young, but that doesn't mean it was the wrong thing to do," KC said. "You can't beat yourself up about it."

Daphne sighed. "I was so naïve."

"Naïve how?" Skylar asked.

"It never occurred to me that the intense feelings Brian and I had for each other would go away . . . that one day they would just be . . . gone."

"No one can ever know that," KC said.

"But *I* would have known that if I'd known him better," Daphne said. "I rushed into it, and then once we were married and I had Emma, I lost who *I* was." Tears started sliding down her cheeks again. "I was so stupid to let it happen."

Skylar narrowed her eyes. "What do you mean? Let what happen?"

Daphne didn't reply.

Skylar's eyes became dark. "He didn't . . . *hurt* you, did he? I swear to God, if he ever touched you—"

Daphne quickly shook her head. "No, never. It was just that when we met, I was on my way to *becoming* someone, you know? I had a real future, and then—poof—it was gone." *I was gone.*

"That's not true, Daphne. You have a wonderful daughter you adore. That's *huge*," KC said. "You have to be proud of that."

Daphne wiped a tear from her cheek. "I know, and I am, but we all know I used to want to be something *in addition to* a mom. Brian was never going to be on board with that, but I was too blind to see it."

Skylar nodded slowly. "Ah, now I get it."

"He's old-fashioned?" KC said.

Daphne laughed weakly, her eyes still wet. "He never even changed a diaper. Can you believe I married a man like that?"

"I think a lot of women marry men like that," Skylar said. "They don't discuss the division of labor before kids enter the picture, but when they realize they aren't on the same page as their husbands, it's too late and they're stuck doing all the work."

Daphne nodded slowly. "That's exactly what happened to me." *I can't believe I let it happen to me. I thought I was smarter than that.*

"Did you ever, you know, ask him to help?" KC asked.

Daphne squeaked out a laugh. "If it were only that easy."

"I'm sorry, that was a dumb question," KC said.

Daphne smiled and put a hand on KC's arm. "That's okay. It's just, or I should say it *was* just, hard. I was so young, and I didn't know what I was doing, and I think I just gave up battling him because it didn't seem worth wrecking my marriage for. I decided it was better to . . . keep the peace." *I always kept the peace.*

"Do you think it would have wrecked your marriage if you had spoken up?" Skylar asked.

Daphne frowned. "I don't know, but at the time I thought it would. So I gave up on the career thing and put all my energy into being a good mother, but when I look back now, I realize that while I love my daughter, that decision probably contributed to the deterioration of my marriage because I stopped being *myself,* stopped being the Daphne Brian fell in love with, and the Daphne who fell in love with Brian." *I miss that person.*

"You're still Daphne to me," KC said. "It's been wonderful hanging out with you again."

Daphne closed her eyes. "You're just being nice. You know I'm not the same. I'm a fragment of who I used to be."

"None of us are the same as we were in college," Skylar said. "We're adults now, Daphne. We've all changed."

"But at the core, where it really matters, you two seem the same to me," Daphne said. "I don't think you could say that about me."

KC shook her head. "You're being too hard on yourself."

"I think what you're feeling is totally normal," Skylar said. "Not that I have any experience with divorce, but I have several friends who do, and you'd be surprised at how often the word *failure* creeps into the conversation. Failure for having chosen the wrong person. Failure for not trying hard enough to make it work. Failure for not living up to society's expectations."

Daphne sighed. "I don't know anyone in Columbus who's divorced. I feel like a pariah at Emma's school sometimes. Some of the other mothers, the way they look at me . . ." Her voice trailed off. "It's like they think there's something wrong with me."

"They're probably just resentful because they're not happy in their own marriages," Skylar said.

Daphne frowned at the thought. "You think so?"

Skylar shrugged. "You never know, but I wouldn't be surprised. No one knows what's going on behind closed doors in a relationship, so who is anyone to judge when two people decide to pull the rip cord?"

"Amen," KC said. "I don't like people who judge. Except real judges, of course. They're cool."

"What about your friends out there?" Skylar asked. "They support you, right?"

Daphne felt her cheeks flush, then picked up a handful of sand. "I don't really have any close friends, just people I know from

Emma's school and around the neighborhood. There's Carol, a nice older lady who lives across the street, but she's the only one." She'd never officially admitted that before, but there was no use hiding it now. There was no use hiding any of it now.

Skylar and KC exchanged a look but didn't say anything. They understood.

Daphne watched the sand slide through her fingers. "Everyone thinks he left me, and I guess technically he did, but I knew a long time ago that it wasn't working anymore, maybe even before he did."

"How long?" Skylar asked.

"Years," Daphne whispered.

"Oh hon," Skylar said.

"I'm so sorry you had to go through that," KC said.

Daphne sighed. "I knew it wasn't working, but I was *committed*, you know? And we had Emma, and all her activities, and there was so much to do to keep the household running that I wouldn't let myself face it . . . I couldn't bring myself to face it. It was almost like I was subconsciously waiting for Brian to be the one to wave the white flag and say he wanted out, and one day he finally did."

KC and Skylar remained silent.

Daphne took a deep breath. "I know it's for the best that we're not together anymore, I really do. But I'm still . . . and I know this probably sounds crazy given everything I just told you . . . but I'm still hurt that . . . that I was so easily replaceable," she whispered the last words.

"Oh sweets," Skylar said. "Don't feel that way."

"I can't help it. It's bad enough that everyone thinks he left me. Now he's found someone else first, and I feel like a cliché because I gave up my career to be a stay-at-home mom. I was an honor student at Northwestern, and now I'm working part-time in a flower store."

"I love flowers," KC said.

Daphne gave her a weary yet grateful smile. "I love *you*," she said.

Skylar held up a finger. "First of all, it doesn't matter *who* pulled the trigger. If it wasn't working, it wasn't working, and prolonging the inevitable would have only hurt you both more."

"Exactly. Who cares who blinked first?" KC said. "Who would even know something like that?"

Skylar held up another finger. "And *second* of all, who cares if he found someone else first? That has nothing to do with you. It's not like he left you *for* this Alyssa woman." She hesitated. "He didn't leave you *for* her, right?"

Daphne shook her head. "No, he didn't meet her until after we split up. I'm sure of that, but it's still hard to watch. I just wish I'd found the strength to leave, to rebuild my life instead of behaving like a passive bystander in it. If I'd done that, I don't think I would care so much about where Brian's going because I'd be focused on where *I'm* going. Instead, I feel stuck."

"I'm sorry if the moms are being catty about it," KC said. "I've seen that side of parenting, and I'm not a fan."

Daphne groaned. "Tell me about it. The gossip in our town is terrible. It's like high school, only meaner, because people aren't talking about your prom date, they're talking about your *marriage*."

KC nodded. "I witnessed my share of the chatter when I entered the picture at Josh and Jared's school. Divorces, affairs—everyone knows everyone else's business. Suburban gossip can be fierce."

Skylar made a face. "Remind me never to move to the 'burbs. Don't any of these women have jobs?"

"I'm sure some of them do, but they're not the ones I interact with," Daphne said.

Skylar pointed at her. "Now you know who your new friends need to be. Women who have too much going on to be digging through other people's laundry baskets."

Daphne laughed weakly. "Trust me, I've been thinking that for a long time."

"Why didn't you tell us any of this before?" KC asked. "If I were this upset, I probably would have brought it up while we were still at the airport."

Daphne smiled and wiped a tiny tear from her cheek. "That's because you're you. The truth is, I didn't bring it up because I didn't want you two to see me this way."

"What way?" Skylar asked.

Daphne laughed and gestured to herself. "*This* way. Hysterical, insecure, racked with self-doubt, an emotional train wreck."

"But we're your *friends*, Daphne," KC said. "You shouldn't have to pretend around us. We take you as is, remember? The Three Musketeers, together forever?"

Skylar nodded. "She's right, you know. We love you no matter what."

"I guess I just didn't want you two to see how differently my life has turned out than what . . . than what I expected it would be," Daphne said.

Skylar shook her head. "We care about *you*, not your résumé." She looked at KC. "Is your life résumé the way you expected it to be at this age?"

KC shook her head. "Not even close. As we just saw in Daisy the diary, my plan was to be a lifer in the Peace Corps, remember? Look at me now. I drive a *Mercedes*, for crying out loud. And while I do love being married to Max, dealing with his drug-addicted brother is another story. I can't say *hosting an intervention* was on my bucket list, but—boom—there it is."

Skylar tapped KC's arm. "Forget what I said earlier about refraining from gossip. That sounds juicy, so I'll be following up on it later."

KC smiled and looked at Daphne. "See? No one's life goes exactly the way they think it will when they're in college. We all have hiccups and detours along the way. That's what makes it interesting."

Skylar nodded. "Definitely. Anyone who tells you otherwise is probably hiding a dead body in the basement."

Daphne laughed, softly but sincerely. "You guys are so great. I'm sorry for turning our first night here into a sob show."

Skylar held up a hand. "Stop that. From now on, no apologizing for your feelings, okay? If you want to cry, then cry. If you want to laugh, then laugh. If you want to complain about your ex-husband, then complain about your ex-husband. This trip is about celebrating the fact that we've been alive for four decades, and I don't want any of us to feel like we have to put on an act and make our lives look like something they're not."

"Well put," KC said with a smile. "I can totally picture that on a greeting card."

Daphne smiled. "I wish I shared your sunny take on the whole *turning forty* thing. Right now I just feel like a middle-aged woman with a broken past and nothing to look forward to."

Skylar stood up and clapped some sand off her hands and backside. "Okay, I realize that ten seconds ago I said I wanted us to speak freely on this trip, but that might be the biggest load of crap I've ever heard." She held up a finger again. "*First* of all, you're not middle-aged. As you yourself pointed out over dinner, you're still in your thirties; is that not correct?"

Daphne nodded.

"Good. Now, thirties is hardly middle-aged, and anyone who would suggest otherwise is an idiot." She held up a second finger.

"And *second* of all, as we also discovered during dinner, your eyes are still functioning like they did when you were a teenager, is that not also correct?"

Daphne nodded again.

"Good. More evidence that you're not ready for a senior living community anytime soon. And for the record, only those whose eyes aren't working *at all* couldn't see how gorgeous you are for a woman of any age; is that not correct as well?" She looked at KC.

KC agreed. "I was shocked to hear you haven't been dating. I figured you'd have men chasing you down the street, or the cul-de-sac, or wherever it is that you live."

Skylar clasped her hands together. "Good, we're all on the same page. Daphne, you are intelligent, genuine, and more beautiful than you've ever been, so for the love of God, let's get you back on track to living the life you deserve, which is one filled with love, friendship, happiness, and—for this week at least—lots of mango sangrias, margaritas, and rum punches. Are you with me?" She held her hand down to Daphne.

Emotionally exhausted but no longer despondent, Daphne looked at her friends and felt an enormous wave of relief begin to wash over her. She'd been so scared of revealing her true feelings, yet now that she had, she wondered what she'd been so afraid of. They loved her then, and they loved her now. *I'm still the same person to them,* she realized. *Maybe I'm not as lost as I think I am.*

Feeling drained yet hopeful, she held out her hand to Skylar. "All right, I'm with you. That sounded like another greeting card, by the way."

"Maybe I should look into that as yet another side business," Skylar said. "Apparently I'm full of creativity this week."

KC jumped up. "You're full of something, that's for sure."

"Watch it, pip-squeak," Skylar said. "I could squash you like an ant just by sitting on you."

Skylar and KC each took one of Daphne's hands, then pulled her up to a standing position. As KC wiped the sand off her backside, Skylar stood in front of Daphne and put her hands on Daphne's shoulders. "Are you feeling better now? Even a little?"

Daphne nodded, then smiled as she wiggled her feet back into her flip-flops. "I am." *I really am.*

"Good." Skylar slipped an arm around her and gently nudged her back toward the beach house. "Now let's get some sleep. Tomorrow night I'm not taking any excuses about how tired you two are."

"Uh oh," KC whispered from behind them.

"I heard that," Skylar said without turning around.

"What happened to your selective hearing?" KC asked with a groan.

"What did you say?" Skylar put her hands behind her ears, then looked over at Daphne and winked.

# Chapter Six

When Daphne woke up the next morning, she yawned and stretched her arms overhead. Slowly the deliciousness of her new surroundings washed over her. *I'm in an extravagant house on spectacular St. Mirika. With Skylar and KC.*

That was quickly followed by another realization. *I broke down last night. They know now. But it's all right.* The budding sense of hopefulness she'd felt on the beach last night was still there. *I'm going to be okay.*

Then a third realization hit her, this one not as easy to swallow. *Tomorrow I turn forty. Forty! Wow.*

She stretched her arms again, then froze. Perched high on the far side of the ceiling, over near the glass doors leading to the deck, was a small gecko.

"Hey little guy, what's your name?" Daphne said softly. She held a hand to her ear, pretending to listen, then made up a name for her new friend.

"Fred, did you say? It's nice to meet you, Fred. I'm Daphne, and I'm going to be forty years old tomorrow. What do you think of that?"

She chuckled to herself. *What is wrong with me?*

Whatever the impetus, it felt good to laugh. She pulled the duvet to one side and gently swung her legs to the tile floor. She wiggled her feet into a pair of disposable slippers she'd found the night before in the closet—they looked just like the ones she'd seen in hotel rooms and were wrapped in a tidy band made of thick white card stock—then shuffled into the bathroom to get ready to face the day.

As she brushed her teeth and looked at her reflection, she realized how much better she felt than she had just twenty-four hours ago. Something was missing now: a weight she'd been carrying around for so long that she'd forgotten what it felt like not to have it dragging her down. She hadn't planned to confess her struggle to come to terms with her failed marriage, but breaking down and opening up to her friends had lifted an enormous burden off her psyche. It was liberating.

She set the toothbrush down on the sink and spoke silently to the woman in the mirror. *This is your last day in your thirties. You're on a beautiful tropical island with your two best friends. You'd better make the most of it!*

There was no use fighting it. Like it or not, at this time tomorrow, she'd be forty. She was still dreading it, but not nearly as much as she'd been just yesterday. She was smart enough to recognize that for the mental victory it was. *At least I don't need reading glasses yet.*

After finishing up in the bathroom, she returned to the bedroom to check her phone. Her face lit up at the notice of a text message from Emma, the first she'd received since before she left for the airport. With the message was a photo of Emma and Brian on a chairlift, waving at the camera through snowflakes, silly grins on their pink faces.

*Hi Mom, having a great time! Hope you are too. Happy early birthday if this reaches you!*

She smiled at the message and briefly held the phone close to her heart. It had been a long time since Emma had sent her a friendly text like that. She typed a quick reply, then set the phone down on the desk, trying not to think about who had taken the photo.

She looked up at the ceiling. "Hey, Fred, my daughter's on vacation with my ex-husband and his new fiancée. Isn't that *great?*"

She chuckled again to herself. *I think I'm losing it. But at least I'm laughing and not crying, right?*

She finished dressing, then glanced up at the gecko one last time and waved good-bye before shutting her bedroom door and making her way down the hall.

．　．　．

"Good morning, sunshine, did you sleep okay?" KC said in a hushed voice from the kitchen, then put a finger to her lips and jutted her chin toward the living room. Daphne turned her head and saw Skylar hunched over her laptop, headset on, her dexterous fingers once again flying over the keyboard.

"Yes . . . got it . . . yes . . . got that too. Wait a minute, Jason, could you please repeat that last number? Hmm . . . okay, yes this time around, but that can't happen again. No really, it can't, trust me."

Daphne glanced at KC, who responded with an "I have no idea" gesture.

Skylar kept talking. "You've *got* to get me a meeting with Alfonso next week, okay? Yes, yes. Got it. And what about Germany? We have an analyst call in two weeks. Without that report, they're going to be at our throats. Julie, did you hear that?"

"She never stops, does she?" Daphne whispered.

"I guess not," KC whispered back. "Want some coffee?" She held up her mug. "They've got one of those superdeluxe machines that brew one delicious cup at a time. I was about to go enjoy this on the deck and admire the view. Come join me!"

Daphne smiled. "Sounds heavenly. You go ahead, I'll make myself a cup and meet you out there."

KC pointed to the half-and-half and sugar she'd left out on the counter, then carefully made her way past Skylar. She quietly opened the French doors leading outside as Daphne tiptoed into the kitchen. She pulled a white ceramic mug from one of the cabinets and set it under the nozzle of the coffeemaker, then pressed the button. As she watched it brew, she listened to bits and pieces of Skylar's side of the conversation and wondered what the discussion was about. It had been ages since Daphne had been in an office environment, so much of the jargon sounded like a foreign language to her.

"Have they finished the RFP yet? If not, they're going to drag down the entire CRM implementation . . . The data for that IBU is in the cloud. Yes, check the content management system for Asia Pac . . . How's the pipeline visibility for Germany?"

Daphne stirred sugar into the mug, then picked it up and watched her friend. Skylar's brow was furrowed in concentration, her mouth tense. In Daphne's mind, Skylar's corporate life had always seemed so glamorous, especially when compared to her own suburban existence, but right now it didn't look all that appealing.

She took a sip of her coffee. *Is that what my life would be like if I'd gone down that route? Would I be working right now too? On my vacation?*

She tiptoed toward the glass doors leading to the deck, which KC had left slightly ajar. Skylar looked up and gave her a weary smile as she passed. Daphne thought she looked tired. And a little stressed.

Daphne smiled back, then gently shut the doors behind her.

. . .

"Maybe it's because I've had a good night's sleep, but I think it's even prettier here today than it was yesterday," Daphne said as she settled into a deck chair next to KC.

KC propped her legs up on a bench. "Probably because you had a good cry too. Remember what Eleanor said yesterday about how rain makes you see things in a new way? Tears are a form of rain, in my opinion."

Daphne flinched. "Can we maybe not talk about my meltdown? Or at least not yet? It's eight o'clock in the morning."

KC grinned. "Meltdown, that's cute. Spoken like a true mom."

Daphne smiled weakly, then gazed out at the clear water. "*Anyhow*, I think the water has a little blue in it today. Yesterday it was more green. The sand looks just as white, though. Stunning, isn't it?"

KC reached over and clinked her mug against Daphne's. "Here's to another day in paradise, and yes, I realize I kind of just plagiarized a Phil Collins song. Who knows what other adventures await?"

"In all seriousness, thanks for being there last night," Daphne said as she sipped her coffee. "I know that wasn't one of my finer moments."

"Nonsense. It was one of your *finest* moments."

Daphne gave her an incredulous look. "How so, exactly?"

KC set her mug down and sat up straight. "Do you know how many people go through their entire lives pretending everything is okay when it's not, burying their feelings, never being able to confide in anyone? It's toxic to keep all that bottled up inside, but people do it because they're terrified to admit that their life isn't perfect."

Daphne frowned. "I never thought about it that way. I guess I knew *I* was doing it, but it never occurred to me that other people were doing it too."

"I'm proud of you for having the guts to pull the curtain back a little bit." KC pointed to the cloudless sky. "And it's only rained once. Remember what Eleanor said? Think how enlightened we're going to be by the end of the week. Geniuses, probably."

Daphne laughed. "I guess we'll see."

"So are you still up for a workout on the beach? We should go before it gets too hot."

Daphne grimaced. "I want to, but I'm kind of scared."

KC waved a dismissive hand. "Don't be scared. It will be fun, I promise. I'm not out to kill anyone. And afterward we can walk to that hut with the banana on top and get a smoothie."

Daphne glanced down the beach and had an unsettling thought. If they did their session on the stretch between here and the smoothie shop, there was a decent chance Clay from yesterday and his bachelor-party friends would see them at some point. She wasn't thrilled at the idea of *anyone* seeing her suffer through a sweaty exercise session, much less a group of men in their twenties.

She blinked. *Why am I thinking about this? What is the big deal? Although, it was kind of fun talking to him.*

She swallowed and casually pointed in the other direction. "I'll do it, but I'm thinking it would be cool to check out a new part of the beach. Maybe we could do the boot camp down that way?"

"Sure, I'm easy." KC took another sip of her coffee, then kissed the mug. "Have you noticed that even the *coffee* tastes better here than at home?"

Daphne smiled. "I think that's because the machine that brewed it probably cost more than my car did."

"Perhaps, but part of me thinks tiny fairies sprinkled St. Mirika with magic dust that makes everything here beautiful and yummy." She used her fingertips to make pretend droplets fall from the sky.

"Good morning, ladies, sorry for having to begin our first full day here with another work call, but it is what it is." Skylar's voice suddenly boomed from inside the house, then returned to a normal decibel as she stepped out on the deck. "Wow, it's already getting warm out here."

"Everything okay at the office?" KC asked. "That call sounded a little tense."

Skylar shrugged. "A minor crisis, but nothing I haven't been through before."

"You were right about your work demeanor," Daphne said. "You sound so professional on the phone. It's impressive."

Skylar did a little curtsy. "Well, thank you, my love. I do my best."

"We were just talking about doing a beach workout, then heading over to check out that smoothie place," KC said. "You in?"

Skylar shook her head. "I was *planning* to, but . . ."

KC raised her eyebrows.

Skylar laughed. "Okay, I'm totally lying, I wasn't planning to, and yes, I know I shook your hand, but in court I would swear that was under duress. Plus, I've been doing supported squats all morning."

"Supported squats?" Daphne said with a cough. "As in . . . sitting down?"

Skylar winked at her. "Indeed. I might be able to join you for the smoothie part, though."

"If you're breaking our deal, does that mean I'm off the hook for shopping?" KC said.

Skylar gestured toward the glass door. "Anyone want some more coffee while I'm in the kitchen?"

Daphne and KC both raised their hands. "I assume you didn't hear my question about the shopping?" KC asked.

"You assume correctly," Skylar said. "Two coffees, coming right up."

. . .

KC adjusted her baseball cap, this one purple with "NU Soccer" embroidered in white across the bill. She clapped her hands together and began to twist her torso back and forth as Daphne was laying out a large beach towel on the warm sand—and wishing she could lie there with it.

KC pointed about thirty yards down the beach. "Let's start with some light stretching, and then we'll do some easy shuttles from here to that rock. Sound good?"

Daphne stood up straight, gave her beach towel a yearning glance, then lifted her arms out to either side. "We've already established that I don't have much of a choice in this particular matter, so I think that's a superfluous question."

KC squinted at her. "What's *superfluous?*"

"Unnecessary. What's a shuttle?"

"Just a light jog. We'll do ten up and back, no break in between."

"Does up and back count as two?"

KC laughed. "No. Now let's get these vibrant bodies of ours moving. Did you put sunscreen on? Your skin looks a little pink."

Daphne adjusted her ponytail. "Trust me, I practically took a bath in the stuff. And for the record, I prefer *rosy glow* over *pink.*"

KC grinned. "Okay, just checking. The sun is a wonderful life force, but it can be dangerous. I'm liking that your argumentative side is making a comeback, by the way."

Daphne smiled as they began to jog. *I'm liking it too.*

. . .

Forty-five minutes later, Daphne feared her legs were going to give out. She felt the sweat dripping down her face as she jogged in place, tapping her palms to her knees as KC counted out loud. She couldn't remember the last time she'd been this exhausted. In addition to the shuttles and running in place, they'd done multiple sprints, squats, sit-ups, planks, and lunges.

She looked over at KC, her breath heavy. "Are we almost done? I think I might actually collapse in a heap, right here on the sand." *At least I wouldn't be sobbing this time.*

KC grinned at her. "Almost done, pal. Just twenty more. Come on, you can do it. Watch me. Knees high, knees high."

Daphne lifted her tank top and used it to wipe the sweat off her face. "I feel like we're in one of those commercials they show for exercise videos at three in the morning. Not that I watch TV at three in the morning, of course."

KC laughed, but didn't stop. "That's it, just like this. Keep it going, keep it going."

Daphne did her best to imitate her diminutive friend, who never seemed to run out of energy. "How can you be so cheerful right now? I'm dying!" she squeaked out.

KC didn't slow down. "You'll get the hang of it. That's it, knees high, knees high. Count down with me now, we're almost done."

Together they counted backward from ten, then KC clapped her hands together. "That's it, Daphne; you did it! Nice job!"

Daphne immediately put her hands on her hips and began to walk in small circles, trying to catch her breath. "Oh my God, I'm so glad that's over."

KC trotted over and put a hand on Daphne's shoulder. "Seriously, Daphne, you did amazing. You're in much better shape than I expected, given the way you were talking."

Daphne gave her a look. "You think I'm in *shape*? I think I just almost died."

KC laughed. "Says you. It will be easier tomorrow, I promise."

"Tomorrow? Are you crazy? There's no way I'm doing that again tomorrow. I'm already afraid I'm not going to be able to walk tomorrow."

KC shook her head. "I wasn't planning for us to do *this* tomorrow. The key to staying fit is to mix things up so you don't get bored. So we can do another workout like this again later in the week. Tomorrow . . . I was thinking we could go for a nice run along the beach, or maybe a hike."

Daphne began walking back toward the house. "Are you trying to kill me? Is that your plan? I always had a suspicion that you never really liked me."

KC quickly caught up to her and pinched the flesh above her hip. "You finally figured that out, did you? But really, you did great just now, and I love how it's brought out the fiery side of you."

"Just think what a bitch I'd be if we lived in the same town."

KC laughed and adjusted her baseball cap. "I'd have you playing soccer before you knew what hit you. Now let's go see if Skylar's done with her call. I'm dying for a smoothie!" She picked up her beach towel and shook it out, then rolled it into a log and trotted ahead toward the house.

.  .  .

A half hour later, Daphne, Skylar, and KC were sitting on a bench at the smoothie place—officially named Bananarama, to Daphne's delight—each with a fresh, cold drink in hand.

"Delicious," KC said as she took another sip. "I have zero idea what's in this, and you know what? I don't care."

"What's yours called?" Daphne asked. "Skylar and I both got a Mango Madness."

"That's island speak for *no leaves*," Skylar added.

KC licked the side of her cup. "Mine is Taste Explosion. That's a pretty accurate description of what's going on in my mouth right now."

Skylar studied her mostly orange-colored smoothie. "Can you imagine if these had alcohol in them? Maybe that's another business we should explore along with the mango sangrias." Then she looked at Daphne. "So you survived the workout?"

Daphne groaned. "*Survived* being the operative word. It wasn't pretty."

"Please, you did great." KC lightly punched Daphne's arm.

"Ouch." Daphne covered the spot with her hand. "I'm fragile, remember?"

KC laughed, then looked at Skylar. "Maybe you can go for a run with us tomorrow?"

Skylar shrugged. "We'll see. I may have another conference call."

"For real?" Daphne asked. "Or are you just avoiding the torture chamber?"

"I take offense at that," KC said.

Skylar sipped her smoothie. "Depends on what I hear from a few people on my team later today. But I'd rather not think about work right now. I suggest we go back to the house and relax on the beach for a while, then shower and head to the center of town for some lunch and shopping."

"Shopping?" KC did not look thrilled. "What about our deal that was declared null and void?"

"C'mon, tomboy, throw me a bone, okay? I promise it won't be that bad. Plus, we're going dancing tonight, remember? Maybe you can find something fun to wear. And I *definitely* want to see you in something girlie for Daphne's birthday dinner. I'm thinking pink. And flowers. Maybe even a bow. Although I'm kidding about the bow."

KC ran her fingers over the bill of her baseball cap. "Can I wear this with a dress?"

"Only if you want to be eating alone. Daphne, what say you? You up for a trip into town?"

Daphne nodded. "Sounds good to me, although just to warn you, I may need to sit down on a bench at some point, or maybe lie down when we get back. My body is already rebelling from what I just put it through." She put a hand on her lower back and grimaced.

Skylar smiled and stood up. "Lying down is what the *beach* is for, my dear. Now let's get a move on. The golden tan I don't have is waiting for me to claim it."

Together they headed back toward the house, flip-flops in hand, their feet ankle deep in the clear water. The sun was hot but not unbearably so, a cool breeze dancing across the shore. There were a fair number of people sunbathing on the soft sand and frolicking in the gentle waves near the smoothie hut and neighboring area, but the farther they got from the hotels marking the center of town, the less crowded the beach became. For a stretch it was just the three of them, and they strolled in a brief yet comfortable silence. As she admired the quiet beauty surrounding them, Daphne thought about what had happened as they'd covered the same route after dinner, how she'd finally opened up—and the sky didn't come crashing down.

She glanced up at the handful of clouds swirling above them. Were they due for another rainstorm soon? *I hope so.*

"Any word from Emma?" KC asked Daphne.

"I got a text. Sounds like she's having fun, although it makes me nervous that she's in a different state without me."

"Try not to worry so much. She's with her *father*, not a gang of convicted felons. It's not like she's going to get into any trouble," KC said.

"I know, but still, it's hard. As I'm sure you've noticed, when it comes to Emma, I'm kind of a worrier."

"I can't believe you have a teenage daughter," Skylar said. "Did you freak when she got her period?"

Daphne coughed out a laugh. "You have no idea. I'm still a little traumatized."

KC gestured toward the ocean. "Remember how traumatic going swimming used to be before we started using tampons?"

"I've never used anything but tampons," Skylar said.

KC looked at her. "Even in the beginning? In the beginning I was way too scared to try them."

Skylar shook her head. "I have older sisters, remember? From day one they refused to let me use a pad, said it was like straddling a surfboard."

Daphne laughed. "That's a pretty accurate description. A little too graphic for my taste, but accurate."

"My sisters don't sugarcoat things," Skylar said. "Hard as it may be to imagine, I'm the soft one in my family."

"Hey, check it out." KC pointed down the beach to what appeared to be a game of touch football.

The trio came to a stop about thirty feet away from the action, which looked a little rowdy and not all that organized, yet quite fun. A pair of wireless speakers set on a beach towel played reggae music, providing a tropical, low-key backdrop that belied the very American competition playing out on the sand.

"Babe alert," Skylar said under her breath.

"Which one?" KC asked.

"Take your pick," Skylar said with a little whistle.

Daphne scanned the group. Of at least a dozen men running here and there, none caught her eye until she spotted a familiar face.

It belonged to Clay Hanson.

She immediately smoothed a hand over her ponytail and found herself wishing she didn't feel quite so . . . frumpy. Skylar was wearing a pretty green sundress and looked as put-together as ever, but she and KC were still in their sweaty workout gear. She knew it was silly to care about her appearance, but she did.

Sure, Clay was a few years younger than she was, but there was just something about him that made her want to look . . . *attractive.* Or at least more attractive than she felt right then.

She glanced at the tote bag she was carrying. It contained sunscreen, two bottles of water, her wallet, a visor, a pair of sunglasses, and a beach towel. As always, she'd brought an assortment of practical items with her, *mom* items that were of absolutely zero use to her right now. No lip gloss or blusher, not even a hairbrush.

"Now *that* guy's hot," Skylar said in a hushed voice.

Daphne looked up from her bag and wondered which one Skylar was talking about. Her eyes surveyed the section of beach the group had carved out as their playing field. A dozen or so shirtless men running across it, barefoot on the sand, most of them appearing to be in pretty good—if not extremely good—shape. Only a couple of them had any trace of a beer belly, and just one of them appeared to be losing his hair. She wondered which ones were married, or if any of them had children. By the time Daphne was in her late twenties, she had a daughter in school, but she knew that wasn't typical.

The guys were playing seven on seven, all of them horsing around and clearly having a ball, acting like overgrown versions of the kids they weren't anymore. They were using a bright green Nerf ball, the likes of which Daphne hadn't seen in years, and which brought back a few childhood memories of her own. During her elementary school years, flag football with a Nerf ball had been a popular lunchtime activity, right up there with Red Rover, dodgeball, jump rope, and marbles. She'd never been very good at flag football or dodgeball, but she'd *dominated* at marbles.

"If they were playing volleyball, I'd swear we'd died and gone to heaven," Skylar said.

"Good call," KC said.

Daphne snapped back to the present. "Are you referring to that scene in *Top Gun*?"

Skylar smiled and pushed her sunglasses on top of her head. "You bet I am."

"Best scene ever," KC said.

"There's a surfeit of toned skin out here, I'll give you that," Daphne said.

KC looked at her sideways. "Does that have anything to do with surfing?"

Daphne laughed. "Just means there are a lot of fit bodies in front of us."

"Should we go around them?" KC pointed to the water, then looped her finger up toward the houses. "I'd hate to interrupt their game."

Skylar put a hand out to stop KC. "What's the rush? I say we stay and enjoy the view for a while."

KC laughed. "Okay then, stay and enjoy the view it is."

"I'm not opposed to that," Daphne said with a slight smile. *What's the harm in looking?*

"Nor *should* you be opposed to it," Skylar said. "Let's get a little closer."

The three of them inched their way toward the group, not wanting to draw attention to themselves. Once they were in earshot of what the players were saying, it became apparent that the chatter had much more to do with heckling than discussing the score or rules of the game.

"Come on now, Bates! My grandmother could have caught that!"

"I'm sorry, Wilson, did you say something? I can't hear such a high-pitched voice."

"Eric, dude, could you be any slower? You're like a dial-up Internet connection for chrissake."

KC grinned and put her hands on her hips. "These guys are awesome. They remind me of my brothers. Josh and Jared would fit right in too."

"Awesome and *cute*. I like the quarterback. I wonder what his story is." Skylar gestured to a tall, dark-haired guy in hunter-green board shorts. From that distance Daphne couldn't tell if he was wearing a wedding ring. Then again, given what she'd recently learned from Skylar about married men, that probably didn't mean much.

"They could pass for a boy band shooting a video, although it would be a pretty large band," KC said. Then she looked around the surrounding beach area. "I wonder why they're all here? I don't see any significant others cheering them on."

"Bachelor party," Daphne said.

Skylar and KC both looked at her.

"Is that a guess?" Skylar asked. "Or do you know something we don't?"

Daphne pointed at Clay, then up toward the deck. "I met the tall guy in the blue shorts yesterday when I was taking a walk on the beach. A bunch of them are staying in that house."

Skylar checked it out. "Nice place. I wonder which one is getting married?"

"I have no idea. Clay's the only one I met. He was on the deck by himself."

Skylar turned to watch the game again. "I hope it's not the quarterback."

"We could always just ask them," KC said.

Daphne felt her cheeks turn red. "Oh, I don't think we should."

"Why not?"

"Because they're so much, you know, *younger* than we are," Daphne said.

"So? Who cares?" KC looked puzzled.

Skylar put a hand on KC's shoulder. "I think what she's trying to say is that if we approach a big group of younger guys and ask them which one of them is getting married, it will make us look like cougars."

"Like what?" KC looked even more confused now.

"Cougars." Skylar made a clawing motion with her fingernails. "You know, older women who prey on younger men."

KC opened her eyes wide. "That's really a word?"

"Where have you been?" Skylar asked. "That's been a word for years."

KC frowned. "Well, it doesn't sound very nice."

Daphne nodded. "I agree. I don't like that term. I think it's disrespectful to women."

"I'm not particularly fond of it either, but I didn't make it up," Skylar said with a shrug.

"You date younger men," KC said to Skylar. "So you're a cougar?"

Skylar shook her head. "I date them, but only if they approach *me*. Big difference, at least in my opinion."

"Is there a term for men who date younger women?" KC asked.

Skylar laughed and put her hand on top of KC's head. "Yes, my tiny friend. It's usually called *rich*."

KC pushed Skylar's hand away, but she was laughing. "*Hey now*, I think my husband would take offense to that."

Skylar laughed too. "Then don't tell him."

Now Daphne was also laughing. She glanced up at the sky. *It feels so good to laugh like this.*

Just then a stray football came flying their way. KC bent down to pick it up, then effortlessly tossed it back to the group in a perfect spiral.

"Wow," yelled the blond guy who caught it. "Nice arm." He looked genuinely impressed.

KC smiled and adjusted her baseball cap. "Thanks! I played a little as a kid!" she yelled back.

Skylar chuckled. "Of course you did."

The majority of the players were now looking at Daphne and her friends from afar, Clay included. He clapped some sand off his hands and waved. "Hey, Daphne White, good to see you again!" he yelled.

She waved back and forced herself to yell loud enough for him to hear her, although she could feel her cheeks burning at the attention. "Hi, Clay Hanson!"

"You and he are on first- *and* last-name basis?" Skylar said. "Well done, *Daphne White.*"

"Please behave," Daphne whispered back to her.

Skylar slipped her sunglasses back over her eyes. "Clay *Handsome*, is it?"

"Clay *Hanson*," Daphne said, still in a whisper. "And please keep your voice down."

Skylar smiled without looking at her. "You call him whatever you like, and I'll do the same. All I'm saying is that he's quite the eye candy, and it's been a long time since you've visited the candy store."

KC rubbed her hands together and grinned. "Can I just say I'm *loving* hanging out with you two again?"

• • •

"Halftime!" someone called out, and the game quickly broke up as nearly everyone headed up to the deck, where a large red cooler filled with ice-cold bottles of water—and beers—awaited.

Two players stayed behind. One was the blond who had caught KC's throw. The other was Clay. They chatted with each other for a moment, then turned and began walking toward Daphne, Skylar, and KC. When Daphne realized what they were doing, she swallowed and hoped her friends wouldn't say anything to embarrass her. *He's coming over here!*

As if reading her mind, Skylar patted Daphne's arm. "Don't worry," she said under her breath.

"Thank you," Daphne said, her voice hushed.

"Great game," Skylar said in a normal decibel as Clay and the blond approached.

"Thanks," Clay said with an easy smile. Then he looked at Daphne but pointed the Nerf ball at KC as he spoke again. "I gotta say, your friend here could show you a thing or two about throwing."

"*Both* my friends here could show me a thing or two about a *lot* of things," Daphne said with a smile of her own, one that didn't feel as forced as she feared it would be. "This is KC, and this is Skylar."

"Clay Hanson." He shook both their hands, then gestured to his pal. "This is Doug Bates."

"Ah, *Bates*, the one who runs slower than a grandmother," KC said with a slow nod.

Doug pretended to stab himself in the heart. "Coming from someone with an arm like yours, that hurts."

Skylar narrowed her eyes at Clay, but not in an unfriendly way. "Do you always speak to people using first and last names?"

Clay laughed and scratched the top of his head. "Sorry, force of habit. I meet a lot of people through work."

"What do you do?" Skylar asked.

"I'm in finance. Nothing too exciting. Doug here's the one with the cool job." He patted his friend on the shoulder.

"Oh yeah? What would that be?" Skylar looked at Doug.

"I'm the host of a sports talk radio show."

KC's face lit up. "Did you just say sports talk radio? I *love* sports talk radio!"

"Doesn't he have the perfect face for radio?" Clay said.

"Shut it, pretty boy," Doug said, punching Clay's arm.

"That's my husband's dream job," KC said.

Clay punched Doug's arm back. "It's pretty much *every* guy's dream job. Lucky bastard."

"What can I say? Someone has to do it. So what brings you three to St. Mirika?" Doug asked them.

"Just a girls' reunion," Skylar said. "What about you?"

Daphne glanced at Skylar, amazed at how she was able to pose the question without giving any indication that she already knew the answer.

"Bachelor party." Doug turned toward the deck and pointed at a sandy-blond-haired man standing next to the quarterback Skylar had been eyeing. "That's the betrothed over there."

"Which one?" Skylar asked casually.

*She's so smooth,* Daphne thought. No wonder she was so good at her job.

"See Scott, the tall, dark-haired guy who was playing quarterback? It's the one standing next to him. His name's Perry," Doug said.

"*Perry?* That's fancy," Skylar said. With the guys' backs briefly turned to them, she discreetly gave Daphne's arm a little squeeze, then leaned toward her and whispered. "I'm calling him *Hot Scott.*"

Daphne smiled. For now at least, the quarterback was still in the game. *This is fun.*

Clay turned around. "It's a family name. We rib him about it all the time." Then he gestured toward their makeshift football field. So you three want to join us for the second half? We could use some fresh legs out there."

"Fresh legs?" Skylar gave him a skeptical look. "I don't mean to sound rude, but from what I saw, it didn't look like anyone was running all that hard."

"They were running harder than you were," Daphne said to her.

"I'll take that," Skylar said with a shrug.

Doug laughed. "Wanting fresh legs is code for *some of the guys want to stop playing and start drinking.*"

"I think 'some' is probably an understatement," Clay said.

"They want to start drinking already? But it's not even lunchtime." KC looked a little horrified.

Skylar patted her shoulder. "We're on island time, Missy Franklin. Relax. No one here's training for the Olympics."

"So what do you say?" Clay asked KC. "We all saw that arm, so you can't pretend you don't know how to play."

KC grinned and raised her hand. "Okay, I'm in! Can I play quarterback?"

Doug snatched the Nerf ball from Clay, kneeled down, and handed it to her. "You took the words right out of my mouth—well, not exactly—but you know what I mean. It would be an honor." Then he looked up at Skylar and Daphne. "What about you two? Up for a scrimmage?"

Daphne swallowed. She was decently coordinated but hadn't played touch football since . . . how long had it been . . . *elementary school*? "Um . . ."

"Come on, Daphne," Clay said. "It will be fun. You can be on my team."

"Go ahead." Skylar gave her a nudge. "I'll watch. That will keep the numbers even."

KC pinched Skylar's waist. "Way to weasel out of it."

Skylar laughed. "I'm just being helpful. No one likes to play with odd numbers, and besides, I'm not dressed for it. Now go, scat." She gave Daphne another push.

"Okay, why not?" Daphne smiled weakly. *I hope I don't regret this.* She was proud of herself for trying something new—while simultaneously terrified that she'd make a fool of herself.

"Come on up to the deck, we'll introduce you to the crew." Clay waved the three of them toward the house. A few of the guys were already drinking beers, but most were drinking bottled water. Clay raised his voice. "Everyone, this is KC, Daphne, and Skylar."

An assortment of greetings filled the air as the guys waved back.

"Where'd you learn to throw like that?" Perry called to KC.

"I have brothers." She held up three fingers.

Skylar put her arm around KC. "Don't underestimate this one. She's tiny, but she's also not human. It's only a matter of time before some government scientist shows up and hauls her away for research."

KC leaned her head against Skylar's shoulder. "Aw, thanks."

Doug pointed to KC and Daphne, then to Skylar. "These two are going to join the game in the second half, and this one wants a beer." He looked at Skylar. "That was an assumption about your wanting a beer, but a correct one I hope?"

"Very correct," she said with a strong nod. "You're good. If you ever want to get out of the radio business and explore the world of sales, give me a call. I'm always looking for talented people."

Doug laughed. "I'll keep that in mind."

"Good. Now beer me, please," she said.

Scott quickly leaned over the railing and handed Skylar a frosty bottle. "I gotcha. Skylar, was it?"

"Yes, and you are . . . ?" She looked up and took the bottle with a casual smile and a subtle bat of the eyelashes, again providing no hint that she was already well aware of his name. Daphne watched her friend in action and felt like she was taking a clinic in how to remain calm, cool, and collected in any social situation. *I need to learn from her.*

She glanced at her tote bag and again wished it didn't look so . . . practical, if not downright maternal. At least it didn't have a sippy cup and little plastic bags filled with Cheerios inside.

Doug clapped his hands together a few times and shouted. "Okay people, let's get moving. Lactic acid's a bitch; can't let it build up."

KC smiled up at him, her eyes bright. "You know what lactic acid is?"

He tapped his temple. "I'm a radio personality. My entire profession is based on knowing just enough to make people think I know a hell of a lot more than I actually do."

She put her hand up for a high five. "My husband would love you."

After a few minutes most of the players had come down from the deck to reassemble the teams and prepare to start the second half. Daphne, who was now standing next to Clay, bit her lip. "I hope I'm not too much of a weak link." She pointed to KC, who was already on the beach, jogging in place and stretching. "If you haven't already noticed, Mia Hamm over there's the athlete of our trio."

"Hey, don't be stealing my nicknames," Skylar said to her.

Daphne turned her head. "Have you already called her Mia Hamm this trip? I've lost track."

Skylar took a sip of her beer. "Well, if I hadn't yet, I would have at some point this week. That one's definitely in my rotation."

Daphne laughed. "You and your rotations."

Skylar winked at her. "Don't be knocking my systems."

Clay gestured toward the rest of the group. "I don't think you have much to worry about. Half the guys are still recovering from last night, and the other half are in terrible shape. We're getting old."

Daphne smiled to herself. *That's what* you *think.*

Ignoring the last part of his comment, Skylar calmly took a sip of her beer. "What did your gang do last night that requires recovery?" She directed the question to Clay but turned her gaze to an approaching Scott, who was among the last to arrive from the deck.

"We went to the Castaway," Clay said.

Skylar raised her eyebrows. "How was it? We were supposed to go, but these two pansies said they needed their beauty sleep." She gestured to Daphne and then to KC, who was now jogging in place about twenty feet away.

"It was fun, definitely the most happening spot in this part of the island," Scott said. "I'm sure we'll end up there again tonight if you want to come check it out."

"Then maybe we'll see you there. Even if I have to drag these two by their ponytails, we're going out tonight. They already promised me. *Right*, Daphne?"

Daphne protectively reached for the back of her neck, imagining what that would feel like. "Right."

"Can I grab you another brew or some water before we kick off again?" Scott asked Skylar as he pointed toward the deck.

Skylar smiled at him. "A water would be lovely, thanks. I'll join you."

As Scott and Skylar made their way up toward the house, Clay watched after them for a moment, then looked at Daphne. "She's a spirited one, isn't she?"

Daphne nodded. "You have no idea. You do *not* want to get on her bad side."

"Well, for the record, I think it worked," he said.

She turned and looked up at him. "You think what worked?"

"The beauty sleep you got last night. Now come on, let's go play some football." He jogged onto the beach.

Before she could react, KC yelled and waved for her to join them. "Come on, Daphne!" Doug was standing next to her now.

Daphne kept her head down as she walked quickly toward the sandy field, hoping no one could see how much Clay's comment had just made her blush.

Or how good it had made her feel.

. . .

Daphne and KC played the entire second half of the game, which lasted a hair over thirty minutes before everyone decided to throw in the towel and head back to the deck—and the cooler of beers sitting on it. Daphne successfully met her modest goals of (a) not getting hurt and (b) not embarrassing herself. She also had much more fun than she expected to. Once the game got going, she didn't feel self-conscious about the age gap between her and KC and the guys, and she was surprised by how friendly the players on both teams were to her. She caught three passes and only dropped one, so for her, it was a resounding victory, even though her team lost.

While Daphne was thrilled just to have made it through the game unscathed, KC, on the other hand, stole the show from the opening drive. Her athletic prowess impressed not just Doug, but anyone who knew anything about football. Not only did she throw multiple touchdowns from the quarterback position, but on the last play of the game she discreetly changed roles with Doug to move to wide receiver. Under normal circumstances she wouldn't have been able to outrun anyone on the other team—except for Daphne, of course, whose job to that point had been to watch for a quarterback sneak. The surprising switch caught the other team on their heels, and Daphne on the wrong part of the field, or, more accurately, the wrong part of the sandpit. Terminology notwithstanding, the momentary confusion allowed KC to run down the beach unimpeded—and catch the winning pass unguarded. Once she was safely inside the end zone, she chucked the green Nerf ball high in the air, then plowed straight into the water, diving headfirst under a wave in celebration. Her team quickly followed, all of them splashing and hooting and hollering. The team began to pump their fists and chant: "KC! KC! KC!"

Clay and Daphne stood on the beach with their fellow teammates, watching the celebration erupt.

"She's like a goddamn hummingbird," one of the guys said.

"Amazing," another guy said.

Clay nodded. "I get tired just watching her. Where does she get all that energy?"

Daphne made the universal "I'm clueless" shrug. "She's been bouncing off the walls since the day I met her. Sometimes I think she has caffeine in her veins instead of blood."

Clay laughed. "You and she have been buddies a long time?"

She nodded. "We lived in the same dorm freshman year. Skylar too."

"Ah . . . so you're all Northwestern brainiacs," he said with a slow nod. "That explains a lot."

She cocked her head to one side. "Explains a lot about what?"

He smiled. "I'm just messing with you."

She swallowed and felt her neck get a little hot. "What about this group? How did you all meet? Or is it kind of a hodgepodge whose only connection is the groom?"

Clay put his arm around the guy standing next to him, the one who'd compared KC to a hummingbird. "The bulk of us went to business school together, and a few of the guys, like this chump here, are Perry's buddies from undergrad at Rutgers," he said.

"Do you have a fancy name too?" Daphne asked the friend.

"Hardly. I'm Steve. Doesn't get much more common than Steve."

She smiled. "I don't know about that. What about John?"

He laughed. "My last name's Johnson."

She laughed too. "Okay, you win. I can't help you." *I'm joking around with attractive younger men!*

"She sure showed them how it's done, didn't she?" a female voice called.

Daphne turned her head and saw Skylar approaching them, gesturing toward the water. "Check out our girl," Skylar said.

Daphne's eyes followed Skylar's arm. KC was now perched on top of Doug's shoulders, horsing around and hollering like one of the guys.

"I want to be like her when I grow up," Skylar said.

Clay laughed. "Me too."

"Me three," Daphne said.

As they stood there watching the revelry continue, Daphne realized that it had been a long time since she'd been surrounded by so much lightheartedness. It felt great.

# Chapter Seven

After hot showers and lunch at a tiny beachside café, the three friends went window shopping along the main drag marking the center of town—a charming, picturesque area lined with winding cobblestone streets that didn't appear to follow any sort of grid or structured pattern whatsoever. Most of the buildings were quaint one-story structures, with the occasional two-story unit housing an array of assorted businesses. Daphne noticed two law firms, two dentist offices, one accounting firm, and one sign for a shared chiropractic/acupuncture outfit. The rest of the storefronts dotting the sidewalks were a mixture of restaurants, boutiques, combination coffee/dessert shops, and nail salons, their white stucco facades freshly scrubbed and practically sparkling; each roof was topped by the rounded clay caps emblematic of the Mediterranean style, and many boasted matching ceramic pots full of brightly colored flowers on the windowsills.

As they wandered the free-flowing streets and explored the tiny alleys of the hamlet, Daphne felt like she was in another era, light years away from Grandview Heights. Had she really been out of Ohio for only two days?

Most of the storefronts they encountered presented modest, tasteful window dressings. A handful, however, featured bolder offerings inside. One shoe store displayed a particularly outrageous rack of boots.

"Check those out." Daphne pointed to a thigh-high pair made with red, white, and blue snakeskin. The spiked heels looked to be at least four inches long.

Skylar held up a defensive hand. "Beyond tacky. They're clearly going for the shock value."

KC looked down at her midsection. "Those things would go up to my vagina."

Skylar laughed as they moved away from the store. "That brings new meaning to the term *shock value*." She pointed to a sundress on a mannequin in the next window, then spoke to KC. "I can't picture you in those boots, but I bet that little number would look great on you. Let's go try it on."

"Do I have to?" KC asked. "Can't we go in there instead?" She pointed to a store across the street called Ryan's Sports Shack.

"You can't possibly need more workout gear," Skylar said. "C'mon, show some estrogen for once and try on a pretty dress for me?"

KC sighed. "Okay, fine. Will you at least work out with me if I try it on? A dress *up* for a work*out*?"

"Perhaps . . . definitely maybe . . . we'll see." Skylar opened the door to the boutique. "But first, let's see that baby on you."

The three of them ducked inside the pleasant yet slightly cramped shop, and Skylar and Daphne perused the jewelry display while KC took the dress to the tiny fitting room in the back.

"You doing okay today?" Skylar asked, her voice a bit hushed. "You seem to be, but I don't want to push."

Daphne picked up a dangly gold earring and held it to one ear in front of a mirror. "I'm doing much better than yesterday, but given where I was yesterday, that's not saying a lot."

"It'll take time. I'm just glad you finally opened up to us. I knew there was something off with you, right from when we met at the airport, but I wanted to wait until you were ready to talk about it."

Daphne looked at her. "You did?" She thought she'd done a pretty good job of concealing how she was really feeling. Maybe not a spectacular job, but a decent job.

Skylar nodded. "It was pretty clear something was eating at you."

"How so?"

Skylar sorted through a rack of colorful beaded necklaces. "The best way I can think to explain it is that you didn't seem like yourself. You seemed, I don't know . . . *vanilla*."

Daphne didn't respond, but her eyes said, *Could you elaborate?*

"You know, a little bland, a little going through the motions, which is unlike you," Skylar said.

Daphne frowned. Vanilla *was* the perfect word for how she'd been feeling. For way too long. *And I'm supposed to be the one who's good with words.*

Skylar held up a necklace for inspection. "One of the things I've always loved about you is how *engaged* you are, Daphne. I don't mean bouncing off the walls like KC, but that you have a spark about you, you know?"

Daphne nodded slowly. Skylar was right. *What happened to that part of me?*

Skylar returned the necklace and put a hand on Daphne's arm. "I know the old Daphne is in there somewhere—I've seen little glimpses of her today. We just need to figure out how to get her back full-time."

Daphne felt a few tears welling up in her eyes, but for the first time in a long time, they weren't entirely tears of sadness. They were also tears of optimism.

"Please don't give up on me, Skylar," she whispered.

Skylar shook her head. "Never. I'm a bulldog, remember? I don't give up on anything I care about, and I care a *lot* about you."

"Thank you," Daphne said as she wiped a tear from her eye.

"Okay, pals, what do you think?"

They both turned their heads at the sound of KC's voice at the back of the store. She took off her baseball cap and flung it at her friends, then held out her arms and did a little twirl.

Daphne caught the baseball hat and carefully tucked it into her tote bag for safekeeping. She also removed a tissue and discreetly dabbed at the remaining tears.

"Well? Am I a Greek goddess?" KC shimmied her hips side to side, runway-style. The white dress she had on had spaghetti straps with thick horizontal pink stripes.

Skylar chuckled and covered her mouth with her hand. "I know I picked it out, so hate to say this, but you kind of look like a candy striper."

KC looked crushed. "Darn. For real? I was kind of digging it. The stretchy material is supercomfy."

Skylar turned to Daphne. "Back me up here?"

Daphne shook her head. "I'm sorry, but I'm with Skylar on this one. I feel like I'm in a hospital right now."

KC held up her palms in surrender, then turned on her heel and mock-stormed into the dressing room with a laugh. "Okay, fine. But don't say I didn't try!"

"Now we know who to go to if we need some first aid, though," Skylar called after her.

"Wow, she really did look like a teenybopper in that thing," Daphne said. "From the neck down she could have passed for one of Emma's friends."

Skylar began sifting through the dress rack. "We'll find her something. I'm determined to put a little salsa in that señora if it kills me. So speaking of Emma, earlier you said she was in Utah. Is it her spring break?"

Daphne hesitated before replying. "Yes, she's in Park City with Brian . . . and Alyssa." *All three of them. Together. Get used to it.*

Skylar saw the strain on Daphne's face. "I gather this is the first time she's gone on a real vacation with Alyssa?"

Daphne nodded. "The first of many, I suppose. Alyssa's got all kinds of money."

"That might not be a bad thing. Sometimes traveling opens the mind a lot more than a textbook can," Skylar said.

"I know. I just need to get used to the idea that there's another mother figure in her life now. I hate that."

"I'm sorry, hon. You know it'll get easier, right?"

Daphne sighed. "I know. I just want it to get easier faster."

Skylar smiled. "There's that wit. But you'll adapt. That's the roughest part of anything difficult, getting used to it."

KC appeared next to them. "Okay, my personal shoppers, have you found me anything else, or am I off the hook?"

Skylar held up another white sundress, this one strapless and embroidered with tiny blue-and-green flowers. "Try this one. It's supercute."

"You want *me* to try on a *strapless* dress?" KC asked.

"Did I stutter?" Skylar said.

Daphne reached for the dress. "Wait a minute. I think this is the same pattern as my duvet cover at the beach house."

"It is?" Skylar held the hanger up and studied it. "My duvet cover's white with blue swirls."

Daphne nodded. "It's *exactly* the same as mine. This dress could have been made from the same fabric."

KC grabbed for the dress. "That's awesome! I could lie on your bed wearing this and I would be completely camouflaged. Strapless or not, that alone is worth seeing if it fits."

She skipped into the dressing room, and Skylar and Daphne watched her.

"She really is like a kid," Skylar said.

. . .

After an afternoon of shopping and wandering around town, they returned to the beach house, a bit tired, sunned out, and ready for some downtime before dinner. KC ducked into her room for a nap, saying she was too wiped out even to make herself disappear on Daphne's bed wearing her new dress.

Skylar had to dial into yet another conference call and quickly settled at the desk in the living room. "I feel like this is my office," she groaned as she reached for her headset.

"At least you have a nice view, right?" Daphne said.

"That's the spirit." Skylar chuckled and put on the headset. "Now shush, I need to switch gears into professional mode."

Despite all the activity of the day, Daphne wasn't feeling sleepy, so she decided to go for another walk on the beach, this time in the opposite direction. She and KC had explored a sliver of that stretch during their workout, but she was interested to see what else lay beyond the patch they'd covered.

Before leaving the house, she popped into her bedroom to check her phone—which she'd left plugged in on the dresser while they were out shopping—to see if Emma had returned her text from earlier in the day. The screen was blank.

Daphne frowned. While a part of her hoped her daughter's lack of communication was because she was having too much fun on her vacation to even think about her phone, a bigger part of her hoped it was due to poor cell reception. She felt a bit self-centered admitting that to herself, but it was true. She missed her daughter, and she wanted her daughter to miss her back. At least a little bit.

She set the phone down on the dresser, then reached for her straw hat and tote bag and quietly made her way into the kitchen so as not to disturb Skylar's call. She heard snippets as she retrieved a bottle of water from the refrigerator and tiptoed through the living room toward the French doors, the sound of Skylar's fingers flying over the keyboard providing a musical backdrop to the conversation.

"Walk on the beach," Daphne mouthed the words and pointed to the ocean.

"Sounds *bueno*," Skylar whispered with a quick smile, then immediately returned her focus to the conference call. Daphne was amazed at her ability to slip in and out of worlds so seamlessly.

Daphne gently closed the glass doors behind her, then walked across the deck and glanced up at the cloudless blue sky. She'd applied and reapplied sunscreen a couple times already, but she could still feel her fair skin burning in the hot sun. She hunted inside her tote bag for a bottle of sunblock and her sunglasses, sprayed herself down one more time, then put on the straw hat and glasses and made her way down the steps. Once off the deck, she removed her flip-flops to enjoy the feel of the beach between her toes, but it was too hot for her skin, so she quickly trotted down to the shore. The clear green water felt soothing on her bare feet, the wet sand soft.

She took a quick look back at the deck, then set off on her walk.

·   ·   ·

After wandering quietly for a few minutes, Daphne noticed that the houses lining the beach were becoming more secluded, the gaps between them noticeably larger. Soon what she was passing no longer qualified as *houses* so much as mansions. Or full-blown estates.

Each one seemed to be more stunning than the next. The architecture differed from structure to structure, but nearly all of the residences were white. To Daphne the collective effect was reminiscent of the pristine, shingled, white-and-gray houses of Nantucket.

It was simply . . . beautiful.

Daphne stopped and put her hands on her waist, gazing up at one of the mansions. These were clearly the vacation homes of the über rich, toys of those so wealthy there was no need to even consider renting them out. It was hard to fathom that kind of wealth. She was still getting used to the gorgeous place Skylar's boss was kindly letting them borrow. The house she was staring at right then was from another world entirely. She wondered what that type of life would be like. Were the people who owned it happy? The popular refrain said that money can't buy happiness, but Brian had always told Daphne that he wondered if whoever had coined that saying didn't have a lot of money.

*"How could you not be happy if you were rich?"* he would say. She'd never really challenged him about it, but looking back now, she saw the comment for what it was—a reflection of his immaturity, of his relatively shallow values.

Come to think of it, she'd never challenged him on most of what he said. *I used to think he was wise just because he was five years older, but he wasn't even thirty when we met.* Oh, how her perspective on age had changed.

She turned around to look out at the ocean. A memory of Skylar's comment from earlier flickered to life: she'd described Daphne as *vanilla*.

It had stung to hear Skylar choose that word to describe her, but Skylar was right. It had been gradual, but over many years of pouring her energy into her daughter's activities, of struggling to calm the waters with Brian, of smoothing the way for everyone *else* to be happy, Daphne had lost track of what made *her* happy. And it wasn't money.

When she and Brian had met, she'd loved dancing and traveling and taking chances. She loved staying up late and drinking wine and laughing over lively conversation. She loved exploring and wandering and wondering. All the seeds for a picture-perfect future were there, but then everything started to change. Daphne began to wonder what their marriage would have been like, what her *life* would have been like, if he'd just . . .

She balled her hands into fists. *Stop thinking about it. It's over.*

She glanced up again at the extravagant house, then picked up a rock and hurled it into the ocean, farther than she had yesterday. As it sailed through the air, she was surprised to hear herself repeat the thought out loud—as a shout. "It's *over!*"

She watched the rock hit the water, making a small splash that quickly disappeared. Almost immediately the sea regained its smooth veneer, leaving no trace of the rock or its impact. Daphne stood there for a few moments, then checked her watch and decided it was time to head back to the beach house. She took a deep breath and felt a jolt of buoyancy as she exhaled. *It's time for more in my life. No more vanilla.*

Skylar would be proud.

$$\cdot \quad \cdot \quad \cdot$$

"Hey, woman, how was the walk?" Skylar greeted Daphne with a broad smile. She was still sitting at the desk in the living room, her headset now dangling around her neck.

Daphne pointed outside toward the new swath of beach she'd just explored. "Gorgeous. I think we're at the tail end of a ritzy neighborhood. Some of the houses that way are unbelievable."

Skylar closed her laptop, then removed her headset. "So I've been told. That's a glimpse into how the other half lives."

Daphne laughed and looked around the expansive living room. "Like we have it so bad. This place is amazing."

"Hey, I'm not knocking it or complaining in any way. I'm just speaking the truth, which is that I'm well aware that our current digs are hardly extravagant. Some of the estates along that part of the island have their own helipads."

"Well, for *me*, this place is certainly extravagant. But I agree that it's just because I haven't been exposed to the lavish things you have. You're pretty much the only high roller I know." She knew Brian's parents were well-off, but she couldn't imagine their flying all over the world like Skylar did. They were too reserved to actually *enjoy* their money.

Skylar shrugged. "Extravagance is relative. Trust me, my life in New York is far from the upper echelons. You ready for a drink?"

Daphne glanced at the kitchen. "I don't know if I can do alcohol yet. I think I need some coffee, to be honest. I should have followed KC's lead and taken a nap."

Skylar waved a finger at her. "Don't even think about pulling the rip cord early again tonight. You promised, remember? And if there's one thing I admire more than your vocabulary, it's that you never break a promise. It's hard to get you to *make* one, but once you do, I know it's golden."

"I know, I know: enough with the guilt. I'm well aware that I told you I would rally tonight, thus the suggestion of a caffeine infusion. Is KC still passed out?"

"I think she's in the shower."

"When do we need to leave for dinner?"

Skylar glanced at her watch. "In about an hour. Just enough time for you to shower and change and have a cocktail with us on the deck. After your caffeine infusion, of course."

Daphne nodded. "Got it."

"Did I hear someone say something about a cocktail on the deck? I feel like a new person after that power nap."

Skylar and Daphne both looked toward the hall. KC was standing there, her wet hair pulled back into a ponytail. She wore a pair of cutoffs and a bright teal T-shirt that read "St. Mirika!" in white lettering.

Skylar held up her forearm as if to shield her eyes. "What in the name of Holy Jesus are you wearing?"

KC glanced down at the shirt. "Isn't this great? I bought it when you two were in that jewelry store."

"Why is it *shouting* at us?" Daphne asked.

KC laughed. "I have *no idea*, but I love it."

"What happened to that adorable white dress with the flowers?" Skylar said.

"I thought that was for Daphne's birthday dinner."

"Then what about the dress you brought with you?" Skylar asked.

KC shrugged. "I can't find it in my suitcase. I must have forgotten to pack it." She glanced down at her shirt. "No worries, though. I'll just go with this."

Skylar covered her eyes with her palm. "God help us."

KC grinned and raised a hand in the air. "So what about that cocktail? I'm in!"

# Chapter Eight

"What's the plan for tomorrow?" KC sipped her rum punch, then set it down as the waiter handed her a dessert menu. "And you'd better not say shopping. I already paid those dues."

Skylar gave Daphne a look. "What is wrong with her? Who doesn't like shopping? It's like not liking chocolate. Or sleeping. Or breathing. It's just not natural."

Daphne smiled and took a sip of her drink. "Don't ask me. I gave up trying to understand what makes her tick about a week after we met. It was easier just to watch her run around like a wind-up toy."

KC rubbed her hands together. "*So*, what's on the docket? Doug told me about some gorgeous cliffs on the other side of the island. Should we go check them out? Or maybe go zip-lining? Do they have that here? Or parasailing? I've always wanted to try something high-flying like that." She turned toward Daphne, her eyes bright. "Any of those would be a killer way to celebrate your birthday, don't you think?"

"I guess so," Daphne practically mumbled, not wanting to let on how much the idea of anything *high-flying* frightened her.

"I'm exhausted just listening to that list," Skylar said. "Did you know that some people go on vacation to relax?"

Daphne was grateful for Skylar's objection. When she was younger, she hadn't been so scared of heights, had she? She didn't think so.

"Well, we have to do something adventurous to ring in Daphne's fortieth," KC said, then leaned over and patted Daphne's arm. "Maybe we'll kick it off with a nice run on the beach."

"Can we call an audible on that?" Daphne asked. "After today I'm afraid to find out how much my body's going to hurt when I wake up. I'm already feeling it."

"A little soreness is good," KC said. "It's like a receipt for your hard work."

"We'll see," Daphne said. *Is this what it feels like to get old?* She glanced at the dessert menu, wondering how much time she had left before she'd be reaching inside her purse for her own pair of reading glasses.

Skylar tapped her fingernail against her drink. "If *I* have anything to say about it, your muscles won't be the only thing hurting in the morning." She gestured to the waiter for another pitcher.

"Oh no," Daphne said. "More rum punch?"

"Oh yes," Skylar nodded. "More rum punch."

"Oh mama," KC groaned.

"Oh shush," Skylar said.

KC looked at Skylar. "Anyhow, back to tomorrow. What are we doing? You still haven't told us the plan, but I know you have one. You *always* have one."

Skylar paused to let the waiter set a fresh pitcher on the table. When he was gone, she refilled their glasses, then picked up her drink and smiled. "You are correct. I've made arrangements for us to spend the afternoon at the nicest spa on the island."

Daphne's ears perked up. "A spa?" She hadn't been to a spa in ages. *I could use some pampering.*

"There's a pretty famous one on the island called Serendipity, and from what I've seen, it's gorgeous. I booked us each a facial and a massage, my treat."

"You don't have to do that," Daphne said.

"Please. I *want* to. I've been itching for a fancy spa trip myself lately, so it's not like my motives are purely altruistic."

Daphne smiled. "Okay then, you can treat."

"Where is it?" KC asked. "Will it take all day?"

"It's at the Four Seasons on the north shore, but God forbid you spend an *entire day* relaxing, so I thought we could stop at the monkey forest on the way. How does that sound?" Skylar said.

KC pumped her fist in the air. "Now we're talking!"

Skylar pressed a palm against her forehead. "Only you would be more excited at the idea of seeing a monkey than of getting deluxe spa treatments."

KC grinned. "Come on, even *you* have to admit that going to a monkey forest sounds awesome."

Skylar shrugged. "Okay, I'll take that. Who doesn't like a good monkey?"

"How does it work?" Daphne asked. "Is it like a zoo?"

Skylar shook her head. "Not at all. The monkeys run around completely free, no cages or anything. You can even feed them bananas if you want. They sell them right there. I've been to the one in Bali, and it's pretty cool. But you have to be careful with your sunglasses, because the monkeys will jump on your shoulder and take them right off your face."

"For real?" Daphne asked.

"Oh yes. They're not afraid of humans at all. In Bali I saw this guy holding a yellow-and-orange-striped Popsicle, and a monkey ran up and stole it right out of his hand, then bolted up a tree. The monkey must have thought it was a banana."

KC clapped her hands together. "I can't believe we're going to see real monkeys! I might not be able to sleep tonight."

Skylar shook her head slowly. "Once again, I don't know how to respond to that."

KC pointed at Skylar. "Hey, city girl, if you're allowed to dream about having someone travel with you just to make your hair pretty, I can get excited about seeing some monkeys."

"She has a good point," Daphne said to Skylar.

Skylar laughed and touched the sides of her head. "I have a lot of hair. It's hard to deal with."

KC did a little dance in her seat. "Monkeys! Woo, I'm so excited!"

Skylar looked at her askance yet again, then picked up her dessert menu. "Okay Curious Georgia, let's order something sweet, then get out of here. We need to change venues so you can re-create that move you just did on an actual dance floor. The night is young, *we* are young, and the Castaway is awaiting."

•   •   •

The Castaway was hopping. As the trio approached the entrance, they were greeted with the unmistakable music of a Jamaican steel drum, whose sound Daphne had always thought had the mystic ability to elevate the mood of everyone within earshot. The inside area of the bar was long and a bit cramped, especially near the front door, but the entire backside of the structure was open, leading onto an expansive deck area off the beach. A dance floor front and center was surrounded by cushioned chairs and love seats, the talented three-man band tucked away in a corner. A string of white paper lanterns lined the inside walls and also framed the outdoor area, wrapping the entire place in a warm, festive glow.

"I already love it here!" KC snapped her fingers and began to bob her head from side to side.

Daphne inconspicuously glanced around to inspect the demographics. The place wasn't packed, but both the inside and outside areas were quickly filling up with revelers. Inside, most people were tucked up close to the bar, chattering loudly over cocktails and rows of shot glasses. On the deck area, some couples and small groups of friends were already having fun on the dance floor, while others huddled together and watched from their seats. Still others stood by themselves or nestled in small groups, and nearly everyone swayed gently to the music. The Castaway was inviting and friendly, and as Daphne scanned the crowd, she saw faces smooth, wrinkled, and somewhere in between. She was also hard-pressed to find one that didn't have at least a hint of a smile on it.

Including hers.

Skylar ran her hand over KC's ponytail. "I completely agree. The vibe is groovy, and I don't throw that word around lightly. Now, who wants a drink? I've heard this joint has the best rum punch on the island."

KC raised her hand. "I'm in. I'm not gonna lie. I'm loving the rum punch."

Daphne shook her head. "I'm good for now."

"You sure?" Skylar gave her a look that asked, *Are you doing okay?*

Daphne smiled. "I'll have one in a little bit, I promise. For now I'll take a water."

"Okay, be right back. Why don't you grab us a place to sit if you can find one."

Skylar squeezed her way toward the bar, and as soon as she was gone, KC pinched Daphne's waist. "All good with you? You look a little uncomfortable."

Daphne smiled. "It's been a while since I've been in a scene like this, but I'm fine, really. I'm just a little tired. I should have been smart and taken a nap like you." She thought it ironic—and somewhat humorous—that her friends were now worried about her state of mind when she was finally feeling a little better about it. *I should have opened up to them a long time ago.*

"Power naps are the fountain of youth," KC said. "Twenty minutes and I feel like a new person. Sometimes, when I *really* need one, I don't even make it to the bedroom. I just lie facedown on the living room carpet."

Daphne laughed. "What?"

KC pointed to the floor. "Yep. Facedown on the carpet. Max thinks I look like a corpse, but I swear it works like a charm. You should try it sometime."

Daphne laughed again. "I'll keep that in mind." She looked out at the deck. "I can't remember the last time I went dancing. Maybe our girls' weekend in Chicago? I used to love to dance." *I used to be pretty good at it too.*

"I hear ya. Seems like I only dance at weddings these days, but I'm feeling the urge to shake my booty tonight."

Daphne put her arm around her. "Are you going to do one of your trademark moves?"

KC snapped her fingers in the air twice. "It is not beyond the scope of possibility, my friend. I guess we shall see."

"We shall see what?" Skylar returned, carefully holding three glasses of rum punch. She handed one to both KC and Daphne, then took a big sip of her own to keep it from spilling.

"What's this?" Daphne asked.

Skylar batted her eyelashes. "I'm sorry, did you not want one? I don't have the best hearing."

Daphne laughed and shook her head. "You're evil."

Skylar shrugged and lifted her drink in the air. "I'll take that. To the Three Musketeers, back together at last."

"To my last night in my thirties." Daphne raised her glass too. "Tomorrow it's all over."

Skylar rolled her eyes. "Oh please. We've been over this like a thousand times. It is *not* over. In fact, it is *far* from over. Mark my words, ladies. Forty is the new black."

KC coughed back a laugh. "Huh?"

"You heard me, Peppermint Patty."

"I thought the expression was *life begins at forty*," Daphne said.

"I like to be original," Skylar said as she pointed to KC's glass. "Now, consume."

KC lifted the glass and studied it. "What exactly is in rum punch that makes me love it so much?"

"Rum," Skylar said. "That's all you need to know. Now, what were you saying? Something about we shall see?"

"Remember those random dance moves I used to do at parties when I was a bit, um, inebriated?" KC asked.

Skylar cocked her head to one side. "Is that a fancy way of saying when you were *schnockered*?" She elbowed Daphne. "What's the SAT word for a more agreeable phrase?"

"Euphemism," Daphne answered immediately.

Skylar snapped her fingers. "Yes, *euphemism*. Is that a euphemism for when you were three sheets to the wind, which by the way is a euphemism for *drunk*?"

KC grinned. "Whatever the word, you know I've never been much of a drinker." She took another sip of her rum punch. "This is the most alcohol I've had in a long time. And I'm not gonna lie. It tastes pretty darn good."

"That's like the third time you've said a variation of that exact same thing," Skylar said.

Daphne smiled. "I love how entertaining KC gets when she's tipsy."

Skylar sipped her own rum punch. "I love it too. Remember the time she did a full-on *backbend* at the SAE formal?"

"I'd pay to see that again," Daphne said.

KC laughed. "I'd probably get myself thrown out of here if I pulled that move. I'd probably throw my back out too, come to think of it."

Skylar gestured toward the young couple making out in a corner. "I beg to differ. While watching you get punted from a bar at age forty would most definitely be the highlight of the trip, I suspect the threshold for what's considered appropriate behavior isn't very high here."

"Why exactly did we choose Chicago to celebrate turning thirty?" KC furrowed her brow. "I remember wanting to go to Vegas."

Daphne felt her face flush. "Um, that was me. Emma was so young, and Vegas was so far away . . ."

Skylar put a hand on Daphne's shoulder. "Methinks it was Brian who put the kibosh on the idea, but that's water under the bridge now, correct?"

Daphne gave her a grateful look. "Correct."

Skylar winked and pointed toward the back. "Let's check out the deck."

They wandered outside and surveyed the landscape in search of open real estate. For a few minutes it was standing room only, so they were forced to sway with the crowd, but soon Skylar noticed a couple getting up to leave a cushioned bench. Like a seasoned pro, she pounced the moment they were gone, somehow managing to look dignified as she did so. She took a seat and gracefully crossed her legs, then smiled and patted the open spots on either side of her.

"The view's much better from here," she said.

Daphne plopped down next to her, but KC remained standing.

"Do we have to sit?" KC said. She began hopping side to side like a boxer. "I'm kind of itching to dance. I love this music."

"Then go for it." Skylar gestured to the dance floor. "No one's stopping you."

KC stopped hopping and let her arms fall to her sides. "You won't dance with me?"

"I will, but not yet. I want to soak in the scene first." Skylar's head turned as if on a swivel. "This place is a gold mine for people watching. I love the way everyone lets loose on vacation."

"If you've got moves on the dance floor like you do on the gridiron, I'll dance with you," a man's voice said.

The three of them looked to KC's left. Doug from the football game approached, a big smile on his face.

"Hey, teammate!" KC gave him a high five. "Fancy meeting you here."

"What can I say? Word got out that you would be here, so how could I *not* come?"

KC glanced behind him. "Where are your buddies?"

Doug pointed over his shoulder with his thumb. "At the bar. Where else would they be?"

"All of them?" Skylar craned her neck through the crowd. The *Is Hot Scott here?* went unspoken, but Daphne didn't need to hear it to know that's what she was asking, just as Skylar didn't have to hear the *Is Clay here?* Daphne was thinking.

Daphne smiled to herself. *I love that we don't have to say it out loud.*

The playfulness and subtext of their communication was like going back in time for her, each new interaction quietly nudging her dormant persona back to life.

"About half of them are here," Doug said. "The rest of the crew are still at the bar where we had dinner. They may come by later." He turned to KC. "So what about that dance, champ?"

She grinned. "You don't have to ask me twice."

The two of them disappeared into the crowd, but Doug was so tall that Daphne and Skylar could see the top of his head bobbing up and down in the middle of the dance floor.

"I wish I had half her energy," Daphne said. "I'm proud of myself for even being here right now, and she's out there cutting a rug."

"You *should* be proud of yourself for being here," Skylar said. "We're all wired differently, so for certain things you can and should only compare yourself to yourself. I work with some people who never sleep more than four hours a night, and they're completely fine. I know I can't function like that, so I don't try. I need at least six hours to get by."

Daphne pressed a palm against her chest. "I could never live with just six hours. I don't do well without sleep. I was a zombie when Emma was a baby." Her mind began to drift as she remembered that phase of her life. Brian needed to work in the mornings, so it went without saying that Daphne was the one to take care of the moonlight feedings and rocking sessions—even on the weekends. It was during those quiet hours that the first seeds of doubt began to take hold, when she began to wonder if her marriage wasn't what she'd thought it was going to be.

Now she knew better. Now she knew he should have stepped up. She also knew she should have spoken up.

"Daphne." Skylar snapped her fingers. "Earth to Daphne."

Daphne blinked. "I'm sorry, got lost in my thoughts there. Did you say something?"

"I asked if Emma is having fun on the ski trip? Have you heard from her?"

"Not since this morning. I don't think she has very good reception there."

"I'm sure she's having a great time." Skylar put her arm around Daphne's shoulder and squeezed. "I'm *also* sure she's missing you a little bit, even if she's too cool for school to tell you so."

Daphne smiled, grateful that she didn't need to explain. "Thanks. I think I'm going to the restroom. Watch my seat?"

"I'll try, but if Hot Scott makes his way over here, I won't try that hard."

Daphne laughed. "Fair enough." She stood up and smoothed her sundress, then reached for her purse.

Skylar lowered her voice. "Here comes your birthday present."

"What?"

"Babe alert, two o'clock."

Daphne glanced to the right and saw Clay and Scott emerging onto the deck. Scott was unquestionably good-looking, but it was the sight of Clay that got her attention. Tan and with a slight stubble now, there was something about him that made her just a little bit . . . uncomfortable. Or was *nervous* a better word choice? Anxious?

As Daphne stood there mentally evaluating appropriate adjectives, Skylar gave her a nudge from behind. "Don't be shy, go say hello."

"You think I should?"

"Of course. And send his buddy my way while you're at it."

"I'll try," Daphne said.

"Don't try, *do*. There is no *try*."

Daphne gave her a look. "Didn't Yoda say that? I'm pretty sure Yoda said that."

Skylar sighed. "You are such a nerd. Will you get going already?"

"Okay, fine." Daphne took a deep breath and smoothed her dress again, then headed in the direction of the restroom. *Smile. Be friendly. Loosen up. You can do it. He thinks you're pretty, remember?*

She weaved her way through the crowd, her eyes scanning the dance floor as she walked. She spotted Doug and KC among the sea of people but now didn't see Clay and Scott anywhere. She turned back to look at Skylar, who was gently nodding her head to the music, clearly content to be sitting by herself. At least for now.

"Careful there, neighbor."

Daphne turned around and nearly bumped into Clay. He had one hand high in the air, and she had a feeling he'd put it there to keep her from knocking the drink out of it.

"Oh gosh, I'm so sorry. I didn't see you."

He laughed. "Talk about stating the obvious. Have you been here long?"

Daphne shook her head. "We just came from dinner. KC's dancing with Doug, and Skylar's sitting over there. Doug said some of your crew was here, but I wasn't sure if that included you." She gave him a half smile. *Another feeble attempt at flirting, but at least I'm trying!*

He smiled. "I told you this place was fun. Isn't it great? I love the energy here. Everyone's so chill."

"Skylar calls it the vacation vibe, although it could just be the alcohol. Speaking of which, KC's pretty funny right now. She doesn't usually drink very much."

Clay held up his beer in a toast. "You're a *great* dancer, said the tequila."

Daphne laughed. "That's good. Did you make that up yourself?"

He shook his head. "I stole it from a buddy. You know what they call a margarita?"

She cocked her head to one side. "I do not. What *do* they call a margarita?"

"A snow cone of bad decisions."

She laughed again, but before she could say anything more, an attractive young blonde appeared out of nowhere and grabbed Clay's arm. She didn't look a day over twenty-five.

"*There* you are, big guy. I was wondering where you'd wandered off to. Come dance with me." She began pulling him toward the dance floor.

Daphne blushed. *I can't compete with that.*

She held her arm out to let them pass. "Don't let me hold you up, I was just on my way to the ladies' room. If you see KC out there, tell her we have a rum punch waiting for her when she gets thirsty."

"Will do. Good to see you, Daphne." Clay gave a quick wave as the blonde dragged him into the crowd.

Daphne watched them for just a moment, then turned and headed straight for the restroom, which had two stalls. Surprisingly, one of them was open. *Thank God,* she thought as she pushed open the door. Waiting in the restroom line at a crowded bar was one thing from her younger days that she did not miss.

After exiting the stall she washed and dried her hands, then hunted around in her purse for her lip gloss. She glanced in the mirror and smiled politely at the two women huddled together at the adjacent sink. She didn't mean to eavesdrop, but it was impossible not to given their proximity. From the conversation Daphne inferred they were about a year removed from college.

"Going back to work's gonna blow. This week has been off the *hook*," the first woman said.

Her friend stuck out her tongue. "Don't get me started on how much I'm dreading walking into that office. I hate my boss. She's such a bitch."

"I saw your post about her on Facebook. Sounds like a nightmare to work for."

"You have no idea. As soon as I can line up something else, I'm out of there."

As Daphne opened her lip gloss, she realized that she felt a bit sorry for the women, despite their youth. Actually, *because* of their youth. Granted her own career hadn't progressed past the bottom of the totem pole, but she couldn't imagine not knowing better than to criticize *anyone*, much less an employer, in a forum as public as social media. She made a mental note to set Emma down and explain the permanence of a digital footprint.

She stole another glance at the women as she applied a dab of color to her lips. Both of their complexions were unlined. Flawless, actually. Not a wrinkle between them. Daphne couldn't help but wish her own skin still looked that good. Not that hers looked *bad* by any stretch of the imagination. It just looked . . . older.

Their conversation continued. "Did she really sleep with him again?" the first woman asked. "I thought she said she was done with being treated like that."

The second woman shrugged. "He's an ass, but she's in love with him. She keeps hoping he'll change."

The first woman sighed. "Why is it so hard to find a good guy? I just want to get married already and be done with it. I'm so sick of the dating game."

"Me too. If it were up to me, I'd have a ring on my finger by now."

Daphne put her lip gloss away and slung her purse over her shoulder. As she turned to leave, she took a last glance at her reflection in the mirror and remembered when she used to talk like that, when she used to dream about the day a dashing Mr. Right would come along, sweep her off her feet, and carry her into the future she'd been dreaming of since she was a little girl.

*Be careful what you wish for*, she wanted to tell them.

．　．　．

"How'd it go with Clay Handsome?" Skylar asked as she handed Daphne her drink.

Daphne plopped down on the seat next to Skylar. "It went. He's not alone, so I aborted."

"Let me guess. A pretty young thing?"

Daphne nodded and took a big sip of rum punch.

Skylar crinkled her nose. "Sugar. What about Hot Scott?"

Daphne glanced around the deck. "I didn't see him, but I imagine he's not alone either. Pretty young things are a dime a dozen here. Although I see a handful of gray heads too, which I've got to admit makes me feel less like a senior citizen. When I get home, maybe I need to start going to Bingo parlors like KC."

Skylar rolled her eyes and stood up. "I'm pretending I didn't hear that. As for the boys, oh well: easy come, easy go. I'm activating Plan B."

Daphne gave her a curious look. "And that would be . . . ?"

Skylar pointed to the bar. "Alcohol. Need I say more?"

Daphne laughed. "You needn't."

"Hold down the fort, will you? Barreling my way to the front of the line might take a while."

"I'll do my best." Daphne took another sip of her drink and again surveyed the deck area, which was now packed with partygoers—and pulsating. "But don't blame me if I fail miserably. This place is getting kind of rowdy, and I don't want to end up with a black eye trying to save your seat."

"You're almost forty years old. I'm sure you can manage to save my seat."

Daphne smoothed a hand over her hair. "*Thank you* for reminding me of that. That's *just* what I needed to hear at this exact moment in time."

"Anytime, babe." Skylar blew her a kiss, then turned and slipped through the crowd. Daphne turned her attention back to the spot where she'd last seen Clay. While she'd been in the ladies' room, the band had been replaced by a DJ, and the dance floor, which had gradually expanded to cover most of the deck, was now so full she couldn't locate him. And despite Doug's height, she'd long ago lost track of him and KC. She scanned the entire area again, then gave up and took another sip of her drink.

When the song ended, the DJ, who had been playing hip-hop, changed gears and began to play a slower piece of reggae music. In response, the population on the dance floor collectively slowed down its pace, but there was little attrition. Daphne peered through the crowd, wondering what had happened to KC, but she still couldn't see her.

She took another sip of her rum punch, then closed her eyes and softly rocked her head back and forth to the music. *KC will be fine. I will be fine too.*

Daphne loved reggae music. There was something so soothing about it, so happily mellow, that it always made her smile and feel like everything was going to be fine. Perhaps it was because she usually only heard it playing at barbecues, which by their nature are, typically at least, inherently void of major stressors. Whatever the association, reggae made her feel relaxed and happy, which was exactly what she needed right now.

The rum punch was also helping her unwind and enjoy herself. Outside of the occasional glass or two of wine (perhaps three on those nights when she'd dabbled with the online dating sites), she wasn't much of a drinker anymore, and while she had drunk less than her friends tonight, she was beginning to feel the effects of the alcohol. However momentarily, the edges were softened, the nerves calmed, the awkwardness of her encounter with Clay soothed.

She smiled, her eyes still closed. *Things are good. I'm on gorgeous St. Mirika with my dear friends and having a really nice time. Who cares if I have crow's feet.*

"Excuse me, is someone sitting here?"

Daphne opened her eyes and saw a slender brunette standing in front of her. She looked to be in her early twenties. She also looked like she was about to cry.

Without thinking, Daphne pushed her purse to one side and patted the empty seat next to her. "Not anymore. Please, sit down. Are you okay?"

The girl pressed her palms against her eyes and sighed. "I'm so embarrassed."

Just moments ago Daphne had felt intimidated by the age gap between herself and a good chunk of the female patrons at the Castaway, but all that melted away at the sight of this teary-eyed young woman. Her maternal instinct kicked in with a force that surprised her.

"What's wrong?" She put her hand on the woman's svelte arm.

The young woman slowly removed her palms from her face, but her birdlike shoulders remained slumped. "I feel so stupid," she said softly, not making eye contact.

"Why? What happened?" Daphne asked.

The woman didn't reply right away, but it was clear she was collecting her thoughts, so Daphne waited patiently for her to respond.

After a moment the woman took a deep breath, then wiped a tear from her cheek and began to speak, still without making eye contact. "I met this really cute guy here last night, and he seemed kind of interested, so I was hoping to run into him again tonight. That's basically the reason I came here, to be honest. But . . . but . . . he's with someone else. I just saw them together."

Daphne made a sympathetic face. "I'm so sorry. Men can be so fickle." Her brain suddenly recalled a similar situation from her freshman year in college. It had been two decades, but she still remembered it vividly because of the anguish she'd felt. She'd had her eye on a cute sophomore in her American history class, and she went out of her way to sit next to him whenever she could do so without being too obvious. After a handful of brief yet flirtatious conversations—mostly initiated by her—he'd asked her over to watch a movie at the off-campus apartment he shared with two buddies. When she arrived, he opened up his refrigerator and offered her a beer, which turned into several, and they ended up making out on the couch until his roommates came home. It was all quite innocent, but it was dreamlike to Daphne. She barely knew him, but their evening together cast a spell over her that left her giddy and literally unable to eat, something that had never happened to her before. That same night she'd begun making plans in her head for all the fun things they would do together—picnics, dinners, date nights, more movies on the couch—all under the intoxicating haze of romance.

The very next afternoon, as Daphne was still floating in the warm memories of his kisses, she spotted him walking arm and arm with another girl—and not in a platonic way. She was crushed.

More than twenty years later, she still remembered what that felt like, how hurt and humiliated she'd been. She also remembered the jarring realization of how quickly she'd begun planning a future with someone who had already left her in his past.

How eager she'd been to find her Prince Charming at such a tender age.

"I'm sorry," she said again to the devastated young woman sitting next to her in Skylar's seat.

The brunette gave her a weary smile. "Thanks for being so nice. I'm Janine, by the way."

"I'm Daphne. And there's no need to thank me. We've all been there. It stings now, but eventually it goes away, I promise." Daphne couldn't even recall that young man's name now. Was it Jim? John? Maybe James? She remembered that it had been something nondescript, and while she'd found him dreamy at the time, over the years both his name and face had been absorbed into the massive blur that was now *the past*.

"Are you here with your family?" Janine asked. "I'm on spring break from Florida State."

Daphne smiled and shook her head. "Not this trip. I'm with two girlfriends. My daughter's with her dad this week. I'm . . . divorced." *There. I said it. And the world didn't end.*

Janine's eyes got a little bigger. "You're here with two *friends*?"

"Yep, from college actually. We met in the dorms."

"That's so cool. I hope when I'm, um, older, that I still do fun things like that."

Daphne laughed. "I'm not *that* old."

Janine blushed and pushed a loose strand behind her ear. "Oh, I didn't mean to . . . um . . . you know . . . "

Daphne smiled. "It's fine, really, I'm just giving you a hard time." She knew Janine wasn't trying to insult her, and while Daphne *was* feeling quite maternal at the moment, it was clear that Janine viewed her as a mother figure and not a contemporary of any sort. Then again, back when Daphne was in college, she would have thought the exact same thing at the sight of an older single woman at a bar. She probably would have been horrified, to be honest. When she was in college, she thought twenty-five was old. Truly old, as in time-to-hang-it-up old.

She snickered to herself at the memory. How could she have ever thought twenty-five was old?

She took a sip of her drink and looked at Janine. The young woman was nice-looking, there was no denying that, but her little black dress was a little too tight, her makeup a bit too heavy. She'd come to St. Mirika to enjoy her spring break with her friends, but here she was, fretting over a boy she'd just met and would probably never see again. She was trying too hard and wasting her time, but she didn't know it . . . yet. *She'll learn.*

Daphne remembered how she used to do the same thing when she was younger. She kept barking up the wrong romantic tree and could never understand why it didn't turn out the way she wanted it to. Over time, with the benefit of hindsight, she'd realized that's what a lot of young women do. Not all of them, of course, but a *lot* of them. In college Daphne often put so much mental energy into trying to figure out what guys wanted that it never occurred to her to focus on what *she* wanted from a relationship, to consider if the men she was chasing would make *her* happy. Now she understood that it was free spirits like KC and Skylar who were the happiest of all. KC and Skylar never cared a lick about what other people— male or female—thought of them, and finding "the One" at such a young age, if ever, was never on their radar. In college KC was a tomboy who loved to play soccer and wear baseball hats, and she was still that person today, currently on the dance floor and having a blast with a guy a decade her junior who was clearly thrilled to be her dance partner. Eighteen-year-old Skylar was an ambitious honors student who loved to banter with many boys and kiss even more of them, but first and foremost she focused on herself. Now she was running a global sales operation, dating multiple men, and still setting her own rules.

"Where are your friends?" Janine asked Daphne. "I lost mine."

Daphne gestured inside, then toward the dance floor. "One's at the bar; the other's somewhere out there."

Janine looked surprised. "The dance floor?"

Daphne nodded. "She may have a few years on you, but KC will outlast you *and* all your friends. Trust me."

"That's cool. She sounds fun."

"Yes, KC is definitely cool *and* fun." Daphne felt a stirring of pride at her friend's perpetual youthfulness, just as she had during the football game earlier. And, by association, she began to feel a little bit of pride in herself. After all, while not on the dance floor, she *was* in a bar right now. And she *had* played football earlier in the day. She was also enjoying herself along the way. There was definitely something to be said for that.

"How long are you here?" Janine asked.

"Just a few days." Daphne smiled at her, and while she envied her radiant skin and cascading hair—as she had the young women in the restroom—she didn't envy the insecurity that emanated from her. With even more clarity, Daphne realized just how much she'd grown up since her college days.

She also realized something else. *I don't want to be that age anymore.*

Instead of mourning the air-brushed memories of her lost youth, she was now seeing that while she'd certainly had fun in that period of her life, it hadn't been without its bumpy patches, and she was glad it was over. For better or for worse, Daphne now knew who she was at her core, even if she'd allowed herself to stray from it during the time she'd been married to Brian. But her personal detour was a different story, one that she knew she needed to address. Janine, however, was still navigating those internal waters, still trying to figure out who she was.

Daphne had already done that. Now it was time to get her back.

She took a sip of her drink and smiled at Janine. "Actually . . . we're all here to celebrate our fortieth birthdays." She felt a sense of relief as she said the words. She'd stepped across the line, spoken her impending age out loud for the first time.

Janine looked shocked. "Forty? For real? I never would have guessed."

Daphne smiled. "Thanks. Mine is tomorrow, actually. Kind of hard to believe, but I'm slowly getting used to it."

"Happy birthday," Janine said. "Really, you look amazing. My mom's forty-three, but she looks way older than you."

Daphne laughed again. No wonder her maternal instinct had kicked in around Janine. She wondered what Skylar would think of her new friend: Where *was* Skylar exactly? She should have been back by now. Daphne craned her neck toward the entrance to the bar but couldn't see her. *Where is she?*

"Oh God, there he is," Janine whispered.

Daphne turned back to look at the young woman, who was now shielding one side of her face with her hand.

"The guy you were with last night?" Daphne asked her.

Janine nodded, not looking up. "I wasn't *with* him, but I kind of wanted to be, if that makes sense. I thought we were having fun, you know, flirting and dancing, and we even kissed a little bit, but then we kind of lost each other in the crowd."

"Which one is he?" Daphne knew men didn't often "lose" women they were interested in.

Janine kept her eyes averted, her hand still shielding her face. "Tall, green T-shirt, tan cargo shorts. Please don't be too obvious."

Daphne casually scanned the dance floor until her eyes rested on the man in question. She covered her mouth with her hand to stifle a gasp . . . and a laugh. It was Scott. Hot Scott. *Okay, this is bizarre.* There was no question about it: she was caught in a generational time warp. Daphne bit her lip. *Oh jeez.*

Out of respect for Janine's feelings, she tried not to show her amusement at the situation, but she found it pretty . . . amusing. *Don't laugh. It will crush her if you laugh.*

"Hey, hot stuff, I'm sorry that took so long." Skylar reappeared from the crowd, holding a small cardboard box filled with fresh drinks.

Daphne squinted at the drinks. "Did you get a job here?"

Skylar smirked. "The line was crazy long, so I decided to stock up. There's no way I'm waiting in that thing again." She smiled down at Janine. "Looks like you made a new friend in my absence. Hi there, I'm Skylar."

"This is Janine," Daphne said. "She's here on spring break with her girlfriends."

"Nice. I like to think I'm on a spring break with my girlfriends too. You want a rum punch, sweetie?" Skylar held up the cardboard tray.

"Did I take your seat? I'm so sorry." Looking a bit embarrassed, Janine stood and reached for her purse. "I should try to find my friends anyway."

"Don't go on my account," Skylar said. "We can all fit. Come on, stay put and have a drink with us. You look like you could use one."

Janine sat back down and gave Skylar a weak smile. "Is it that obvious?"

"Kind of, but then again I work in sales and have a freakish ability to read people." Skylar sat down and handed Janine a glass. "What's up?"

"Boy trouble," Daphne said.

"*All* boys are trouble." Skylar surveyed the deck. "Is the culprit here?"

Daphne looked at Janine. "Can I tell her?"

Janine nodded softly as she took a sip of her drink.

Daphne shifted her eyes to the dance floor. "Tall with dark hair, green T-shirt, tan cargo shorts. He was kissing Janine here *last* night, but tonight he's here with another girl."

Skylar's eyes followed Daphne's, then flickered with recognition when they landed on Scott, who appeared to be dirty dancing with a young blonde about Janine's age. She quickly looked at Daphne and gave her a *Got it* nod. The amused look on her face showed she shared Daphne's outlook on the peculiarity of the situation. Janine was in knots over the tenuous love triangle, but for Skylar the triangle—make that *square*—was hardly a source of drama. Quite the contrary, and Daphne knew they would laugh about it as soon as Janine was out of earshot.

Daphne stole a quick glance at Janine. She looked sad, disillusioned, and, well, a bit clueless. Just as Daphne had been at her age. *Score another point in favor of being older.*

Skylar sipped her drink. "I'm sorry he kissed and bailed, but better that than to *sleep with you and bail*, right?" She gave Janine a sympathetic smile, and Daphne again admired her friend's compassion. Just a few minutes ago Skylar had been planning to put a few moves of her own on the man in question, and here she was comforting a woman roughly half her age about him.

Janine half smiled, then set down her unfinished drink and stood up. "I guess so. I think I'm going to go back to the hotel."

"You sure?" Daphne asked. "What about your friends?"

She pursed her lips. "They won't miss me, trust me." Her eyes darted to the dance floor.

Daphne and Skylar exchanged a glance, and then they understood.

Skylar narrowed her eyes at the crowd. "Is the blonde he's dancing with one of your friends?"

Janine nodded slightly.

"Ouch," Daphne said. That had to hurt.

"Does she *know* you like him?" Skylar asked.

Janine nodded again. "I think so. I mean, she was here last night."

"So she saw you two kissing?"

Janine swallowed, and her cheeks flushed red. "I wouldn't say we were *kissing*, exactly. I, um, I kind of tried to kiss him, but he didn't really, um, reciprocate very much. I was . . . I was pretty drunk." She looked mortified, and Daphne's heart broke a little for her. "I didn't tell my friends about it."

"Kiss or no kiss, if she knows you like him, then she's not your friend," Skylar said.

Janine wiped a tear from her eye. "I think she's just drunk right now and doesn't know what she's doing. She's usually really sweet, I swear."

Skylar scratched her cheek. "Then you're a nicer person than I am. Then again, a lot of people are nicer than I am."

Daphne put her arm around Skylar. "I think you're very nice."

Janine laughed weakly. "You two have been really kind, thank you." She turned and gave them a slight wave, then left.

After she was out of earshot, Daphne shook her head. "Poor thing."

Skylar sipped her drink. "Girls can be so horrible to each other at that age, especially when alcohol and douchey men are involved. I remember once freshman year at Northwestern I was at this party, and a girl I'd become friendly with in one of my classes made out with a guy she *knew* I had a crush on, like almost right in front of me. And she didn't even *like* him. I think she just did it to get back at her boyfriend. I never spoke to her again, although I don't think she even knew how much I hated her because we didn't run into each other that much after the semester ended, but in my mind she was blacklisted forever. I got even, though."

"You did? How?"

Skylar smiled and pointed to herself. "Years ago she applied for a position at my company, and *I* got to interview her. Trust me, she didn't get the job."

"Remind me not to get on your bad side," Daphne said. "You play hardball."

Skylar sipped her rum punch. "I don't care how drunk you are, or how much the world has changed since we were in college, or any of that crap. It's pretty black and white. You don't engage with a guy if you know your friend likes him, period." She held up her palm. "To people like that I say *unsubscribe*."

Daphne laughed. "You unsubscribe from people?"

"All the time. Life's too short to deal with unstable personalities." She scanned the area for KC. "Where's Serena Williams?"

"Still on the dance floor, I suppose. I haven't seen her since you went inside."

"There she is." Skylar pointed through the crowd.

"Where?" Daphne's eyes followed in search of KC yet saw nothing but a mass of pulsating bodies. The DJ was back to playing hip-hop, and the crowd was now practically jumping up and down in unison.

"At the bar on the other side of the dance floor."

Daphne raised her eyebrows. "There's *another* bar here?"

Skylar stood up. "Apparently so. I wish I'd known that before I wasted half the evening waiting in line for these drinks. Let's go find the little one."

Daphne glanced at their bench. "Do you think we should give up our seats? They're kind of comfortable."

"All good things must come to an end. Besides, I promised KC we'd dance with her."

Daphne put a hand on her own chest. "You promised KC that *we'd* dance with her? I don't remember being part of that discussion."

Skylar grabbed Daphne's arm and pulled her up. "You are now. Let's go."

They carefully skirted around the swarm on the dance floor and spotted KC sitting on a stool at a small outdoor bar at the very edge of the deck. To her right was Doug. They were both holding a drink and laughing.

"There she is," Skylar said.

Daphne squinted. "Are my eyes playing tricks on me, or is that an empty shot glass in front of her?"

Skylar smiled. "Your eyes are still working just fine. I'm so happy to see that right now."

When she noticed her friends approaching, KC grinned and held her arms open wide. "*There* you are. I was wondering what had happened to you."

Daphne laughed. "What happened to *us*? This is the first time we've moved since we got here."

Doug put his hand on the top of KC's head. "The captain here's a little tipsy."

"The captain?" Daphne raised her eyebrows.

"As in captain of the football team," he said.

Skylar held up her drink. "Nice. I may add that to my arsenal of nicknames."

KC stood on her tiptoes and hugged Skylar and Daphne. "I'm having so much fun on this vacation! Skylar, thanks so much for organizing it rock-star-style! And Daphne, thanks so much for finally getting that pretty face of yours out of boring *Ohio* to come hang out with us!"

Skylar looked at Daphne and mouthed the word "hammered."

KC hugged them even tighter. "Have I told you two how much I mean to you?"

Daphne laughed. "What?"

Doug chuckled and pointed to the empty shot glass. "That was our third."

"Three shots?" Skylar's eyes grew wide. "The woman's smaller than my twelve-year-old niece."

Doug held up his hands in a "don't shoot" gesture. "She insisted. She said we were celebrating our victory in the football game."

"We were *celebrating*!" KC pumped her fist. "We are *champions*!"

Skylar looked at Daphne and mouthed the words "She's going to die tomorrow."

Daphne laughed. It had been nearly twenty years since she'd seen KC like this, and she was thoroughly enjoying it.

"Guess what!" KC said in a voice way louder than necessary. "Doug said he's *never* seen a girl throw a football as well as I did today. And I'm *forty*!"

Skylar gave Doug a little nudge with her elbow. "Don't you love how she just owns that?"

He smiled and nodded. "She's the best. I've never met anyone like her."

"We should figure out how to bottle her positive attitude and sell it," Daphne said.

Skylar whistled. "Can you imagine? We'd make a fortune. Yet another business to start when we get home."

"We'd make a fortune on what?!" KC yelled. "On being *champions*?!"

Skylar put an arm around her. "We're right here, peanut. No need to shatter any eardrums."

"Hey, people, we wondered where you'd gone off to."

They turned and saw Clay approaching the bar, followed by Scott. Daphne waited to see if the blonde from earlier was trailing behind Clay, but she didn't spot her. *It's probably only a matter of time before she resurfaces.* Scott appeared to be solo as well. For now, at least.

Not wanting to experience that awkwardness again, Daphne touched Skylar's arm and gestured toward the other side of the deck. "Maybe we should take KC back to where we were sitting," she said in a hushed voice.

Skylar gave her a strange look and kept her voice at a normal decibel. "Why would we do that?"

"We wouldn't want to, you know, *intrude*," Daphne practically whispered.

"Since when are attractive women an intrusion?" Suddenly Scott was behind them, one hand on Daphne's shoulder, the other on Skylar's.

Daphne gave him a sheepish look. "How did you hear that?"

"It's a gift. I can't see twenty feet in front of my face, but I can hear a pin drop in the other room."

"Skylar has superhuman hearing too!" KC yelled.

Scott smiled at Skylar. "Yet another thing we have in common."

"What was the first thing?" Skylar asked him.

"I'll tell you later. First things first." He turned and gestured to the bartender. "Anyone need a drink?"

"I'll take a brew," Clay said.

"Those are the magic words," Doug said with a nod. "Grab me one as well."

Skylar nodded too. "You don't have to ask me twice. A rum punch would hit the spot."

"I'm in," KC raised her hand.

Skylar pulled KC's hand down. "I think the muppet here's had enough."

Scott looked at Daphne. "What about you, Daphne? What's your poison?"

Daphne smiled and pointed to the rum punch she'd been nursing. "I'm good, thanks."

As Scott leaned toward the bartender to order, Daphne turned her head and scanned the crowd. *If she comes back, she comes back.*

Doug put his arm around KC but spoke to Skylar. "Think this one is going to make it out of bed tomorrow? She might have a monster hangover."

"I'll make it!" KC shouted. "Just watch me!"

Skylar shrugged. "We'll see. Our only formal plan for the day is to go to a spa, so all she really has to do is go from lying down in one place to lying down in another. How hard can that be?"

"What about the monkey forest?" KC frowned. "I want to feed them bananas!"

Skylar smiled. "That's right, we're going to the monkey forest too. Can't forget the monkeys."

KC pumped a fist in the air. "We're going to the monkey forest tomorrow! And it's Daphne's fortieth birthday! Can you *believe* that? Doesn't she look *amazing*? She's so *pretty*! Isn't she *pretty*?!" She reached up and began to pet Daphne's hair.

Daphne felt her face turn beet red. Doug clearly knew their age, but until now Scott and Clay hadn't, at least not officially. *I guess that cat's out of the bag.*

Clay looked at Daphne. "Forty? Really? I never would have guessed."

Daphne did her best to mimic Skylar's trademark *What can you do?* shrug, although part of her wanted to run onto the beach right then, dig a big hole in the sand, then jump into it and hide. But Clay didn't have to know that, right? She added a smile to her shrug. "As Skylar says, forty is the new black." *Maybe I am learning from Skylar.*

Clay laughed. "Well, whatever color forty is, it suits you."

"Thank you." *I'm beginning to think so too.*

The DJ began playing "Dancing Queen" by ABBA, and KC suddenly jumped up from her barstool, wobbled slightly, then steadied herself. "Okay, people, this is a tune that simply *must* be danced to! Who wants to join me? Skylar, you promised."

"Okay, let's go," Skylar said, setting her drink on the bar. "Who can say no to ABBA?"

Scott put a hand on Skylar's lower back. "Show me the way," he said.

"Let's rock this thing." Doug pointed toward the dance floor.

As they all made their way toward the pulsating crowd, Clay caught Daphne's eye, then jutted his chin toward KC, who was waving her arms in the air. "I think the tequila's been whispering in someone's ear," he said.

·   ·   ·

After what seemed to Daphne like hours but in reality was just a handful of songs, KC finally ran out of steam. When the band stopped to take a short break, she put one hand on her hip and raised her other in the air. "Okay, I think I just hit the wall."

"Thank God." Skylar immediately bolted off the dance floor in the direction of the exit. "I hit that thing like three days ago. Let's get out of here."

Daphne quickly followed her. "I thought you'd never say the word."

"I'm pretty beat too," Clay said.

"Anyone want a roadie?" Doug asked, pointing to the bar.

Clay shook his head. "I'm good, thanks."

Skylar pointed to the beach. "I'm walking home if anyone wants to join me."

"You guys are really leaving?" Scott ostensibly asked the group, but he was clearly looking at Skylar.

"Why don't you go find your friend?" Skylar said over her shoulder. "She seemed fun."

"What friend?"

"The sorority girl who was hanging off your arm earlier. I bet she'd love to dance with you."

Scott laughed. "She's a kid."

Skylar shrugged, still not looking back. "I could say the same about you."

"Ouch."

She turned around and put her hands on her hips, then smiled at him. "You want to walk us home?"

"You have anything to drink there?"

"Perhaps."

He smiled back. "Then yes."

"Okay, then walk us home." She intertwined an arm with KC's on one side and Doug's on the other, then gestured with her head for him to follow. "Let's hit it, people."

Daphne watched Scott trot to catch up with the group, figuratively as well as literally chasing her friend. *Bravo, Skylar.*

"You ready to go?" Clay asked Daphne.

"More than ready." She placed her hands on either side of her head. "My ears are ringing."

In a staggered formation, the six of them made their way down the beach. A number of people were milling around, many of them fellow refugees from the Castaway. As they approached the shore, Daphne turned back for another look at the bar, which had thinned out a bit but was still quite crowded.

"I wonder what time it will finally quiet down?" she said to Clay.

"Not for hours. We were there pretty late last night."

"This is plenty late for me. I'm glad our house is close enough to the action to be fun, but not too close to keep me awake all night."

"Are you a light sleeper?"

"Light enough." She didn't feel the need to tell him that she had earplugs in her travel bag. And an eye mask. *He knows how old I am. That's enough information for one night.*

Daphne and Clay eventually caught up with the others. Skylar glanced back at the fading lights of the Castaway, then looked at Doug. "What happened to the rest of your crew?"

"God knows," Doug said. "Attrition is pretty normal for a group our size."

Scott, who was now walking on the other side of Skylar, put a hand on her shoulder. "I can't say I have a problem with it."

Ignoring his overture, Skylar yawned and stretched her arms over her head. "I haven't danced that much in ages. I may fall asleep before I make it home."

"Aw, don't say that," Scott said. "You promised me a nightcap."

Daphne glanced at Skylar to see her reaction to his comment, but Skylar didn't seem to have one. At least a visible one. *She's so good,* Daphne thought.

Before Skylar could respond, out of nowhere KC bolted ahead of the group.

"Oh sweet potato, what is she doing *now?*" Skylar asked.

"She's like a superhero," Doug said with a wistful smile as he watched KC go.

Daphne laughed. "She *is* like a superhero. Can you believe she pulled out the Running Man and the Robot on the dance floor?"

Doug kept smiling. "I get happy just thinking about that. I love how she doesn't care about looking like an idiot. Not that she's an idiot, of course. You know what I mean, right?" He scratched the back of his head. "Oh hell, that came out wrong. Did that make me sound like an asshole?"

"You *are* an asshole," Scott said.

Clay laughed. "Takes one to know one."

Skylar patted Doug on the arm. "No worries, I totally get what you're saying. Now let's catch her before she tries to swim to Florida." She quickened her pace, as did Doug and Scott, leaving Clay and Daphne trailing behind.

Daphne waved good-bye at them. "No more running for me. I've had enough exercise for today."

Clay laughed. "You're putting your foot down, are you? Just saying no?"

She smiled up at him. "I guess I am. Not really by choice, though. Sad as it sounds, I'm just too tired. Maybe I should go to California and follow KC around for a few weeks. That would whip me into shape."

"Where do you live now?"

"Columbus. About as far from the beach as it gets. I guess that's not really true, but it's far enough. What about you?"

"I'm in New York, but plenty of my buddies from business school work in Chicago, so let me know if you ever need me to pick you up a purple sweatshirt. Or maybe a purple license plate holder? I know you Wildcats love your purple."

She smiled. "Thanks, I'll remember that. Oh my gosh, look! KC's doing one of her best moves!" She pointed about fifty feet ahead of them.

KC, who had finally stopped running, now had stretched her arms straight over her head. She remained that way for a moment, then proceeded to bend backward until her hands reached the sand. Skylar, Doug, and Scott stood a few feet away, buckled over in laughter.

"Is she really doing a *backbend*?" Clay squinted down the beach.

Daphne clasped her hands together and smiled. "I knew it was only a matter of time before she pulled that one out of her pocket. I'm surprised it took this long, to be honest. After I found out she'd been doing shots, I figured we'd see a backbend right on the dance floor."

"I take it you've seen her do this before?"

Daphne pushed a loose strand of hair away from her eyes. "Oh yes, many times. In college that was her go-to party trick, or one of them, at least. I'm sure it doesn't surprise you that she had multiple party tricks."

He chuckled. "No, I can't say that it does."

"I can't believe she can still contort her body that way. Doesn't it look painful?"

Clay made a strained face and put his hands on his lower back. "I think I'd end up in traction if I attempted a stunt like that."

Daphne put her hands on her lower back too. "You and me both. The girl has superhuman DNA, that's the only way to explain it. Either that or she's been lacing her oatmeal with steroids all these years."

Clay chuckled again. "I doubt that. Her voice is way too high." He glanced at his watch. "Hey, it's after midnight, so it's officially tomorrow. May I be the first to wish you a very happy birthday?"

She covered her face with her hands. "Oh my gosh, I can't believe I'm forty." *But it feels kind of good to say that out loud.*

He put his hand on top of her head. "Come on, you look great for *any* age, and you know it."

She removed her hands and smiled. "You're just saying that to be nice." *But I'm thrilled you said it.*

He gestured toward the multiple thatched-roof bars and restaurants peppering the beach. "I respectfully beg to differ. Come have a birthday drink with me?"

"Now?" *Weren't we just talking about being tired and going to sleep?*

"Why not? The Pirate's Cove is right over there. We had a few drinks there our first night on the island. It's a fun little spot."

"What about them?" Daphne pointed down the beach. KC was up and running again, barely a dot on the horizon now. Skylar, Doug, and Scott were trailing behind, a trio of silhouettes in the darkness.

"They're all adults—they'll find their way back. Come on, Daphne, it's your *birthday*."

She pressed her palms together and stared briefly into the moonlight. She hated to ditch her friends, but then again, KC wouldn't last much longer anyway, and given the obvious chemistry between Scott and Skylar, it was probably only a matter of time before they wanted to be alone together. And besides, wasn't that part of the reason Daphne had come to St. Mirika in the first place? To focus on herself, for once? To stop being locked in the past? To let go of her expectations about what life *should* be like and finally start . . . *living it? No more vanilla!*

Clay was nice and smart and funny. And very good-looking. And he was asking to buy her a birthday drink. On the beach. Just the two of them. Maybe it meant nothing, but what did that matter? She tried to squash the internal chatter. *Stop worrying so much! Just have fun! Take a chance for once!*

"Daphne? You there?" Clay waved a hand in front of her face. "What do you say? Can I buy you a drink to ring in your birthday?"

She hesitated for just a moment, then smiled. "Okay, sure, why not?"

"That's the spirit. Let's go."

They walked up the sand to the Pirate's Cove. A small bamboo roof covered a handful of round wooden tables surrounding a sliver of a dance floor. A string of red lights encircled the rows of intermittent bamboo poles on either side that served loosely as a fence. The place was barely a quarter the size of the Castaway, and Daphne was immediately drawn to its cozy charm.

"What's your poison, pirate?" Clay asked her as they approached the tiny bar.

She held up her palms. "I have no idea. What kind of poison do pirates drink on their birthdays?"

He picked up a laminated list of drink specials and studied the options. "Hmm. How about a Treasure Chest? Or a Booty Drop?"

She gave him a look. "There's really a drink called *Booty Drop*?"

He pointed to the menu. "Swear to God. I couldn't make up something that bad."

She smiled. "Okay then, I'll try a Booty Drop. Why not, right?"

"Do you want to know what's in it?"

"Not really. I prefer not to know, actually." *I'm scared to know, actually.*

He arched his eyebrows. "Going in blind, are we now? Are you always this adventurous?"

She smiled. "Not really. Maybe." *I want to be. I used to be.*

"I like your attitude. Why don't you grab one of those high tables, and I'll order the drinks."

"Sounds good." *I'm liking my attitude too.*

She climbed onto a wooden stool and observed her surroundings. The place was about half-full and hummed with conversation, but it felt downright subdued compared to the mayhem they'd just experienced. The demographic here was also noticeably older than that of the Castaway, and Daphne felt like she'd left—make that *escaped from*—a college fraternity party to join an adult cocktail party. Civilized, calm, and pleasant. She loved it. *This is much more my style.*

As if on cue, soft island-style music began playing in the background. Daphne smiled, and for the first time wondered *why* she'd been so fixated on turning forty. Yes, it was a big milestone, but the earth was still rotating. She was also pretty sure the sun was going to come up in a few hours. Maybe she'd let this birthday take on too much symbolism? Maybe it was time to stop being so afraid of starting over?

Clay approached with their drinks. He took a seat and handed her a glass, then raised his to hers. "Happy birthday, Daphne White. Here's to a long and happy life."

She clinked her glass against his. "Thank you, Clay Hanson." *Clay Handsome.*

Without realizing it, Daphne found herself studying him as they each sipped their drink.

"What?" he finally said, touching his cheeks and chin. "Do I have something on my face?"

She laughed and shook her head. "No."

"Then what?"

She took a deep breath. *Just say it.*

"To be honest, I didn't expect to be ringing in my birthday with the likes of you."

Clay narrowed his eyes. "The likes of me? Am I that unappealing?"

She blushed. "I'm sorry, that came out wrong. It's just that . . ." She looked down.

"Do you think there's a warrant out for my arrest or something?"

She laughed and regained eye contact. "I highly doubt the police are on your heels. What I was trying to say is that . . ." *Do it!*

She took another deep breath, then continued. "What I was trying to say is that I haven't been out for a drink with anyone since my ex-husband and I split up. Not that this is a *date* or anything, but I'm just feeling a little out of my comfort zone even being here. I'm sorry, I'm rambling."

"When did you get divorced?"

"We separated over two years ago, but the divorce wasn't final until recently."

"Do you have kids?"

"A daughter, she's fifteen."

"For real? You look way too young to have a fifteen-year-old daughter."

She laughed and pushed a strand of hair out of her eyes. "Tell that to her."

"You haven't been on a date in more than two years?"

She blushed and cast her eyes downward. "No."

He finished his drink and set the glass on the table. "Then let's call this a date."

"What?" She looked up at him.

"You heard me. I'm a man, you're a woman, we're having a drink, *on the beach in St. Mirika*, I might add." He gestured to himself and then to her, then pointed toward the ocean. "I say we label this a date."

She felt her cheeks flush and stared at the table again, too flustered—and thrilled—to respond. *Is this really happening?*

Before she could say anything, the unmistakable roar of thunder shook the Pirate's Cove. They both looked out at the ocean, then up at the sky.

"It's going to pour," Clay said. "Happens all the time here."

Daphne gazed wistfully toward the water again. "So I've heard."

"Do you like rain?"

She tapped her fingertips on the table. "I didn't used to, but the rain here is different. It's so warm, and soothing. I find it . . . enchanting."

"Your hands are enchanting," he said. "Very elegant."

Caught off guard by the non sequitur, she stopped tapping and looked at her fingers, suddenly self-conscious. "Thank you," she said softly.

"And for the record, I wasn't just saying all that to be nice," he said.

She slowly looked up at him. "You weren't just saying what?" She practically whispered the words.

"When I said that you look great for any age, or that you look way too young to have a fifteen-year-old."

She felt her cheeks turn a deeper shade of pink. Acknowledging her age was one thing. *Discussing* it was another.

"Am I making you uncomfortable, Daphne White?"

"A little. Maybe we can change the subject?"

He put a hand over hers. "Sure. How about we talk about how I was serious when I said we should call this a date?"

She swallowed and felt her insides stir at the touch of his skin on hers. *Oh my gosh. This is really happening.*

He began to move his thumb over her hand. "Does it make you nervous that I find you attractive? You seem nervous."

She swallowed and pulled her hand away from his to pick up her glass. "A little."

He chuckled. "You're totally nervous right now. It's cute."

She took a sip of her drink. "So . . . what happened to the girl?"

"What girl?"

"The blonde one you were with at the Castaway?" *The pretty one hanging off you like a necklace?*

He shrugged. "She was nice enough, but not for me."

Daphne sipped her drink again. "Is that so?"

"That is so. Plus, if you hadn't noticed, I've had my eye on someone else tonight."

She gave him a playful look. "Hmm. Interesting." *He likes me!*

He stared at her. "Yes, interesting. I know you're older than I am, Daphne, but if it's not obvious by now, I don't care about age. To be honest, I like you *because* you're older. It makes you different." He began to stroke her forearm with his fingers, and she felt a flurry of tiny sparks flashing throughout her body.

He kept stroking her arm. "That younger woman tonight? I'd be lying if I said I didn't find her attractive, but with you . . . let's just say there's something appealing about dealing with . . . a more sophisticated buyer."

She laughed. "So I'm a harder sell?" *If you only knew how unsophisticated I feel right now.*

"In a way, yes. Now dance with me." He set down his drink and reached for her hand, then pulled her onto the tiny dance floor. He put his hands around her lower back, and together they began to sway to the reggae music. Just one other pair shared the space, a married couple Daphne guessed to be in their fifties. They gave Daphne and Clay a friendly smile before returning their attention to each other.

"The way you carry yourself is elegant, like a ballerina," Clay said. "I noticed that right away when I saw you on the beach yesterday."

"I used to take dance classes when I was younger," she said.

He pulled her closer to him. "I can tell. It's sexy."

She looked up at him. "So you like a challenge? Is that what this is about?"

He tucked a free strand of hair behind her ear, then returned his hand behind her lower back. "Let's stop overanalyzing it, okay? I find you attractive, period."

She smiled. "Really?"

"Yes. From the moment I saw you, I was interested, and that's only grown as I've gotten to know you a little bit. You're pretty, and you're fun to talk to, but I don't want to talk right now." He pulled her even closer, then leaned down and gently touched his lips against hers. She was too surprised to resist, not that she wanted to. As she'd just admitted to him, she hadn't kissed anyone in years. Her body responded accordingly. *Please do that again.*

The tiny sparks she'd felt had been one thing, but the heat that was now buzzing inside made her a bit dizzy. His lips were warm and soft, and her body instinctively pushed against his.

"You're so beautiful," he whispered into her ear.

*You smell so good.* She inhaled deeply to breathe in his scent. She was entranced by it, and she wanted to drink it in.

"Mmm . . . so hot." He nuzzled her neck, then kissed her shoulder before moving back to her lips.

They kissed for a bit longer, then Clay began to caress the back of her neck with his hand. She caught her breath. *Oh my God that feels so good.*

Suddenly aware of what was happening in a very public place, she opened her eyes and glanced around to see if anyone was watching them. The older couple was gone now, and as far as she could tell, no one else there was even looking in their direction, which helped make her a bit less self-conscious. The alcohol also served to dim the glow of self-awareness. She tried to remember the last time she'd behaved like this in public, much less on a dance floor, but her memory didn't reach that far back.

Her mind was also too distracted at the moment to focus on anything besides how good his hands felt on her, how good his lips felt on her. *Please kiss me again.*

"I love your body," he murmured. "And your posture. I thought maybe you were a yoga instructor."

She laughed. "Definitely not."

"Well, whatever you're doing, it's working."

She smiled but didn't respond to the compliment. If he only knew how her muscles already ached. She really needed to start exercising more often, especially now that she knew guys like Clay Hanson were paying attention.

Just then they heard another roar, followed by the crashing din of raindrops hitting the roof.

"There it is," Clay said as he looked up. "Don't you just love that sound?"

Daphne closed her eyes and nodded. "It's beautiful."

He leaned down and spoke softly into her ear again. "*You're beautiful.*"

"I could listen to the rain all night," she said, her eyes still closed. *I could stay like this all night.*

"Can I spend it with you?"

She pulled away from him and opened her eyes. "What?" Had he read her mind?

He gave her a suggestive smile and pulled her back toward him. "You heard me."

She did her best not to giggle like a teenager, but she couldn't help herself. "Is this how it works now? I've been out of the loop for a while."

"You tell me." He began caressing her shoulder, then lightly ran his fingers up and down her arm.

She closed her eyes again, so glad she'd worn a sundress, savoring the touch of his hands on her skin. She pressed her cheek against his firm chest, listening to the drumming of the rain on the thatched ceiling above them.

They swayed like that for few minutes before he spoke again. "Please take me home with you," he whispered into her ear.

The question sent a sizzle down her spine. The familiar yet unfamiliar sensation of attraction, mixed with anticipation, stirring something warm inside her. *I forgot what this feels like.*

Their bodies pressed together, they continued to slow dance. The rain poured around them in sheets, nearly drowning out the soft sound of the music.

After a few moments, she spoke quietly in his chest. "Okay." *Come home with me. Make me feel alive again.*

He lifted her chin with his fingertips and smiled down at her. "Is that a yes?"

She glanced out at the beach. Her friends were long gone by now, and for the first time she wondered if any part of the group's separation had been intentional. If it had been, she was grateful to whoever had orchestrated it. She turned her eyes back to Clay and felt her lips turn up at the corners. Then she nodded ever so faintly. "That's a yes."

· · ·

When Clay and Daphne reached her beach house, soaking wet from their walk home in the rain, all the lights were off save for a small one on the back deck. The inside was still and quiet. Daphne peered in the window, then turned toward Clay and put a finger over her lips.

Clay eyed her with suspicion. "Do you want me to be quiet so we don't wake them, or so they don't know I'm here?"

Daphne tried not to giggle but couldn't help herself. "Both. Will you take those off?" She pointed to his flip-flops before awkwardly removing her own. "I think you got me a little tipsy."

He arched an eyebrow. "So you're saying I'm taking advantage of you?"

She reached for the door handle. "Only if you want to." *Please take advantage of me.*

He laughed and scratched the back of his head. "I'm not sure how to take that. That's hardly a glowing invitation."

"Any invitation is better than no invitation, am I right?" She quietly opened the glass door and stepped inside the dark house.

"Touché," he said as he followed her.

"Oh my gosh, it's dark in here," Daphne whispered.

He put a hand on her lower back and kept his deep voice hushed as well. "I like dark. Lead the way to the bedroom so I can get you out of that wet dress."

"Scared I might catch cold, are you?" She reached behind her and took his hand, then carefully led him through the living room toward the hall, tiptoeing across the tile floors. *I can't believe I'm doing this. I'm so glad I'm doing this.*

"I feel like we're sneaking into your parents' house," he said. "If we get caught, are you going to be grounded?"

Daphne giggled again. "Shh." She couldn't remember the last time she'd *giggled*. She also couldn't remember the last time she'd tiptoed in the dark while holding hands with a man she barely knew. *This is so much fun.*

When they reached the kitchen, she noticed two empty bottles of wine on the counter—and two used goblets in the sink. She pointed to them and was about to say something when Clay pulled her toward him and kissed her deeply, stroking her hair as he did so. When they finally broke apart, he gently touched her cheek.

"I've wanted to do that since I first saw you," he whispered.

She smiled up at him but didn't say anything, trying to catch her breath. Her mind, at the moment, was consumed by a single thought. *Please do it again.*

"You had to know that," he said.

"I wasn't sure." *I hoped, but I didn't know.*

He put a hand over his heart. "You're killing me."

She put her hand over his. "That's a criticism of *me*, not of you. I'm sort of out of practice at this, if you couldn't tell."

He slipped his hands around her lower back, then leaned down and kissed her bare shoulder. "Maybe that's why I'm so attracted to you."

She smiled up at him. "You find it attractive that I can't even tell when a guy's flirting with me?" *I find that sort of . . . pathetic.*

He grazed her forehead with his fingertips. "I find you attractive because you don't try too hard. A lot of women my age . . . they try too hard."

She cast her eyes downward. A vision of Janine from earlier suddenly flashed before her. *I used to be like that. I don't want to be like that ever again.*

She knew now that by default women Janine's age were beautiful and attractive. They didn't *have* to try. *Youth really is wasted on the young.*

"You smell so good." He nuzzled her neck. "What perfume are you wearing?"

She shook her head. "I'm not. Must be my shampoo, or maybe the body lotion I put on? I just grabbed whatever was in the bathroom."

He stroked her cheek again. "*Another* example of not trying too hard. It's what makes you so sexy." He lightly tugged at the strap of her sundress. "I think this is sexy too. Simple, yet beautiful."

She glanced downward. "You like it?"

He put his finger on her chin and gently lifted it. "Very much. However, as nice as it looks on you, I think it would look much nicer crumpled up next to the bed."

She laughed, then quickly covered her mouth and lowered her voice. "That's a pretty good line, I'll give you that. Did you get it from the same guy who gave you the tequila jokes?"

"I actually came up with it all on my own, so take that as a compliment. Now can we please go make out?"

Daphne smiled and put a finger to her lips, then gestured for him to follow her down the hall. As silently as was possible for a man his size, Clay tiptoed behind her. A sliver of light shone underneath the door to KC's room. Skylar's room, located at the far end, was completely dark. When they arrived in front of her room, Daphne reached for the doorknob, but Clay stopped her before she touched it. He turned her shoulders, then gently pressed her back up against the door.

"You're so sexy, Daphne."

Before she could respond, he leaned down and moved his lips softly along her neck and shoulder. "You're driving me crazy," he whispered.

Again she felt intoxicated by his scent, by the tingling sensation of his mouth against her skin, by the seductive sound of his breathing. *The feeling is mutual.*

After a few moments he lifted his head, stared intensely into her eyes without speaking, then quietly opened the door and pulled her inside.

# Chapter Nine

When Daphne woke up, the first thing she saw in the soft morning light was Fred. The gecko. Perched on the ceiling directly above her. She smiled at him. *Hi, Fred. Can you see me?* She was about to stretch her arms over her head, then caught her breath as the memory of the night before hit her. Along with the realization that she wasn't wearing pajamas. *Oh my gosh.* She slowly turned her head to the right. Clay lay on his back, sound asleep, breathing deeply. She bit her lip. *Oh my gosh. What do I do now?* She shut her eyes tight, then opened them and looked back up at the ceiling, trying not to laugh. *Fred, tell me what to do!*

She lay there frozen, literally paralyzed with uncertainty over what to do at that exact moment, not to mention how to act when Clay woke up. It had been more than fifteen years since she'd spent the night with anyone other than Brian. And while she'd had her share of make-out sessions before she got married, she'd never *slept* with a man so quickly before. Was there a next-morning protocol she was supposed to follow? She didn't know it back then, and she certainly didn't know it now. *Does this mean I'm slutty? Or am I kind of cool?* She smiled to herself. What she *did* know was that she'd enjoyed herself the night before. A lot. Clay had made sure of that.

She flushed at the memory and glanced up at Fred again. *My green friend, today I will consider myself cool.*

She hadn't expected to sleep with Clay. When she agreed to bring him back to the beach house, she thought they'd continue what they'd begun at the Pirate's Cove, make out a little bit, nothing all *that* serious. But things changed once he closed the bedroom door. At first she'd been nervous to be alone with him, but her anxiety didn't last long. The intensity with which he'd kissed her lips, neck, and shoulders; the compliments he'd breathed into her ears; the gentle way he'd caressed her skin: one by one her inhibitions began to slip away, and then it just . . . happened.

She'd relished every minute of it, especially the way he'd wrapped his strong arms around her and grazed the top of her head with his lips as they finally settled in to get some sleep.

"You're beautiful," he'd whispered before drifting off.

She closed her eyes, the hint of a smile still on her face. *I slept with Clay Handsome.*

Just as she began to replay the steamy highlights in her head, she felt a tingling in her throat, followed by an uncontrollable need to cough. *No! Not now!*

She reached her hand to her neck and squeezed gently, as if that might somehow prevent the inevitable. She knew what was coming, but she didn't want to wake him up. She wasn't ready to face him, not yet. She willed the sensation to go away, but it only grew more intense, and soon her eyes started watering. She thought about trying to exit the bed without making much commotion, but now it was too late. She sat up and grabbed the pillow, then coughed into it.

She gently let go of the pillow and looked at Clay again, then slowly removed the comforter from her chest and—as quietly as she could—got out of bed. She desperately wanted to brush her teeth, check her face, and put something on! She choked back a laugh at the sight of her and Clay's clothes—still damp—lying in a heap on the floor. She scooped them up, tiptoed into the bathroom and gently closed the door, then carefully hung them over the shower railing, remembering the lusty rush with which they'd been removed, and was delighted to realize she wasn't the least bit disturbed by the mess. *Apparently we had more important things to do.*

She pulled her nightie off the hook on the door, then quickly slipped it over her head. *That's better.* As she reached for her toothbrush, she evaluated her appearance in the mirror. Besides a tiny smudge of mascara under one eye, her face looked pretty good, or at least as good as it could after only a few hours of sleep—and more than a few rum punches. She carefully removed the mascara with a Q-tip, then pulled her hair back into a ponytail and splashed cold water over her cheeks and forehead, hoping the noise of the running faucet wouldn't wake Clay—and simultaneously wondering if there was any chance he'd sleep through the sound of a flushing toilet.

She chuckled to herself at the absurdity—and unfamiliarity—of her behavior. She'd been married for more than a dozen years, yet here she was, acting like someone half her age. For not the first time this trip, she felt as if she'd gone back in time.

When she was ready to reenter the bedroom, she reached for the door, took a deep breath, and mentally prepared herself to see Clay sitting up in bed, wide awake. Or worse, gone. *Please don't be gone.*

She felt a shudder of dread at the thought that he might have taken off once she left the room. Seeing him after their intimate night together would be awkward, of course, but returning to an empty bedroom? That would be much worse. She hesitated. *He wouldn't do that, would he?*

Holding her breath, she gently nudged the door open with what she hoped was a relaxed look on her face, or at least a semi-normal expression, given all the thoughts running around in her head. Assuming Clay was still there, she had no idea what she was going to say to him. While half her brain was still reliving the feel of his lips on her skin, the other half reminded her that she'd just slept with a complete stranger. Her eyes immediately darted to the bed. Clay was sound asleep on his back, still breathing deeply. She exhaled. *Thank God.*

She quietly walked toward the dresser and picked up her phone to see if there were any messages from Emma, but the screen was blank. She set it back down, then turned around and carefully approached the bed, watching Clay's chest rise and fall softly with his breath. Suddenly a strange thought occurred to her, one that caught her by surprise and—momentarily, at least—trumped her anxiety about having just slept with a man she barely knew. *I'm so glad you're not Brian.*

Before she could ponder the significance of that thought, Clay slowly opened his eyes. He furrowed his brow as if registering his surroundings, then slowly turned his head and made eye contact with her. She gave him a shaky smile and waved. "Good morning."

He yawned and smiled back. "Good morning to you too. And happy birthday."

She put a hand over her mouth. "Oh my gosh, I totally forgot today is my birthday." *What a way to ring it in.*

"I'm that good?" He sat up and patted himself on the back. "Well done, Clay."

She laughed, grateful for the break in tension. "Glad to hear you're not lacking in the self-confidence department." Then again, he had no reason to. She blushed at the memory of how he'd made her feel, how attentive he'd been to her desires.

"What time is it?" he asked.

She glanced at the clock on the nightstand, then crossed her arms in front of her and leaned her weight on one hip. "Just after eight." *Is he planning to leave?*

"I wonder how your buddy KC's feeling today," he said.

"Not great, I imagine. If she's even awake, that is."

"That was quite a gymnastics expo she put on there."

"Yep." Daphne had no idea what to do next, so she just stood there in front of the bed, her arms crossed. *Should I climb back in bed? Would he want me to do that?*

She didn't see any obvious signs of regret in his eyes, but then again, she was hardly an expert at reading the facial expressions of men, especially ones waking up naked in a virtual stranger's bed. *Should I bring up last night?*

Her mind raced for something, anything, to say, but she came up with nothing, so she remained silent, again wishing she had a guidebook for appropriate post-one-night-stand behavior. *Don't make this awkward.*

Clay glanced up at the ceiling. "Nice gecko. We have one in our house too."

"I named him Fred," Daphne blurted, then immediately regretted having done so. Talking to a gecko was odd enough. Naming him was worse. But *telling* anyone about it? That bordered on peculiar, with *peculiar* being a generous euphemism for *weird*.

Clay chuckled. "Nice. I named ours Gordon."

Daphne let out a tiny gasp. "You're joking. You named a gecko too?"

"Not joking. Isn't Gordon the perfect name for a gecko? Doug wanted to call him Mervyn, but I won the house vote."

"Gordon is clever, better than Fred. I'll give you that. But Mervyn is pretty good too. My neighbors in Columbus have a dog named Mervyn, and it always makes me laugh to greet him." She smiled at the thought. *Hi, Mervyn.*

He laughed, and she felt the tension between them soften a bit more. *What was I so freaked out about? Just go with it.*

She decided to climb back in bed with him, but the moment she took a step forward, he sat up and pulled the duvet cover to one side. "I'd better get going," he said, swinging his legs onto the tile floor.

She froze. "Oh yes, of course." She felt the awkwardness come rushing back and pointed to the bathroom. "Your clothes are hanging in there. Just to warn you, they're still a bit damp."

.   .   .

While Clay was in the bathroom, Daphne quietly poked her head outside her bedroom door and peeked down the hall toward the kitchen. *Why am I so embarrassed?* She wondered why it bothered her that her friends would soon know that Clay had spent the night. Unless KC had been the one drinking wine with Skylar, which Daphne highly doubted, Scott had probably slept over too. *Stop worrying. They'll be proud of you. So should you.* She glanced back at the shut bathroom door and sighed. She knew what was really bothering her. *Couldn't he have* pretended *he wanted me to crawl back in bed with him? Even for just a few minutes?*

Yes, Skylar and KC would be happy that she'd spent the night with Clay, but there was no getting around how quickly he'd jumped out of bed and said he had to "get going." No matter what her age, no woman wanted to hear those words from a man she's just slept with for the first time. She winced. *What if I was terrible?*

She took a deep breath, then stepped into the hall and quietly closed her bedroom door behind her. As she padded toward the kitchen, she braced herself for the inevitable encounter with her friends, but the spacious room was empty, the lights off, and the living room equally still. She turned around and looked back down the hall. Both Skylar's and KC's doors were closed. Maybe they were still sleeping? If Daphne had had as much to drink as KC, she'd be in a coma for at least half the day, but KC's body operated on a different level. It wouldn't surprise Daphne if KC were already out for a run.

Skylar, on the other hand, was more of a wild card. How late she—and Scott?—would sleep was anyone's guess.

She decided to make some coffee and go sit out on the deck. She reached into the cupboard for a mug, and as she stood in front of the machine watching the liquid drip into the cup, she heard footsteps behind her. She turned around and saw Clay standing there, fully dressed, albeit in clothes that were decidedly more rumpled than when he'd worn them just a few hours earlier.

"Want some coffee?" Daphne pointed to the fancy machine. She hoped it wasn't superobvious how uncomfortable she felt, but there was no getting around the reality of her mood.

Clay shook his head. "Thanks, but I'm not much of a coffee drinker. I was thinking about hitting the smoothie stand."

"Did I hear someone mention the sweet nectar that is *coffee?*"

Daphne looked to her right and caught her breath at the man she saw strolling into the kitchen . . . and wearing nothing but a pair of striped boxer shorts.

"Doug, hi," she said in a near whisper.

"Mornin', Daphne. Hey, Clay." He yawned and scratched his cheek.

Daphne felt her blood run cold. *No!* Doug knew how drunk KC had been last night. *How could he take advantage of her like that?* She quickly turned toward the coffeemaker, unable to look Doug in the eye, furious at him, at herself, at all of them. *I shouldn't have left them alone. How could Skylar have let KC do that? She didn't know what she was doing. We should have protected her.*

"Daphne?"

It was Clay speaking to her now, but she still couldn't bring herself to turn around.

"Yes?" she said in a strained voice.

"Doug and I are going to sit on the deck for a few minutes before I take off, okay?"

"Sure, no problem. I'll bring his coffee out when it's ready. You sure you don't want anything?" she called over her shoulder, trying to keep her speech steady.

"Water would be great, or juice if you have it."

"Okay, got it." Acting on autopilot, she fumbled around for a second mug and a juice glass, then awkwardly pressed the button on the coffee machine. She opened the fridge and removed a carton of orange juice, then filled up a glass for Clay before brewing another cup of coffee. Her mind continued to race. *What should I do? How could this have happened?*

When the second cup of coffee was ready, she set all three drinks on a tray with cream and sugar fixings and two spoons, then carefully walked toward the deck, with the tray visibly trembling. She prepared herself for how to address Doug. *Don't be rude to him. He's not the married one here.*

When she stepped outside and looked toward him and Clay, she nearly dropped the tray. KC was on the deck too. She was dressed in workout gear and leaning against the railing, stretching her quads one at a time by pulling her heels up against her backside. Doug and Clay were seated at the teak picnic table.

"There's the birthday girl!" KC stopped stretching, then bounced over to Daphne and took the tray from her. She set it down on the table, then gave Daphne a huge hug. "*Happy birthday*, my friend!"

Daphne hugged her back, bewildered by her positive mood given the circumstances. "Thanks. Um, did you already work out?"

KC let go of her and nodded. "Yes, ma'am. Had to sweat out all those cocktails. My body's not used to alcohol cruising through the bloodstream like kids on a slip-and-slide."

"How do you feel?"

KC adjusted her baseball cap. "I feel fine *now*, but I'm not gonna lie. When I woke up at six o'clock, I wasn't feeling so hot. But Doug made me drink a *ton* of water before I went to bed, so that helped a lot." She blew him a kiss. "Thanks, pal. I owe you one."

"No problem. After the show you put on last night, I felt I owed you a little TLC." He picked up the coffee mug and took a sip, then lifted it toward Daphne. Thanks for the tasty cup of joe, it's exactly what I need right now."

Daphne smiled as much as she could manage. "You're welcome. All I did was push a button."

"Well, you did a damn fine job," Doug said.

"You also poured a mean glass of juice," Clay said.

"Thanks." Daphne smiled at him too and tried her best to hide how rattled she was by the entire situation. Didn't anyone else feel horribly awkward right now? Or was a casual *morning-after* scene like this par for the course for single people? Or was the correct word *unattached* people? *Unmarried* people? She'd been out of the game for so long, she didn't even know the current nomenclature. Then again, KC wasn't any of those things, and she seemed completely comfortable at the moment. *What is going on? Why are they acting so normal?* She felt as if she were watching a movie in a foreign language—with no subtitles.

"Is one of those for me? I feel like I've just risen from the grave."

Daphne whirled around. Skylar emerged from the house wearing a short robe and slippers, her long auburn locks pulled up into a haphazard bun that somehow looked simultaneously messy and chic.

"Hi, Skylar," Daphne said, then pointed at the tray. "You can have mine if you want." Right now all she wanted to do was go inside and escape this weirdness . . . and maybe go back to bed. Or back to Ohio.

"On your *birthday*? Don't even think about it." She wrapped her arms around Daphne and squeezed her tight. "Happy birthday, sweets. I love you lots." Then she added as a whisper into Daphne's ear, "Good for you, by the way. He's dreamy."

"I'm so confused right now," Daphne whispered back.

Doug stood and held up his mug. "Take mine, Skylar. You like cream and sugar?"

"Right now I like anything that has caffeine in it." She walked up to Doug, and Daphne's jaw dropped at what happened next.

"Thanks, babe." Skylar stood on her tiptoes and gave Doug a quick kiss on the cheek before taking the mug and sitting down on a bench. "Mmm, come to Mama," she cooed to the dark liquid.

Daphne stood there, her mouth still slightly agape. *Huh?* She hoped her expression hadn't telegraphed her bafflement, but she highly doubted it. *Skylar and Doug? What?*

KC, who still didn't seem the slightest bit perturbed, proceeded to stretch out her calves against the railing of the deck. "Hey, Skylar, how would you feel about postponing our spa day?"

"Please tell me you're joking," Skylar said without looking up from her coffee. "Why in God's name would we do that?"

KC jutted her chin toward Doug. "Because my bestie here just invited us to join him and his buddies on a catamaran!"

Daphne stiffened. What did Clay think about this invitation? More importantly, what did *she* think about the invitation? Until now she'd assumed Clay would be gone with the juice in his glass.

Skylar arched an eyebrow. "A catamaran? Tell me more."

KC pointed to Doug. "He'll fill you in. I'm going to pop in the house for some water. Anybody else need anything?"

*Maybe an explanation of what the heck is going on?* Daphne asked with her eyes, but KC didn't seem to notice. While she was immensely relieved to know that KC hadn't cheated on Max, she was still trying to process that Skylar and Doug had ended up together. And where was Scott? What had happened to him? *Where are the subtitles?!*

Doug pointed toward the ocean. "We chartered a big one, includes drinks, lunch, the works. You're more than welcome to join us, we have plenty of room."

Skylar sipped her coffee. "Okay, let's do it. As long as I'm *above* the water, I'm good."

"Sounds like you're more of a land person?" Clay asked her.

"I'm a prefer-not-to-drown person," she said as she gestured toward Daphne. "Ms. Thesaurus over there would know the correct word choice."

Doug and Clay looked at Daphne, and she felt her face flush.

She swallowed before responding. "I . . . I think the adjective she's looking for is *hydrophobic*," she said without smiling. She was too off-kilter to even fake a smile at this point.

"See? Beautiful *and* smart," Skylar said, and Daphne shot her a thankful look. Even in adulthood, there was a fine line between feeling smart and feeling like a nerd. And right now she needed a confidence boost.

KC returned with a tray of waters and proceeded to pass the glasses around. "What do *you* think, birthday girl? It's your special day, so it's up to you."

Daphne cautiously turned toward Clay in search of an answer in his eyes, but he wasn't looking in her direction. She took a deep breath and prepared to say no, but when she spoke, she heard her voice saying the words, "Okay, sure." *Why not? How often do I get invited on a catamaran?*

KC pumped her fist. "Awesome! I'm totally going snorkeling, if that's an option." She swung her head toward Doug. "Is that an option?"

Doug nodded. "Definitely. We'll cruise up to a cove on the north shore of the island, go swimming there and have lunch, then circle back down here. It's going to be a blast."

"Then it's settled," Skylar stood up, clapped her hands, and headed toward the house. "We'll do the spa thing tomorrow. Let me go arrange it. What time do we have to leave? I need to make a couple work calls first."

Doug looked at his watch. "We leave at ten sharp and return at four. The boat is picking us up in front of the beach house. Meet us there?"

"Deal." Skylar made her way toward the glass door to the living room. "I hate to drink and run, my friends, but I'm doing it anyway."

KC jumped up and followed her. "I need to call Max. He's going to be so jealous!"

Doug followed them inside to retrieve the rest of his things, leaving Daphne and Clay alone on the deck.

"Should be a fun day," Clay said. "I've heard that cove is off the charts."

Daphne looked at the deck floor, acutely aware of his chosen words, or lack of flirtatious undertones therein. She also couldn't ignore the physical distance between them. "Definitely. I've never been on a catamaran," she said.

He stood up and gestured down the beach. "I guess I should go home and get in line for a shower. Will you tell Doug I'll see him back at the house?"

"Will do. See you soon."

He gave her a quick kiss good-bye, but she knew it felt forced—for both of them. As she watched him climb down the steps of the deck to the beach, she briefly wondered if last night had been a mistake. But only briefly. *It wasn't a mistake. It was fun. Don't take it so seriously. Just be yourself. Be yourself and enjoy.*

She remembered the early morning ride to the airport just a couple days ago, when she'd been so worried about what her friends would think of her, of who she had become. Now after such a brief time on St. Mirika, away from Columbus, she no longer felt like that tormented woman in the car. *Who am I now?* Was this a new version of her old self? Or someone else entirely? She turned toward the ocean and stared out at the horizon.

Whoever Daphne White was becoming, or *returning to*, she was glad to have her here.

# Chapter Ten

Doug left a few minutes later. Daphne waved good-bye and calmly waited until he'd walked down the steps of the deck onto the beach, then quietly closed the French doors, turned around, and looked at her friends.

"Well?" Skylar called from her desk.

Daphne pressed her hands against her cheeks. "I totally slept with him!"

"I *knew* it!" KC yelled from a stool at the kitchen island. "Nice work!"

"Am I a slut now? Or should I be proud of myself?" Daphne half laughed, half whispered. "I'm not sure which way to go."

Skylar placed her headset on the desk and held up a finger. "Give me five seconds to finish this e-mail . . . okay . . . sending . . . done!" She set down the headset, then stood up and walked toward Daphne, her arms extended. "I'm so proud of you, *dahling*. I knew you could break that dry spell. And God no, you're hardly a slut. Anyone who would suggest otherwise is a complete idiot."

"Agreed," KC said with a firm nod. "You were due for a little horizontal tango."

Daphne laughed, then took Skylar's hands and pulled her down with her so that they were both seated on the plush couch. "What about *you*? Did you really hook up with Doug?"

Skylar shook her head. "Oh God *no*. He took one of the empty bedrooms. We were pretty drunk after we broke out the good stuff, so he decided to crash here." She pointed to the empty bottles on the counter.

"What happened to Scott?" Daphne asked. "The last I saw, he was putting on a full-court press."

Skylar shrugged. "After that drama at the Castaway, I kind of lost interest. Then Doug mentioned that he has a girlfriend, so I unsubscribed for good. Scott's a hottie, but I don't play that game, even on vacation."

Daphne pointed at KC. "And *you*, little lady, nearly gave me a heart attack."

KC put a hand on her chest. "Me? Why? What did I do?"

"Because I thought Scott was with Skylar last night. So when I saw Doug cruising around in his underwear this morning, I thought *you* had hooked up with him."

KC cracked up. "Yeah, right. Can you imagine? Max would have loved that."

Skylar shrugged. "I told him to put on some clothes."

"You have no idea how freaked out I was," Daphne said. "Thank God it was all a misunderstanding."

"Anyhow, back to you and Clay," Skylar said. "How was it?"

Daphne blushed. "Um, good, I guess."

"How good?"

Daphne smiled and looked down. *It was amazing.*

"Don't be shy now," Skylar said. "Was it one-sided? We're too old for one-sided sex."

"Amen!" KC called from her barstool.

Daphne laughed. "No, it wasn't one-sided. To be honest, he was quite concerned about making sure I, um, enjoyed myself." She felt a shiver run through her at the memory.

Skylar snapped her fingers. "Yet another benefit of being older. Men know we won't put up with sexual selfishness like we did in our twenties. Remember those days? Good riddance."

"That's quite a tongue twister," KC called. "*Sexual selfishness.* I can picture the protests now. Stop the sexual selfishness!" She pumped a fist in the air.

Daphne smiled at KC, then looked back at Skylar. "It was kind of awkward this morning, though." *A lot awkward, actually.* "I had no idea how to act, or what to say, literally no idea. I kind of just froze up."

"It's always awkward the next morning," Skylar said. "I wouldn't sweat it. I'm superproud of you."

"*So* proud of you!" KC lifted her water glass in the air. "Daphne got some!"

Daphne frowned. "I kind of wish Doug hadn't invited us on the catamaran trip. I didn't want to say no, but I don't think Clay was too thrilled about that. I kind of got the feeling that he would have preferred to leave things as a 'one and done,' you know?"

"I wouldn't overthink it one way or the other," Skylar said. "You're never going to see him again after this week anyway, so I say just relax and try to have fun. Plus, there will be enough people on the boat to provide a buffer if things get a little weird. Big picture, you bedded a hot guy, and you get to go on a catamaran on your birthday."

"A win-win!" KC called.

"You sound like my neighbor, Carol. That's one of her favorite expressions," Daphne said.

"Your old-lady neighbor uses the expression 'bedded a hot guy'? Skylar asked.

"Sweet! Sounds like we need to visit Columbus," KC said.

Daphne laughed. "I mean she likes the expression 'win-win.'"

KC made a lasso motion with her arm. "I think we should focus on the bedded-a-hot-guy part of this conversation. That bar was overflowing with girls in their twenties, but look where Clay woke up this morning. Yes, that would be *here*. You totally roped him in. I love it!"

Daphne blushed, but she could feel the hint of a smile on her face. "Actually, he kind of roped *me* in. It was after midnight, so he said he wanted to buy me a birthday drink."

"Handsome *and* chivalrous. I love that too!" KC said. Then she turned to Skylar and pretended to cast a fishing line. "And *you*, turning down Scott like that after you'd successfully reeled him in. That was an impressive display of skill *and* willpower. You were both on fire last night!"

Skylar stood up and pulled the tie out of her bun, letting her hair fall loose around her shoulders. "Reeling him in wasn't all that hard, actually. Getting a man interested is all about how you carry yourself. Janine is a perfect example of that. She's a beautiful girl, but the poor thing had desperation written all over her. Guys just aren't attracted to that. That's why so many of them like older women."

"I wish I had your confidence," Daphne said. "I woke up feeling good about last night, but then I half expected Clay to sneak out when I was in the bathroom."

Skylar shook her head. "But he didn't, right? You can't think like that."

"Agreed, negative energy only leads to negative energy." KC jumped off her stool and walked toward them. "The end story is that the birthday girl here had a holiday tryst with a younger man, how exciting!"

"A *hot* younger man, don't forget that critical adjective," Skylar said.

KC nodded. "Indeed. Well done, Daphne."

"Aren't you glad I dragged you to the Castaway?" Skylar said to them both. "I told you we'd have a blast."

"Understatement of the year," KC said. "Although I'm not gonna lie. I could do without the headache right now."

"Do you *ever* lie?" Daphne asked.

KC laughed. "Good point."

·   ·   ·

"There they are, my favorite neighbors." Doug waved from the deck as the trio approached the bachelors' beach house.

"Hey, everyone." KC trotted up the stairs and gave a quick wave to the group. "Long time no see."

A small cheer erupted. "MVP!" someone yelled from the back, and KC took a little bow.

At the sight of all the guys milling around the deck, Daphne's nerves reappeared. Where was Clay? She stopped walking until Skylar nudged her in the back.

"Confidence, confidence," Skylar whispered. Then she interlaced her arm with Daphne's and led her up the stairs. "Gentlemen," she said with a cool nod. "It's nice to see you again. Scott, looking quite dapper, as always."

"Morning, Skylar," Scott mumbled.

Daphne noticed that Skylar didn't seem the least bit fazed that Scott, if not the other guys, probably knew that Doug had spent the night with her, however platonically. Or maybe they didn't know? Did men talk about that sort of thing with their friends the way women did? That line of thought made her wonder if the guys knew where Clay had spent the night. It was all Daphne could do to keep from breaking out into a cold sweat at the idea. Her brain turned with a question she was afraid to know the answer to. *Does everyone here know I slept with him?*

Being more adventurous was one thing. Publicizing a one-night stand was another.

She quickly scanned the rest of the deck for Clay but didn't see him. She did, however, spot three younger women huddled in a corner. She immediately recognized one of them as Janine from the night before. Next to her were two blondes, one of whom had been dancing with Scott when Janine left the Castaway. The other didn't look familiar.

Janine made eye contact with Daphne and gave her a quick wave hello.

Daphne smiled and waved back. *What are they doing here?*

Just then Clay emerged from the house, his eyes scanning the deck. When he noticed Daphne, he turned and walked straight toward her, which both thrilled and terrified her.

"Hey, Daphne, long time no see." He held out a bottle of water. "Can I interest you in some water? I heard you got some exercise last night."

Relieved that he'd made the effort to break the ice, she laughed and took the bottle, then lowered her voice. "Do you think we could keep that on the down low? I hate to broadcast it to the world."

He pretended to look hurt. "I will do my best *not* to take that personally. But you're the birthday girl, so I'll defer to your wishes."

"Much appreciated." She felt her face flush and put the cold water bottle against her cheek, not sure if it was the heat or the memory of what they'd done last night that was causing her temperature to rise.

"Who invited the sorority girls?" Skylar appeared at Daphne's side.

"I was wondering the same thing," Daphne said.

"Scott invited them," Clay said. "They showed up this morning." He gestured toward the house. "I'm going to go grab my backpack. See you on the boat?"

"Sounds good," Daphne said. *What was I worried about? He's not acting weird at all. This is going to be fine.*

Once Clay was out of earshot, Skylar lowered her voice and leaned in close to Daphne. "Drama alert on sorority row, three o'clock. This could get ugly."

Daphne stole another peek at the young women. All three of them were wearing makeup and heels and had their hair down. *Who wears makeup and heels at the beach? Who wears their hair down on a boat?*

"I wonder why Scott invited them?" she whispered to Skylar.

"Why wouldn't he? They're young and nice to look at, and he loves the attention. Plus, he's probably miffed that he ended up alone last night when he easily could have hooked up with one of them. It's textbook game playing for him to have all of us here. Reminds me a bit of my younger self, to be honest."

Daphne put her arm around Skylar. "I love how forthright you are."

Skylar shrugged. "No point in sugarcoating things. All that does is make you fat."

Daphne glanced back at the young women. "So his game is *literally* to put you all in the same boat."

Skylar laughed. "You and your words."

"Hey, people, the catamaran's here! Let's get a move on!" Doug hopped up on the railing and yelled to the group, "Don't forget your swimsuit and shades. Wilson, don't forget your tampons. They have everything else on deck."

"Suck it, Bates!" A stocky man Daphne assumed to be Wilson yelled back.

KC bounded toward Daphne and Skylar. "I'm so excited! I've been on a sailboat before, but never a catamaran."

"Are my favorite neighbors ready to go?" Doug pointed down at them from the railing.

Daphne started rummaging through her oversized tote to check her inventory. "Let's see . . . sunscreen, bug repellent, hat, salty snacks, sugary snacks, energy bars, water, hand lotion, tissues, hand sanitizer, sewing kit, tin of safety pins, mini-first-aid kit, and two tampons just in case of an emergency, although I guess *Wilson* over there has that covered." She looked up at Doug and smiled. "I think we're good."

Skylar peered into the canvas bag. "Good lord, you're in serious mom mode. Do you have a minivan in there too?"

Daphne slung the tote bag over her shoulder. "What can I say? I like to be prepared. Is that bad?"

KC shook her head. "Not at all. It's cute. Very endearing."

Daphne lowered her voice and glanced around the crowded deck. "You think everyone here would freak if they knew I had a teenage daughter?"

"Maybe. The sorority girls probably would. But who cares? *You're* the one who woke up with the hot guy in your bed," Skylar said.

"Shh!" Daphne said.

"It's the truth," Skylar said with a shrug. "Why not own it?"

Daphne thought about it for a moment, then smiled. "You're right, I *did* wake up this morning with a hot guy in my bed. Thank you for reminding me of that." A tiny victory bell rang in a far corner of her brain.

Skylar bowed her head. "You're welcome."

KC pointed at the tote bag. "Can I have one of those energy bars?"

• • •

The catamaran was quite large, so despite the size of their group, once everyone was on board it felt spacious and not crowded at all. At least in Daphne's opinion. Skylar had traveled on many a fancy yacht, so once again *perspective* became the operative word.

After they got moving, three crew members appeared on deck, each holding a tray of rum punches, which were gone in a blink and quickly replaced by a fresh round. The crew also turned on the stereo to play reggae at a decibel that managed to strike the perfect balance between soft and jarring. Again, that was just in Daphne's opinion. She had a sneaking feeling that the younger members of the group might have preferred an uptick in the volume. She remembered those days of ear-ringing dance music, and while she had never been much of a fan, it certainly didn't bother her then as much as it did now.

KC held up her plastic cup for a toast. "Ladies, this is already my favorite day of the trip."

Skylar poked her in the arm. "Who are you, and what have you done with KC?"

"Huh?" KC said.

Skylar pointed to KC's cup. "It's ten thirty in the morning. Even *I* can't drink alcohol at ten thirty in the morning, and I'm a professional."

KC grinned. "When in Rome, right?"

Daphne hunted in her tote bag for a bottle of water. "I think I'll wait until noon to canvas that territory again."

Just then Clay and Doug wandered around from the opposite side of the catamaran, followed by Janine and one of her friends. Both women were barefoot now, the bemused captain having informed them that heels were most certainly not allowed on board.

They were also holding their hair behind them, trying unsuccessfully to keep it from flying in their faces.

Daphne reached for her tote. "Do you need ponytail holders? I think I have some extras in here."

"I want a bag of tricks too," Doug said. "That thing's like a damn Costco."

"Do you have any Rollerblades in there?" Clay peered at the bag. "Or maybe a croquet set?"

Daphne laughed. "Don't be knocking my tote bag. You know if we end up on a deserted island, I'm the one everyone's going to be making an alliance with."

Janine gave Daphne a grateful smile. "I'd love a hair tie, thanks so much."

"Thanks," her friend said with a shy smile of her own. Daphne didn't recognize her, so she wasn't the one who had been flirting with Scott the night before. She glanced around the boat and wondered if that girl was talking to Scott now. Scott was clearly all about talking to pretty women, despite the one he apparently had waiting for him at home.

Daphne handed them each a hair tie. "What's your name? I'm Daphne," she said to Janine's friend. She also introduced the others.

"Becca." The young woman set her drink down and pulled her long locks into a ponytail.

"We hear you're on spring break?" KC said.

Janine nodded. "From Florida State."

"What are you studying?" Skylar asked them.

Becca tucked a few remaining strands of hair behind her ear. "I'm a communications major with a minor in psychology. I'm thinking about applying to law school." The words sounded rehearsed, as if she were trying to impress a potential summer employer rather than engage in casual conversation.

Janine also answered somewhat robotically. "I'm majoring in sociology. I think I might want to be a teacher." She glanced downward as she spoke, essentially addressing the deck floor and not a group of actual people.

Skylar gave Daphne a look, and it was clear what she was thinking. Despite their outward appearance—sexy sundresses and lots of makeup—now that their hair was pulled away from their faces, Janine and Becca looked almost childlike, an impression punctuated by their obvious discomfort in answering such innocuous questions.

"I have a niece who wants to be a teacher too," Skylar said. "She's only fourteen, though, so who knows how long that will last? Last year she wanted to be an astronaut. My sister and her husband are convinced she'll end up a general because she's always telling everyone what to do."

Everyone laughed, yet Daphne couldn't help but realize that Skylar's niece, not to mention her own daughter, were closer in age to these young women than she and her friends were. Daphne had already begun to dread the day when Emma would straddle that delicate line between adolescence and adulthood. Watching her daughter navigate the rocky waters of high school was difficult enough. She wasn't ready for what was to come after that.

After a few more minutes of somewhat stilted small talk, Janine and Becca headed down below to use the restroom. As soon as they were gone, Clay spoke.

"Does anyone else feel old right now?" he said in a hushed voice.

Skylar pushed her sunglasses on top of her head. "No kidding. My niece is more articulate than those two, and she's in eighth grade."

KC laughed. "Be nice now. They're trying so hard to fit in. They've probably never socialized with actual *adults* before."

"Hanson! Bates! Come hither, my henchmen!"

Everyone turned their heads. Perry, the groom, was standing at the front of the catamaran, holding up a drink with one hand, waving Clay and Doug toward him with the other.

"Sorry, ladies, duty calls," Doug said.

Skylar held out her arm to let them pass. "By all means, it's tough work being a bridesmaid."

"We'll catch up with you later," Clay said. He smiled as he walked away, but he didn't specifically make eye contact with Daphne.

"Sure," Daphne said. She wasn't sure if she believed him, but she was thrilled to realize that she didn't really care all that much. She had other things on her mind. *It's a gorgeous day. It's my birthday. I'm aboard a fancy catamaran in the Caribbean Sea—with my best friends in the world right next to me.* However the day was unfolding, Daphne was feeling carefree, something just a few days ago she didn't think possible.

. . .

A few minutes after four o'clock, the catamaran pulled up in front of the guys' beach house, about a hundred yards out from shore.

"Do we *have* to get off?" KC frowned at the small motorboat approaching to ferry them back to land. "I kind of want to stay put."

Daphne raised her hand. "I second that motion."

"Raising a hand is KC's move," Skylar said. "Could you be more original? Come on, ladies, time is a wasting. We've got to shower and get dolled up for Daphne's birthday evening." She gave both Daphne and KC a gentle shove from behind. Not enough to topple them into the ocean, but enough to let them know she'd had enough of the water.

Daphne looked over her shoulder at Skylar as she climbed into the motorboat. "Let me guess, you have a work call before dinner?"

"Perhaps," Skylar said with a shrug.

"It never ends," KC said as she took a seat in the boat.

For Daphne, the day had been glorious. When they'd reached the cove at the north end of the island, most everyone on board had donned a snorkel and dived into the water, which because of the cove formation appeared even greener than the water by their houses, if that was even possible. As promised, the crew expertly led the swimmers to a small group of turtles. After some prodding by KC, Daphne had reached down and gently grazed one with her fingertips.

Janine and her friends had also joined in the fun, albeit reluctantly, and once back on board all three of them quickly disappeared into the bathroom and reemerged shortly thereafter with their faces freshly painted. They were nice girls, but at the end of the day that's what they were . . . *girls*. Scott had spent the early part of the trip chatting them up, but by the afternoon it was clear that even his interest level had waned.

Skylar carefully climbed into the small boat behind Daphne and KC, who were already seated, then pointed toward the shore. "Ladies, a fabulous evening awaits!"

"Are gentlemen invited?"

Daphne looked up and saw Clay looking down from the railing at them. She hadn't spent much time with him on the catamaran, so she was taken off guard by his question. Not that she didn't want to see more of him. Of course she did. But for her birthday dinner? Would Skylar and KC be okay with that? Would it be weird? Should they invite Doug then too? *What does the guidebook say I should do?* She didn't mean to hesitate as her mind jumped about, but she did. A little too long.

"Daphne, say something to him," Skylar finally whispered.

Clay held up a hand. "You know what? On second thought, I don't want to intrude on a birthday celebration. Consider the question withdrawn, your honor."

"I'm sorry, you just caught me a little off guard." Daphne quickly glanced at her friends. "And Skylar already made reservations."

"What about the Castaway?" Skylar whispered. "Maybe we could meet up with him and the guys there later?"

"The Castaway *again*?" KC looked less than thrilled. "I emptied that tank last night."

Daphne gave Skylar a *What should we do?* look, and Skylar responded with one that said *your call.*

The boat started pulling away from the catamaran, so Daphne knew she had to say something. She looked back up at Clay as they pulled away. "Maybe we'll run into you at the Castaway later?"

He nodded. "That works. Have fun at dinner."

She waved good-bye. "Thanks!"

"Bye, Clay!" KC waved to him too. "Say good-bye to my bestie!" Scott and Doug were down below settling the bill with the crew.

The motorboat roared to life, and as it ferried the women back to shore, Daphne frowned and looked at her friends. "That was really awkward."

Skylar leaned over and put her hand on Daphne's thigh. "You did fine. Don't stress."

"Do you *want* to see him again?" KC asked.

Daphne sighed. "I'm not sure. I guess I do, or *did*, but I wasn't getting much of a vibe from him today, so I was kind of thrown off just there."

"That's better than being thrown off the catamaran," KC said.

Daphne laughed. "True."

A few minutes later the boat pulled up to shore, and Daphne carefully climbed out, followed by Skylar. KC was the last to exit, but there was nothing careful about her descent. She leaped into the knee-deep water, then shrieked out in pain upon landing.

"Ouch!"

Daphne and Skylar, who had already reached the beach, immediately turned around to see what had happened.

"Are you okay?" Daphne called out.

"I think I just got stung by a jellyfish!"

Daphne and Skylar began to rush back into the water to help, but KC held up an arm to keep them at bay. "Stop. I don't want it to get you too!" She hopped on one leg toward the shore, then collapsed onto the sand. Her right thigh was red, blistered, and swollen. "Oh my holy hell, this hurts."

Daphne kneeled next to her and took a good look. "That's a jellyfish sting all right. Looks like it got you pretty bad."

KC made a strained face. "Holy frick, this hurts more than when I tore ligaments in my ankle."

Daphne held out her palm. "Grab my hand. You're going to be fine, just try to stay calm, okay? Don't worry, we'll take care of you." She spoke in a soothing voice and began to examine KC's leg. "First we need to get the stinger . . . Okay, here it is. Now don't move, I'm going to get a pair of tweezers." She dug around inside her tote bag for her first-aid kit, then pulled out a tiny pink sleeve containing the tweezers.

"Such a mom," KC said with a grimace. "Who carries around tweezers?"

"I do sometimes," Skylar said. "But for my *eyebrows*, not for treating jellyfish-attack victims."

Daphne carefully removed the stinger, then slid the tweezers back into the sleeve. "I wish I had some vinegar."

KC laughed weakly. "If you did, I would be worried about you. Maybe *you* should have bought that candy striper dress. How do you know so much about jellyfish stings anyway?"

Daphne paused to think. "I saw a documentary about them once."

KC and Skylar exchanged a glance.

"Are you thinking what I'm thinking?" Skylar asked her.

"That episode of *Friends*?" KC said.

Skylar nodded.

KC put a hand on Daphne's arm. "Are you planning to have someone pee on me?"

"Not it." Skylar took a step backward. "Get Doug to do it. God knows he drank enough rum punch today to donate some urine to his *bestie*."

"Is Doug going to have to pee on me?" KC asked Daphne.

Daphne grabbed a fistful of sand and began to rub it over KC's thigh. "Not to worry, no urination necessary. If I remember correctly, this should do the trick." She scooped up some saltwater with her hands and washed it off several times, then reached into her tote bag, pulled out a pink silk scarf, and tied it around KC's upper leg. "The sand should remove any other tentacle stingers, and this pressure will help stop the venom from spreading."

KC looked at her. "Venom? That doesn't sound good."

Daphne shook her head. "It's just a toxin. Your leg will be itchy and sore for a while, but you'll be fine. They were clear about that in the documentary. This is actually quite common."

"Will I be able to play in my tournament next weekend?" KC asked.

"I don't think they mentioned soccer," Daphne said with a smile.

"Did they mention that KC is insane?" Skylar said.

Daphne laughed, and both she and Skylar looked at KC, expecting a witty comeback, but she didn't make one.

"Are you feeling okay?" Daphne asked her.

"I'm . . . having a little trouble breathing," KC said, her face now a bit pale.

Daphne put a hand on KC's shoulder. "Okay, they definitely mentioned that in the documentary. It probably means you're having an allergic reaction to the sting, so we'll need to get you to the hospital. But I don't want you to worry, because you're going to be fine, okay? You're going to be fine." She looked up at Skylar, who was still standing a couple feet away. "Can you go flag a cab while I work on this a bit more?"

"We have a car we can use, it's in our garage," Skylar said. "I'll go get it, will meet you right there, okay?" She pointed to the street behind the sand dune near Clay and Doug's place, then turned and ran toward the beach house.

Once Skylar was gone, Daphne turned back toward KC. "This is nothing to be concerned about, okay? I know I'm not a doctor, but I totally remember that documentary."

KC smiled, but she looked a bit frightened now. "I thought I was only allergic to beets," she said in a near whisper.

Daphne put her hand on KC's arm and gave it a gentle squeeze. "Do you trust me?"

KC nodded her head. "I trust you. And yes, I realize that we just quoted Leo and Kate in *Titanic*."

·  ·  ·

"Skylar, seriously, will you stop tailgating those poor people? You're going to kill us all, assuming this stupid jellyfish venom doesn't do me in first," KC called from the backseat. "Damn this hurts," she added.

"You're hardly dying if you still have the energy to mock me," Skylar said.

"Worst. Driver. Ever," KC groaned.

Daphne turned around from the passenger seat and gave KC a nod of solidarity. "For the record, I'm glad it's not just me. I'm fearing for my life up here."

"Did you hear that Skylar? You are the worst driver I've ever seen, and that's saying a lot for someone who has been in a car with teenage boys behind the wheel," KC said.

Skylar rolled her eyes in the rearview mirror. "I live in New York City, okay? I don't drive much. Plus, I'm trying to save your life, if you hadn't noticed."

"At least keep your eyes on the road, can you please do that?" Daphne looked at Skylar and pressed her palms together in prayer.

"Were you this bad of a driver in college?" KC asked. "I must have blocked it out."

"Trying to save your life," Skylar repeated.

"You should have let Daphne drive," KC said. "The world would be a safer place with you in the passenger seat."

"There it is!" Skylar pointed to the sign for the hospital, then jerked the car to the right and screeched through the entrance at nearly full speed.

"God help us." Daphne closed her eyes.

"I heard that," Skylar said.

"I hope God heard it too," KC said.

. . .

After the nurse took KC inside, Daphne and Skylar settled into the small waiting room, which was nearly empty.

"I hope this means we won't be here that long," Skylar said. "A crowded waiting room is never a good sign."

Daphne pointed at the door leading to the examination area. "Depends on how many doctors are here, or if there's a pressing emergency ahead of you. I took Emma in once for a broken arm, and we were there for seven hours."

"I wonder how pressing an allergic reaction to a jellyfish sting is." Skylar pulled out her phone. "I'm going to look it up."

Daphne stood up to peruse the magazine choice in a rack hanging on the wall. "Jeez, this is slim pickings. Some of these are older than Emma."

Skylar didn't look up from her phone. "I'll stick with WebMD, thank you very much. Oh, bite me."

Daphne turned around. "What's wrong?"

"I missed an important call. They moved up the time, but I didn't see the e-mail because we were on the catamaran."

"Is that bad?"

Skylar stood up and reached for her purse. "It's bad. I need to get back to the house right away. Take the keys, I'll hop in a cab. I'm sorry about this, but if I want to keep from getting fired, it looks like I'm not going to be able to make your birthday dinner."

Daphne gestured toward the door through which KC had disappeared. "No worries, I've had enough birthday excitement this trip to last me until next year. Plus, something tells me you're not the only one who's not going to make dinner."

Skylar's eyes followed. "Poor thing. I wonder how long she'll be down?"

"If it were a normal person, probably a few days or a week. But given that it's KC, she'll probably be out running on the beach before you and I are even awake tomorrow morning."

.   .   .

Daphne rushed toward KC the moment she saw her emerge from the hall with a nurse—and with a noticeable limp. "How are you feeling?" she asked.

KC smiled weakly. "You were totally right. Apparently I'm allergic to jellyfish. Who knew?"

Daphne put a hand on KC's cheek. "Are you in pain? Can I get you anything?"

"She's going to be fine," the nurse said. "Sore and itchy for a few days, but fine."

"More than anything I was worried about missing the tournament next weekend, but they said I should be able to play. Yeah!" KC half pumped her fist, then looked around the waiting room. "Where's Skylar?"

Daphne held up the keys. "Something came up at work, so she went back to the house to make a call. The good news is she took a cab, so she won't be driving us home."

"Oh thank heavens," KC said. "I can't take any more Formula One action today."

Daphne pointed to KC's leg. "So Skylar's most likely out for tonight, and you should probably rest that thing. I'm thinking we cancel dinner, get some takeout, and go home and relax."

"For your birthday? Are you sure?" KC asked.

"Trust me, I'm sure. After all this activity, chilling on the couch for an evening sounds glorious."

"What about meeting up with Clay?"

"That wasn't set in stone, was it? I think a night in with friends is just what the doctor ordered for both of us. And to be honest, I can't think of a better way to spend my birthday."

# Chapter Eleven

After a quiet evening at the beach house, Daphne awoke early the next morning feeling rested, refreshed . . . and *happy*. She looked up at the ceiling and smiled. *I'm happy.* For a few moments she stared at the wooden fan spinning above her, marveling at how silent it was. Fred the gecko was perched on the ceiling again, but not in his usual spot. This time he was closer to the sliding glass doors leading to the deck.

"Hi, little guy. You mixing things up today? It's good to mix things up once in a while." *Just not every night.* While it would have been fun to see Clay again, she'd enjoyed the uneventful time in with her friends.

She tossed back the duvet cover and wiggled her feet into a pair of slippers, then walked over to the dresser to check her phone for a message from Emma. Not expecting one, she was delighted to see her daughter's name on the display.

*Hi Mom, reception is really bad here so just got your last text. I'm having a great time! Hope your birthday was fun. See you in a couple days.*

She typed a quick reply, then set the phone down and smiled, joyful that her daughter was having so much fun. Joyful that *she* was having so much fun. She couldn't put her finger on exactly what it was, but something about today felt . . . *new. She* felt new. Was it because she was forty now? Or because she was no longer so *afraid* of being forty . . . and unattached . . . and without a litany of bylines to her name, much less a Pulitzer?

Maybe turning the page to a new decade, a new phase of her life, a new *outlook* on her life, was exactly what she needed? A blank slate? A fresh start? Or maybe it was a soothing, healing mixture of all of that, like the rain. She couldn't put her finger on it exactly, but she didn't need to. *St. Mirika really is a magical place,* she thought.

. . .

When Daphne ambled into the kitchen a few minutes later, Skylar was sitting at the desk in the living room, quietly sipping coffee and staring at her laptop screen, her headset resting around her shoulders.

"Hey, sweets, how'd you sleep?" She pushed her reading glasses on top of her head.

Daphne yawned. "Like a corpse. I haven't slept that well in years."

Skylar chuckled. "I'm not surprised. You had quite a night to recover from."

Daphne reached for a ceramic mug and set it under the coffeemaker. "An accurate statement. So how's your morning going so far? Any new fires to put out?"

"How did you know? I wouldn't be surprised if I have to head straight back to the airport the morning after I get home."

"Do you want to talk about it? Maybe vent a little?"

Skylar gave her a weary smile. "You're a dear to ask, but trust me, right now I want to do anything but talk about my job. I just want to try and enjoy the time we have left here."

"Remind me again why we made the trip so short?" Daphne asked.

Skylar gave Daphne a gentle tap on the shoulder on her way to brew a fresh cup of coffee. "How quickly they forget."

Daphne nodded slowly. "Okay, I'll take that." *She'd* been the one reluctant to leave home for longer than a few days—and only if it coincided with Emma's spring break. At the time it had seemed so important, so pressing, but now it just seemed . . . foolish.

"It would have been harder for me to get away for much longer anyway, so don't feel bad," Skylar said. "Hopefully the next trip can be longer."

*I hope so too,* Daphne thought.

Skylar gestured outside. "Should we go sit on the deck?"

Daphne glanced down the hall. "Is KC still sleeping? Or is she out running a marathon?"

"I haven't seen her, and I've been up for about an hour. I bet she's still down for the count, especially with that sting in her leg. Even the Energizer Bunny needs to take it easy once in a while."

"Want to walk to Bananarama and get a smoothie after we finish our coffee? We can bring one back for her," Daphne said.

Skylar held up her mug. "You don't have to ask me twice."

• • •

It wasn't even eight o'clock, but the air was already warm and sticky when Daphne and Skylar reached the smoothie hut. And they weren't the only early birds there. As they waited on a nearby bench for the pleasant owner to slide open the window, Daphne found herself surveying the surrounding tables in search of other familiar faces. After just a few days on St. Mirika, she already felt like a member of a community, however small, however ephemeral.

She also felt a little twinge of sadness at the realization that it would be ending very soon.

"I love how calm it is here at this time of day." She watched the clear green waves gently roll up against the empty beach. "Going to the bars and stuff has been fun, but I prefer this so much more. It's just so . . . peaceful."

Skylar glanced up at the cloudy sky. "It's going to pour buckets soon, can you feel it?"

Daphne held out her arms and tilted her head back, eyes closed. "I can't wait. The rain here is so purifying, don't you think?"

Skylar patted her cheeks. "That reminds me, I think I'm getting a purifying facial at the spa today."

Daphne opened her eyes. "I know this might sound a little New Agey, but there's something about the rain on this island, about *everything* on this island, actually, that's helped me learn to embrace life again. Then again, it could just be that I've been hanging around you and KC."

Skylar laughed. "Whatever works, right? I'm all for anything that gets your juices going. Some of the people at my company are so dead inside, it's sad."

"Dead inside how?"

"Hang on a sec." Skylar stood up. Bananarama was officially open, and she was about to become the first customer of the day. She ordered three smoothies, then turned to Daphne. "Depends on the person, but a lot of them are in bad marriages, yet another reason why I'm not sure I'll ever go down that route. Some of them are clearly in the wrong profession, but they feel trapped because they have financial obligations and can't afford to start over. I guess the common thread is that somewhere along the way they got on the wrong path and don't know how to get off it, and as a result they dry up inside."

The smiling owner handed Skylar two smoothies, plus one in a bag for KC, and she and Daphne began the walk home. After a few minutes of silence, Daphne took a deep breath and looked at Skylar. "I became one of those people," she said quietly.

"Was it really that bad with Brian?"

Daphne nodded. "Toward the end, yes. I didn't mean for it to happen. I just . . . became numb inside. I think it was some sort of coping mechanism."

Skylar sipped her smoothie. "Coping mechanism for your marriage? Or for what you gave up for it?"

"For all of it, probably. It helped me, I don't know . . . *manage*. It sounds so cliché, but it was easier to focus on fixing physical things, like remodeling the kitchen or getting the house painted, than to address what really needed fixing . . . our relationship." That evasion seemed glaringly obvious to Daphne now, but for years she just hadn't seen it. Or hadn't wanted to see it.

Skylar stopped walking and put a hand on Daphne's shoulder. "You know what I think?"

Daphne waited for her to continue.

"I think you still have a ways to go, but you've started to become *Daphne* again on this trip,"

Daphne felt a tear form in the corner of her eye. "Really?" *I think so too.*

Skylar squeezed her shoulder. "Without a doubt, and it makes me really happy. You had a one-night stand with a hot guy in his *twenties*, for God's sake! If that isn't living, I'm not sure what is."

Daphne hugged her tight. "Thank you, Skylar," she whispered.

Skylar hugged her back. "You'll get there, don't worry."

They began walking along the beach in a comfortable silence, both of them staring out at the water. All of a sudden Skylar grabbed Daphne's arm and cocked her head toward the sand dune.

"Speak of the devil." They were approaching Clay and Doug's place. The back deck was empty, a handful of empty beer bottles strewn about. "I wonder how late those guys were out last night?" Daphne said.

"A lot later than we were, that's for sure."

"You think they met other women?"

Skylar shrugged as they passed by. "Scott, probably. Clay, possibly. Doug, unlikely. Hey, speaking of women, there's our favorite one." She pointed ahead to their own beach house. KC was sitting on the deck, a steaming mug of coffee in one hand.

"Hey, Wonder Woman, how are you feeling today?" Skylar asked as they climbed the steps.

KC grinned. "*Way* better than yesterday, that's for sure. Leg is still pretty sore, though. I didn't sleep that well once whatever they gave me at the hospital wore off."

"You should have taken more painkillers before you went to bed," Skylar said.

KC held her hands up as if to protect her face. "Those things scare me. I've seen too many horror stories about regular people falling under the spell of addiction after a routine injury."

Skylar rolled her eyes and handed KC the paper bag with the smoothie inside. "*Falling under the spell of addiction?* Who talks like that? Methinks someone's been watching a little too much TV."

"Maybe," KC said as she opened the bag. "But I don't want to take any chances. Thanks for this, by the way. Yummy."

Daphne eyed her with suspicion. "Are you taking it easy like the doctor told you to, or did you just run like fifteen miles?"

KC sipped her coffee and smiled. "I promise you both, the only exercise I've gotten today is lifting this tasty beverage to my lips. I figured a day or two off won't kill me."

Skylar coughed and sat down next to her. "A *day or two*. I have no trouble going a month or two without exercise. Then again, that's probably why you can still shop in the juniors' department and I cannot."

KC pinched Skylar's side. "I bet you'd have trouble going a month or two without working. You can't even go an *hour* or two. There are all kinds of addictions, my friend."

Skylar shrugged. "I tried taking the day off yesterday, and I almost got myself fired."

"Was it really that bad?" Daphne asked.

Skylar took a drink of her smoothie. "I might be exaggerating just slightly. Okay, more than slightly. I wasn't in danger of losing my job at that exact moment. However, our company *was* in danger of losing a major account, which for someone in my position is usually the first step on the road to unemployment. So it was pretty serious."

"But it's okay now?" KC asked.

Skylar finished her smoothie and gestured inside. "Yes. *However*, unfortunately I do need to make a couple calls before we head to the spa. Can you two be ready to leave by ten?"

"What about the monkey forest?" KC said.

"If we want to see the monkeys, it will have to be on the way back. We're lucky they could accommodate us at all after we canceled at the last minute yesterday. So does ten o'clock work?"

KC stood up. "It's perfect. I'm going to call Max and fill him in on my little . . . incident."

Daphne pointed to the beach. "I think I'm going to read on the beach for a while."

"Sounds good to me," KC said. "I'm kind of liking this quiet evening, early morning thing. I had fun the other night, but my liver can't take that kind of abuse too often. Hey, what about those cliffs on the other side of the island? Doug said the views are amazing. Maybe we can do that tomorrow?"

"Let's do it," Skylar said.

Daphne flinched at the thought of how high the cliffs would be.

"I can't believe we leave the day after tomorrow," KC said. "On our next trip let's stay a little longer, okay?"

"Okay." Daphne smiled, then exchanged a knowing look with Skylar. Next trip would be longer, and it wouldn't take ten years to happen. Both of them would make sure of that.

.    .    .

An hour or so later Daphne checked her watch and realized it was time to head back to the house. She closed her book and tossed it into her tote bag, then stood up and began shaking out her beach towel.

"Hey there, stranger."

She turned around, a bit startled by the sound of a man's voice. *His* voice.

"Clay, hi."

He was wearing navy-blue board shorts and running shoes, no shirt. Beads of sweat dotted his forehead and chest.

"You look tired," she said as she folded the beach towel. "Long run? Or long night?"

He laughed. "Both, I guess."

She smiled and adjusted her bag over her shoulder. "That's the way to do it, right?"

"I guess so." He hesitated for a moment, then spoke again. "How was the birthday night out? Did you get into trouble?"

"KC did. She got into a tussle with a jellyfish and lost. That's why we didn't make it to the Castaway."

"A jellyfish? Are you serious?"

Daphne pointed down the beach. "Right when we got off the catamaran."

"Is she okay?"

"She's sore, but she'll be fine. We were a little scared when she started having an allergic reaction, but not as scared as when Skylar drove us to the hospital."

He raised an eyebrow. "Huh?"

Daphne tucked the towel into her bag. "Just be glad you'll never have to ride in a car with Skylar."

"So noted. When are you headed back to the States?"

"The day after tomorrow. What about you?"

"Tomorrow. I can't say I'm looking forward to it." He wiped the sweat from his brow. "I'll be daydreaming about this place from my office, that's for sure."

She sighed and gazed up at the sky. "I hear you. I wish I could stay here forever."

"What do you have planned before you go?"

She regained eye contact with him, the anxiety she'd felt when they'd first met now a distant memory. "We're finally doing the spa thing today, and maybe the monkey forest. KC wants to check out those cliffs you and Doug were talking about, so we'll probably do that tomorrow."

"And tonight?"

"Just dinner." She considered asking him what his plans were but decided not to. *This is the perfect way to say good-bye.*

Before he could speak again, she looked up at the house. "I should probably get going so I'm not too late. I'm already pushing it as it is, and you know how Skylar can be."

She knew she was being a bit abrupt given their history, but drawing out their farewell seemed pointless, and verbalizing what she was really thinking just didn't seem appropriate. She wanted him to know that she appreciated what he'd done for her, how grateful she was for their encounter—however fleeting—for jolting her out of the emotional trance she'd been in for much too long. For making her feel young again. Attractive again. *Alive* again. But she had no idea how to convey any of that without sounding like she'd overanalyzed what to him was probably nothing more than a holiday fling. So instead she said nothing.

After a noticeable silence, Clay spoke. "Well, if I don't see you again, enjoy the rest of your trip."

"You too. It was really nice meeting you." She gave him a hug and kiss on the cheek, then turned and started walking toward the house. As she made footprints in the sand, she wondered if one day, far down the road perhaps, he'd realize the impact their night together had on her.

"Hey, Daphne?" Clay called after her.

She stopped and turned around. "Yes?"

He saluted. "Give my regards to Fred, will you?"

She laughed and returned the salute. "Will do."

. . .

"I'm officially a new person. I may even have to change my name." KC wiggled her arms as they left the spa a few hours later. She turned around and gave an enthusiastic thumbs-up to the sign on the front door. "Well done, Paradise Spa at the Four Seasons. My grateful muscles and I will miss you."

Skylar poked KC in the shoulder. "See? Lying around for a few hours isn't the worst thing in the world."

"I just hope my arms aren't too wobbly to cuddle a monkey," KC said.

Skylar rolled her eyes as she opened the car door. "Trust me, you won't be cuddling any monkeys."

"A girl can dream, right?" KC said as she climbed inside.

Daphne pressed her palms against her cheeks. "My massage was good, but the cucumber revitalizing facial was *amazing*. My skin feels so soft right now." She looked at Skylar. "I could get used to your lifestyle. I mean, the nonwork side of it. The other side would eat me alive."

"You've been the head of the PTA how many times? Trust me, you could handle it," Skylar said.

"I bet you ran a tight ship at that PTA," KC said to Daphne. "You were crazy organized in college, and we've all seen your tote bag."

Daphne blushed. "Maybe."

"Hey, speaking of your *mom* persona, have you been in touch with Emma?" KC asked.

"Not much, the reception is terrible there."

"You doing okay with that?" KC asked.

Daphne smiled. "Actually, *yes*. Once I realized it was out of my hands, it sort of freed me up to focus on other things this week."

"You mean . . . like *yourself?*" Skylar said as she pulled onto the road. "God forbid any mother should do *that*."

Daphne smiled. "You know what I mean. It's hard to separate the two sometimes."

"I hear ya," KC said. "No matter where I am, Josh and Jared are always in the back of my head."

"I can't imagine having to worry about that all the time," Skylar said. "I'm not averse to dating a man who has kids, but I don't know how well I'd handle being a stepmother."

"I think you'd make a fantastic stepmother," KC said. "Especially to girls. You'd be such a great role model, outside of the driving thing, of course. Do you see how tightly I'm gripping this door handle right now? That's the fear of death, my friend."

"Zip it," Skylar said.

Daphne turned around and grimaced at KC in the backseat. "For the record, I'm holding on just as tight."

"You zip it too," Skylar said. "Anyhow, I think any woman who is doing whatever it is that makes *her* happy is a great role model.

Whether it's having a corporate job or being a stay-at-home mom, the important thing is to show kids that it's up to them to choose the life *they* want. Take Daphne here. We all know she could have crushed it professionally, but she chose to dedicate herself to raising Emma, which I think is commendable."

Daphne gave Skylar a grateful look, then cleared her throat. "Actually, I think I'm going to look into some new adventures when I get home."

"Adventures? I like the sound of that. What did you have in mind?" KC asked.

"For starters, I was thinking about signing up for a dance class, just so I could have a hobby of my own, something outside of Emma's world. Plus, being around *you* all week has inspired me to get in better shape."

"I love that idea," KC said. "I love inspiring people!"

Daphne smiled at her. "I also think it's time to dip my toe back into journalism so I can use the part of my brain that I've neglected for too long. I know the industry has changed dramatically since I learned the ropes in school, but I'm kind of excited about learning something new."

"Ready to pop that suburban bubble, are we?" Skylar said.

"*Pop* might be an overstatement, but while I love being a mom, part of me has known for a long time that I need more than that in my life. It took this trip for me to come to terms with it, and to realize that it's okay to want more for *myself* while still loving my daughter to pieces."

"Of course it's okay," KC said. "You have to love yourself too."

"Maybe you should try one of my business ideas," Skylar said.

Daphne looked at her. "You think I should start my own company? What do I know about starting a business?"

Skylar shrugged. "What does anyone know about anything before they try it? You're smart, you could totally do it. *Plus*, I could use some stock options in a hot new venture. I still want to hire my traveling stylist someday."

Daphne laughed. "I think I'll start with submitting an article to a magazine, but I'll keep that in mind. So is anyone up for a walk on the beach before dinner?"

• • •

Early that evening, the three friends were taking a stroll along the shore when the skies erupted for the second time that day. The first downpour had been while they were at the monkey forest after the spa, much to the delight of KC. The rain had briefly cleared the park of the fair-weathered, leaving her free to attract the monkeys with the enormous batch of bananas she'd purchased at the entrance. She'd already set the wallpaper on her phone to a picture Daphne had taken of her, featuring a plump monkey perched on one shoulder, the trademark KC grin on her face.

"I love this rain." Daphne tilted her head back and held her arms open wide. "It's so refreshing."

"Not as refreshing as a rum punch would be right now. Anyone up for cocktails on the beach after dinner?" Skylar said.

"I wonder if Clay and the guys will be at the Castaway tonight," Daphne said. "I ran into him earlier today."

Skylar raised her eyebrows. "Is that so? Interesting that you chose to keep that little nugget of information to yourself."

"We didn't talk for that long." Daphne looked at KC and pointed to her leg. "I told him about your little voyage to the emergency room."

"Did you two talk about getting together again?" Skylar asked.

Daphne glanced back in the direction of the house where Clay was staying. "I decided not to go there. I think I just want to spend as much time with you two as I can before we have to return to reality."

Skylar held up a hand. "I fail to see how you can't do both. It's not like peg leg here or I have plans to sleep in your bed tonight." She gestured to KC, then to herself.

Daphne laughed. "You know what I mean."

"We could always drop by the Castaway later to see if he's there," KC said. "There's no harm in that."

"If I were you, I'd listen to peg leg," Skylar said. "I say you knock it out of the park or go down swinging." She pointed to KC's thigh. "How's the peg feeling, by the way?"

"Okay, not great. I think it will feel better after a couple cocktails."

Skylar rubbed her hands together. "*Now* we're talking. Maybe we should head back to the house for a predinner drink?"

"Sounds good to me," KC said.

The three of them turned around and began walking toward the beach house. After a few minutes KC squinted at two figures in the distance. "Is that Harry and Eleanor? I can't see that far."

Daphne nodded. "I think so."

As they approached the couple, Daphne and KC waved hello. Harry and Eleanor both returned the greeting, but Daphne immediately sensed a difference in their energy—and Harry's appearance. His skin was notably pale, almost ashen, and he was moving quite slowly. But he met them with a warm smile. "There they are. The prettiest ladies on the island, after my wife, of course."

"Ahoy mates," KC said. "This is our friend Skylar, also known as the third Musketeer."

"It's lovely to meet you, dear." Eleanor seemed distracted, but she took Skylar's hand in hers. "Is this your first visit to St. Mirika?"

Skylar nodded. "It's also my first tropical vacation with my best girlfriends in tow, so it's been my favorite."

"Yesterday was Daphne's birthday," KC said.

Harry smiled at Daphne. "Happy belated birthday, kiddo. You don't look a day over twenty-five to me."

"Thank you, Harry. Are you . . . feeling all right?" She didn't mean to pry, but she couldn't pretend she hadn't noticed his condition.

"I've been better," he said.

"What have you darlings been up to since we met you?" Eleanor asked.

Skylar pointed at KC. "That one got herself stung by a jellyfish."

Harry chuckled. "Is that so?"

KC frowned. "Little sucker got me pretty bad."

"She ended up in the hospital," Daphne said. "It turns out she's allergic."

"First beets, and now jellyfish. Who knew?" KC said.

Eleanor interlaced her arm with Harry's. "Big H here was in the hospital earlier today too."

Daphne and her friends all looked at him, his pallid tone suddenly taking on more significance. "Oh my gosh. Are you okay?" Daphne asked.

He smiled and shook his head. "Unfortunately, no. It's my ticker."

"He's on his second," Eleanor said, the shadow in her eyes growing a bit darker.

Wide-eyed, Daphne asked, "You had a heart transplant?"

Harry nodded. "We were hopeful this one would stick, but it doesn't look like that's in the cards."

"We're not giving up, though," Eleanor said. "I'm never giving up."

"She's more optimistic than I am," Harry said. "Always has been, that's one of the reasons I love her."

"I'm so sorry," Daphne whispered.

A hush enveloped the group. Daphne was too stunned to say anything else, and Skylar and KC were equally taken aback. *Harry's dying?*

Eleanor stroked Harry's cheek with her hand, then turned toward Daphne and her friends. "Thanks, love. If there's one thing I'd tell young people like you three dolls, it's just enjoy every day while you can, especially every *birthday*, and don't waste time fussing over things that don't mean squat."

Harry took Eleanor's hand and kissed it. "Well said, my love. Enjoy the party while you can still dance, that's my motto."

Daphne stared at the wise couple standing before her. *He's really dying?*

Eleanor wrapped her arm tightly around her husband's, then carefully looked at the three friends, giving them each a warm smile as she did so. "We'd better get back to the house. It was such a pleasure running into you again. Happy belated birthday, Daphne! Enjoy the continued celebration, and be sure to soak up every minute you have left here, promise?"

Daphne, KC, and Skylar all nodded like schoolchildren. They knew Eleanor was no longer talking about St. Mirika.

Harry gave them a wave as he and Eleanor slowly ambled away. "Have a drink for me to toast this glorious sunset."

·　·　·

"I can't believe he's that sick," KC said on the slow walk back to the beach house. "When we met on the beach the other day, he was so . . . *sprightly*."

"He still is, at least on the inside," Skylar said. "He knows what's important in life. They both do."

"I want to be like that when I'm that age," Daphne said. "Actually, what am I saying? I want to be like that *now*."

"We should all be like that," Skylar said.

KC pinched both their waists. "Does that mean you're up for a workout tomorrow morning? You know what they say—a healthy body makes for a healthy soul. I should probably take it easy, however."

"Maybe. It depends on how late I stay up tonight," Daphne said.

Skylar looked at her. "You have plans we don't know about?"

Daphne bit her lip. "Maybe."

Skylar narrowed her eyes. "Would these *plans* involve a certain Clay Handsome?"

Daphne smiled slightly. "I was thinking it was best to close that book, but seeing Harry like that just now is kind of making me look at things in a different way. Maybe it wouldn't be such a terrible thing if I ran into Clay one last time, right?"

"Of course it wouldn't be," Skylar said.

"Definitely not," KC said.

"You think we should stop by the Castaway later?" Daphne asked them. "Just to check it out? He might not even be there, though."

"But he *might* be," Skylar said. "I say it's worth a flyby."

KC pretended to maneuver the controls of an airplane. "I don't think I have another wild night in me, but I'm happy to play wingman."

Daphne blushed. "I haven't heard the term *wingman* in a long time."

Skylar put a hand on Daphne's shoulder. "I never thought I'd say this to *you*, but maybe it's time you refreshed your vocabulary. Now, let's go get some dinner. I'm starving."

# Chapter Twelve

That evening they had just left the restaurant and were strolling down the sidewalk on Main Street when Skylar froze in her tracks.

"What is it?" Daphne asked, coming to a halt beside her.

"It's my phone. Damn it." Skylar reached into her purse and fished out the vibrating device, then frowned at the text message on the screen. "I knew it."

"Another work emergency?" KC said.

Skylar began walking again. "Yes. I'm sorry, ladies. No Castaway for me tonight. I need to go back to the house for an important call."

"Does it ever stop?" Daphne asked. At the beginning of the week she'd assumed the endless conference calls were related to one particular emergency that needed attention, but now she realized Skylar's job required her to hop continuously from one crisis to the next, with no end in sight and the weight—and heat—of each fire resting firmly on her shoulders.

Skylar tossed the phone back into her purse. "I don't *think* it used to be this bad, but I might just be saying that. I'm so used to it now that I don't realize how all-consuming it is until I'm around people who live relatively normal lives."

"You have spent a lot of this week on the phone," KC said.

Skylar sighed. "I know. I love my job and the lifestyle it allows me to lead, but in moments like this, when I'm supposed to be on *vacation*, I can't help but ask myself if I've traded too much in return. I know that sounds cliché, but it's kind of true."

"How would you change things if you could?" Daphne asked.

Skylar hesitated for a moment before responding.

"I don't know exactly," she finally said. "I've had an amazing career, but I've never been in a committed, serious relationship. Not that it's ever been something I've really coveted, but meeting Eleanor and Harry tonight made me wonder if one day I'm going to regret that, if when I'm their age, I'm going to wish I had someone by my side until the very end, you know?"

Daphne and KC nodded, sensing Skylar wasn't done.

She continued. "I don't necessarily think that having a demanding job and a serious relationship are mutually exclusive, but sometimes I can't help but think that maybe in my case they are, if somehow I've stopped myself from finding the right man without even realizing it. Not that my goal has ever been to get married, but I guess on some base level we all want to love someone . . . and feel loved in return, right?"

Daphne looked at Skylar, her fair skin slightly sun-kissed, her auburn locks flowing down her back, not a strand out of place. Dressed in a silky turquoise halter top and flowy island-chic white pants, she was the picture of success, yet this was the first time Daphne had ever heard her express an ounce of misgiving over the price she'd paid for it. *No one's life is perfect. Not even Skylar's.* Before she realized what she was doing, she walked over to Skylar and hugged her tight.

"Whoa, are you okay?" Skylar asked. "Where is this coming from?"

"I would never unsubscribe from you," Daphne said. "I just think it's about time I told you that."

.    .    .

When they reached the Castaway, Skylar bade Daphne and KC good-bye, then hurried down the beach back to the house.

KC pointed toward the bar. "Okay champ, you ready? Let's do this for Harry!"

Daphne laughed. "I get the sentiment, but that sounded kind of creepy." They began walking toward the deck entrance. Despite her determination to be casual and just have fun, as they ascended the steps, she felt her nerves begin to jitter. *Do I really want to do this?*

"Maybe this is a mistake," she called to KC over her shoulder. The steel drum band was playing again, and the dance floor was filled with bobbing heads.

"Just keep moving," KC yelled back. "Dance while you still can, remember?"

They climbed the steps and joined the scene, which looked exactly same as it had the night they'd been there. Couples snuggling in the lounge chairs, friends bopping together in groups in the center of the room, revelers doing shots at the bar. The stage and the play unfolding upon it remained essentially unchanged, except for the characters flowing in and out like a gentle breeze.

"I think I had enough of this place the other night," KC said. "I'm getting a hangover just remembering my hangover."

Daphne gave her a hopeful look. "So we can go back to the house? I'd much rather relax on the couch than face this scene right now."

KC shook her head. "We have to at least do a run-through to see if he's here. You'll kick yourself if we don't. Besides, Skylar's probably going to be at her desk for a while, so it's better if we give her some space."

Daphne nodded. She knew KC was right: she *would* kick herself if she bailed out now. "Okay."

Beginning at the outdoor bar where KC had downed her tequila shots, they slowly began to survey the landscape for any sign of Clay or his friends. They didn't spot them anywhere on the deck, so KC put her hand on Daphne's back and nudged her inside. The area in front of the long bar was packed, but Daphne immediately noticed a tall man at the far end near the street entrance. His face was obstructed, but she could see the back of his head.

"I think that's Scott," she said to KC.

"Nice." KC snapped her fingers. "Houston, we have contact."

They squeezed their way through the crowd until they reached the area where Scott was standing. KC stood on her tiptoes and tapped him on the shoulder. "Hey, you!" she said with a grin.

He turned around and looked down, a surprised expression on his face. "Oh hi, KC. Hey, Daphne." He gestured toward the young redhead sitting next to him. "This is Ashley."

KC smiled at Ashley, then looked back up at Scott. "Are Clay and Doug here?"

Daphne's eyes darted around the bar. *Is he here?* She recognized a couple other guys from their crew milling about, but not the one she really wanted to see.

Scott jutted his chin toward the back deck area. "They're with their lady friends."

"Their *lady friends?*" KC said.

Daphne felt like she'd been kicked in the stomach. *This was a bad idea.*

Scott pointed back toward the deck. "Last I saw they were dancing. You didn't see them on your way in?"

"No," KC said.

Scott shrugged. "Maybe they took off." He turned back toward Ashley and began to play with her hair as she giggled. Empty shot glasses sat on the bar before them. Daphne wondered what Scott's girlfriend back home was doing right now. Then again, maybe Scott's girlfriend was running her fingers through someone else's hair too. Who was she to judge their relationship from the outside?

"Okay, thanks, Scott. It was nice meeting you, Ashley." KC smiled again, then pulled Daphne by the arm back into the crowd. "You want to keep looking?" she asked her.

Daphne laughed and shook her head. "After *that* revelation? Definitely not. Can we go home now? I miss my slippers."

"You sure you don't want to give it one more shot?"

"Give *what* one more shot? You heard Scott, he's with someone else."

"So? That doesn't mean anything."

Daphne sighed. "Okay, let's walk out the back way. If we see him, we see him. If we don't, at least I tried. Does that work for you?"

KC grinned. "That's the spirit. Harry would be proud."

They made their way back outside, and while KC scanned the crowd, Daphne countered her unease by replaying the conversation she'd had earlier with Clay in her head. *He likes you. He'll be glad to see you, regardless. Don't overanalyze it.*

"There's my bestie!" KC suddenly yelled. "He's on the dance floor macking on some girl. I'm so proud of him!"

"Do you see Clay?" Her eyes followed KC's.

KC peered through the crowd. "Affirmative. He's with a girl too, but they're not swapping spit."

Daphne laughed and looked at KC sideways. "I can't remember the last time I heard the terms *macking* and *swapping spit.*"

KC caught her breath and reached for Daphne's hand. "He sees us. I think he's coming over here."

Daphne scanned the dance floor, then gave KC's hand a squeeze as she spotted Clay emerging from the crowd, a bit disheveled, but not overtly intoxicated like Scott.

"Hey, Daphne, KC. I'm surprised to see you here."

Daphne let go of KC's hand and quickly peered around him to see if a pretty young thing trailed behind him, but he appeared to be alone. "Surprised in a good way, I hope," she said, thrilled to hear the words come out somewhat flirtatiously.

"Of course," he said with a grin. "Always."

"I see my bestie's having a little fun out there." KC pointed over Clay's shoulder.

"He is indeed," Clay said. "And it's about time, if you ask me."

"Good for him. Who shouldn't have a little fun on vacation, right?" Daphne said. This time she made—and held—eye contact with Clay. *Another small victory!*

Just then an attractive brunette appeared out of nowhere and grabbed Clay's arm. "There you are. You disappeared on me." She stood on her tiptoes and gave him a sloppy kiss. "I'm going to the little girls' room. Wait for me here?" Without acknowledging Daphne and KC, she wobbled away on her stiletto heels, leaving the two of them standing there with Clay.

Daphne hesitated for a moment. *Don't give up so easily. You can do this.* She took a deep breath and focused her eyes on Clay. "I see we have a little problem," she said with just the hint of a smile on her lips.

Clay kept the eye contact but didn't speak, and Daphne held her breath. After a pause that was just long enough to be noticeable, his lips slowly curled upward. "Not one we can't take care of."

Daphne felt the squeeze of KC's hand on her torso in a subtle gesture of celebration. Then KC yawned and slowly took a step backward. "My pals, it's been fun, but I think I'm going to get a head start on that walk home. Give Doug a hug good-bye for me, will you, Clay? I assume you'll make sure my girl Daphne gets home safely?"

"You know I will," he said. "Sleep tight."

She gave him the thumbs-up sign, then turned and trotted toward the back exit.

*Best wingman ever,* Daphne thought as she watched her disappear down the steps.

"So . . ." Clay said after KC was gone.

"So . . ." Daphne said with a bat of her eyelashes.

They stood there smiling at each other for a moment, then Daphne nodded her head toward the restroom. "About your friend there . . ."

"She'll be fine." Taking a step forward, he slipped a hand around the small of Daphne's back, and her insides did a little flip-flop. "Besides, you and I have some unfinished business to attend to," he added.

Daphne looked up at him, a suggestive expression on her face. "Is that so?"

He nodded. "It is so. Especially after you ditched me like that."

"You mean last night?"

"Last night and yesterday morning too. Three times in a row would be a little tough on the old ego, even though I'm not that old."

She furrowed her brow. "How did I ditch you yesterday morning?"

He smiled and scratched the back of his head. "You're joking, right?"

"Are you messing with me?"

"Not messing with you."

"Are you drunk?" she asked.

"Have I been drinking? Yes. Am I drunk? No."

"Daphne!" Doug emerged from the crowd and enveloped Daphne in a bear hug. "Is KC here?"

Daphne pointed toward the water. "You just missed her. She said to give you a hug good-bye."

"Coolest girl ever," Doug said wistfully.

Clay elbowed him. "It was never gonna happen, dude. Where's your dance partner?"

"She's getting us some more drinks. I need to drain the weasel." He gestured toward the men's room.

Daphne laughed. "Nice euphemism."

As Doug sauntered away, Clay took Daphne's hand. "Let's get out of here." He quickly pulled her through the crowd toward the back exit, then down the steps to the beach. He didn't let go of her hand until they were nearly at the shore.

Daphne glanced back at the Castaway. "What about that girl?"

"What about her?"

"Shouldn't you at least say good-bye? You can't just ditch her."

He smiled. "Why, because ditching isn't nice?"

"I told you, I didn't ditch you. At least in the morning, I mean." What was he talking about? She'd told him about their trip to the emergency room.

He raised an eyebrow, crossed his arms, and took a few steps back from her. "I beg to differ. If I recall, when I woke up in your bed, you were standing *like this* as far away from me as possible, without actually leaving the room, which made it pretty clear you weren't about to get back into bed until I vacated the premises."

She felt her cheeks blush. That was partially true.

"But . . ."

He kept smiling. "But what?"

"I did that because . . . because I thought you had coyote arm," she said softly.

He laughed. "Did you just say *coyote arm*?"

She swallowed. "You know, when a guy wakes up after a night out and realizes a girl is sleeping on top of his arm? He feels like a trapped coyote and would rather chew off his own limb than—"

He held up his hand. "I'm familiar with the term. But how do *you* know it?"

She shrugged. "I was in college once. I heard stuff."

He took a step closer and put a hand on her shoulder. "Daphne, I did *not* have coyote arm. I had an incredible time with you, for real."

She stared at the sand without replying.

He chuckled. "And I thought you did too, until you started acting like I have the plague. You should have seen the look of terror in your eyes when you came out of the bathroom."

She gave him a sheepish look. "That bad?"

"Worse, like you'd never been afraid of anything more than the idea of being anywhere near me again. You should have heard the heckling I got from the guys on the catamaran. It was pretty clear where I'd just spent the night, but it was also pretty clear you were no longer interested."

She looked down again. "I'm sorry. I didn't mean to do that. When I saw you in my bed, I was . . . pensive."

"I assume that's a fancy word for . . ."

"I'm sorry. I mean I was kind of thinking."

"About what?"

"To be honest, I was thinking how you weren't my ex-husband."

He laughed. "I'm not sure how to take that."

"I mean I was thinking that I was *glad* it was you there and not him. I mean that it was good for me to have gotten over that hump, so to speak."

"Hmm. Interesting word choice."

She smiled. "You know what I mean. Plus, I guess I was . . . nervous."

He reached for her chin and lifted her head. "I make you nervous?"

She nodded. "A little. I know I'm older than you, but I'm kind of a late bloomer in a lot of ways."

He stroked her cheek with his thumb. "You're sexy when you're nervous. Has anyone ever told you that?"

She gave him a tiny smile. "I'm learning a lot about myself on this trip."

"Oh yeah? Like what?"

She sighed. "You'll think I'm silly."

He cocked his head toward the Castaway. "The scene in *there* is silly. Having a conversation with you on this beautiful beach? Not silly."

She took a deep breath before speaking. "Before I came here, I thought I'd screwed up my chance to be happy in life, but now I'm learning that you don't get just one chance, that in a way life is *always* just beginning, that no matter how old we are it's still in *front* of us, every day until the end, so it's important to look forward and not backward all the time."

"That sounds like a lesson everyone could learn."

"I'm also realizing that regardless of where I am, or how I got here, if I don't do what I can to enjoy my life *now*, one day I may wake up and wonder where it all went."

Clay didn't respond right away, and she looked up at the sky, which was quickly becoming covered in dark clouds. *It's so magical here. I'm so glad I came.*

A cracking sound broke the silence. Then the rain came pouring down. Hard.

Clay laughed and glanced around. "How's that for dramatic timing? Think a director's going to appear out of nowhere and yell *cut*?"

Daphne smiled. "I wouldn't be surprised. I love the rain here. It makes everything feel brand-new. Sometimes we all need a fresh start, right?"

"Indeed." He glanced up into the downpour, then back at her. "So . . . speaking of fresh starts, I feel like I got off on the wrong foot with Fred. Would you mind if I came over and tried again? I'd hate to leave St. Mirika knowing I didn't do everything in my power to make a good impression."

She wiped a few raindrops from her eyes, then smiled up at him. "I think . . . I think that could be arranged."

He slipped his hands around her lower back and pulled her close. "Good."

# Chapter Thirteen

Daphne strolled into the kitchen the next morning, her step a bit lighter from her encounter with Clay. Again she'd been the one to wake up first, but this time around she didn't fret about how to act once they were both awake or about how the elusive hookup guide said she should behave. She'd simply leaned over and kissed him on the cheek, then snuggled up next to him and promptly fallen back asleep for another hour until they'd both woken up for good. Now he was probably on his way to the airport, and tomorrow she would be on her way back to Ohio. Back to a future that didn't look so bleak anymore. One that looked quite sunny, in fact. She closed her eyes and smiled to herself. *Thank you, Clay Handsome. Thank you, St. Mirika.*

She didn't see KC or Skylar and wondered if they were still asleep. She knew she'd agreed to another beach workout before they left the island, but she secretly hoped KC was already out on a long run so that she'd be off the hook this morning. Her body had finally stopped hurting from the first boot camp, and she wasn't looking forward to the soreness returning anytime soon. Then again, she *was* looking forward to getting in better shape.

She set an empty mug under the coffeemaker, pressed the button, and watched the black liquid drip into the cup. Soon she'd be standing in her own kitchen, back to sipping coffee from her favorite pink mug. Chipped or not, she was never letting that precious cup go. She smiled at the thought of seeing her daughter.

"Morning, sweets." Skylar walked down the hall wearing her silk bathrobe, her hair wrapped in a towel. "Are you the only one up?"

Daphne turned around. "I'm not sure. Maybe KC's already out on a run?" She looked at the French doors, which were ajar.

Skylar tilted her head toward Daphne's bedroom, then lowered her voice. "I wasn't talking about KC."

Daphne blushed as she doctored her coffee with cream and sugar. "Oh."

Skylar reached for a mug. "Is he still here?"

Daphne gave her a teasing smile. "What makes you think he was here at all?"

Skylar laughed as she set her mug under the coffeemaker. "That would be the writing on your face, babe. It says *I hooked up with a hot guy last night.*"

Daphne giggled too. "He left a little while ago. Had to go home and pack."

"Look at you, all grown up with your first vacation fling under your belt. Welcome to the fun side of being single, my friend."

"Good morning." Skylar and Daphne turned around as KC appeared from the hall, dressed in workout gear, but lacking her typical morning cheer.

Skylar narrowed her eyes. "Who are you, and what have you done with KC?"

KC frowned. "I spoke to Max before I went to bed last night . . ."

They stared at her, waiting for her to continue.

She closed her eyes for a moment, then opened them, a pained look on her face. "Josh's girlfriend is pregnant."

"Oh sugar." Skylar covered her mouth with her hand.

KC sighed, her shoulders slumping. "I can't believe it."

Daphne walked over to her. "That's not a terrible thing, right? Didn't you say they're already living together?"

KC shook her head. "That's Jared. Josh is still in college."

Daphne caught her breath. "Oh."

"He's only nineteen. Oh man, what a mess." KC pressed her hands against her cheeks and walked over to the couch.

"Is she going to keep it?" Skylar asked.

KC nodded and plopped onto the couch. "Looks like I'm going to be a forty-year-old grandmother."

"You'll be the hottest grandma in town, that's for sure," Skylar said.

"Are they going to drop out of school?" Daphne asked.

KC sighed. "Max said they're not, but to make that possible, I think there's a good chance they'll end up moving in with us."

"That's crazy," Daphne whispered.

KC nodded. "Now *that*, my articulate friend, is a major understatement."

"So you may be raising a real baby soon?" Daphne said, remembering how at the airport KC had referred to her cats as babies. *Was that really just a few days ago?*

KC sat there for a moment, then pressed her hands against her thighs and stood up, now wearing a weary smile. "I think that's a definite possibility. Either of you want to join me in a beach run to kick off our last full day here? There's nothing I can do about this disaster right now, so I might as well try to enjoy the time we have left in paradise."

Skylar pointed to the towel on her head. "Sorry, I just showered. I will watch you from the deck, however. Now that you're nearly a *grandmother*, I want to make sure you don't overexert yourself and get injured."

"Don't think you're not coming to the baby shower." KC stuck out her tongue at Skylar, then looked at Daphne. "What about you?"

"You really feel like exercising?" Daphne said. "If I got news like that, I think I'd head straight to bed with a bag of Oreos."

"Now you're talking," Skylar said. "That's a workout I can get on board with."

"God knows I could use a good sweat right now," KC said. "I was also thinking that since it's our last day . . . maybe we could finally check out those cliffs we keep hearing about? Seems more fitting than ever right now, don't you think?"

Daphne paused for a moment, then picked up her coffee and smiled. "I do. Count me in for both the workout and the cliffs."

• • •

"Oh my gosh, they're gorgeous." Skylar gazed up at the cliffs as she shut the car door.

Daphne's eyes followed to the soaring rock structures, which were covered in bright green moss and even higher than she'd feared. A wide staircase snaked up the biggest one, which was then linked to an adjacent and equally tall yet narrower rock by a small suspension bridge.

"Are we supposed to *climb* that?" she asked, her voice a bit unsteady.

"Looks like it," Skylar said

Daphne cleared her throat. "I was under the impression that we'd be looking over cliffs, not climbing to the top of them."

KC pointed to the bridge. "Now *that* looks fun."

Daphne was of a different opinion. As if climbing to the top of the main rock wasn't going to be terrifying enough, to her the thought of also crossing a shaky wooden bridge was quite the opposite of *fun*.

"This doesn't scare you two *at all?*" she asked her friends.

"I'm more scared by the idea of a bad haircut than climbing some rock," Skylar said with a shrug.

KC pointed to the parking lot, then to Skylar. "I'm more scared by the thought of getting back inside *that* car with *her* behind the wheel."

"You're more than welcome to walk home, Grandma," Skylar said.

Daphne swallowed and felt a few beads of sweat forming on her brow. She reached into her tote bag for a pack of tissues, then pressed one against her forehead. *You can do this. Just don't look down.*

KC pointed to a small thatched hut at the edge of the dusty parking lot. "I think that's where we buy the tickets."

The three of them walked over to the booth and got in line behind a white-haired couple who made Daphne think of Harry and Eleanor. She wondered what they were doing right now, and how Harry was feeling. Skylar and KC kept chatting, but Daphne's mind began to wander, so she didn't partake in their conversation. As she stood a couple feet behind her friends, lost in her own thoughts, two men got in line.

"Damn that's steep," Daphne heard one of them say. KC and Skylar were still engrossed in conversation, so Daphne inadvertently began to eavesdrop on the men.

"I jumped off a rock formation like that once, in Greece, right after college," the other man said. "Seems like a lifetime ago."

"College *was* a lifetime ago," the first man said. "We're getting up there, man."

Daphne casually turned around and gave them each a discreet once-over. Both men were tall and appeared to be in their midforties, or perhaps a bit older. One was wearing a dark red base-ball hat that said "Texas A&M" on the front. He was also sporting a platinum band on the ring finger of his left hand. The second man wasn't wearing a hat or a wedding band. Both men were reasonably handsome, yet there was an aura around the one with the bare ring finger that suggested he was feeling a bit uncomfortable in his own skin. Maybe he was afraid of heights too? The thought, however projected, helped soothe her jittery nerves. *At least I'm not the only one less than thrilled right now.*

"Scary how fast the years go by, isn't it?" she said to them with a smile—and an easiness that surprised her. "I've decided to embrace the life-begins-at-forty mentality." *I don't care if you know how old I am. Age doesn't mean squat.*

The man in the baseball hat nudged his friend. "He's recently divorced. If that isn't beginning a new life, I don't know what is."

Daphne looked at the man's friend. "I'm sorry to hear that. How long has it been?"

"It was official the first of the month. This trip is sort of our celebration, sad as that sounds," he said.

His friend patted him on the back. "You're better off without her. You know that."

Daphne held up her bare left hand. "Welcome to the club."

The divorced man gave her a weary smile. "Thanks, if that's even the right word. It's definitely not a club I ever thought I'd join, that's for sure."

She smiled. "Trust me, neither did I. Do you have kids?"

He nodded. "Two teenage boys."

"How are they taking it?"

"I think they're okay with the divorce, but they're not big fans of having to go back and forth between two houses all the time. It makes me feel kind of guilty for causing such upheaval in their lives when they didn't do anything to deserve it."

Daphne adjusted the strap of her tote bag over her shoulder. "You know what? You can't beat yourself up about it. I have a teenage daughter, and for a long time I felt guilty, like I'd failed for not being the picture-perfect mother." She pointed her thumb behind her. "My wise girlfriends here have helped me begin to let go of that destructive mentality—finally—and realize that being divorced and being a good parent aren't necessarily mutually exclusive. Emma knows her dad and I both love her, and that's what really matters."

"See? Kids are resilient," his friend said, then looked at Daphne. "They'll come around, right?"

"Your boys will get used to it," she said to the divorced man with a nod. "And eventually, you will too."

"You willing to put money on that?" He laughed a bit awkwardly. He was clearly doing his best to put on a good face, but the tired look in his eyes showed how much was going on beneath the surface. Daphne knew that look all too well. She'd seen it countless times in the mirror.

Surprising herself yet again, she put a hand on his arm and gave it a gentle squeeze. "It gets better. I promise." Then she lowered her voice and leaned toward both men. "There were days when I didn't want to get out of bed, and that is a sad thing when you're the only one in it."

The divorced man laughed. "I wish I had your attitude," he said. "You're so confident. And insightful too."

Daphne laughed too. "Confident and insightful? Those are two adjectives I don't often hear to describe myself, but thank you for the compliment."

Just then KC turned around and put her hands on her hips. "I feel like I'm missing a good conversation here. Am I missing a good conversation here?" Skylar was now at the ticket window.

"Depends on whom you ask," Daphne said. "I think it's pretty interesting, but my new friends here might beg to differ."

The guy in the hat gave the thumbs-up sign. "We were just talking about being in bed, which in my opinion is always a topic worthy of discussion."

"I concur with your opinion," Daphne said with a firm nod.

"So you're one of the wise friends?" the divorced man asked KC.

"I'm KC." She grinned and held out her hand. "I'm not sure how *wise* I am, but I just found out that I'm going to be a grandmother in a few months. Does that count for anything?" She pointed to the guy in the baseball cap. "I dig your hat, by the way. Go, Aggies!"

He chuckled. "I'm Phil. And I find it hard to believe you're going to be a grandmother."

"*Step*grandmother," Daphne said. "She wasn't having babies in high school or anything."

"True, true," KC said, then turned to the divorced man. "And you are . . . ?"

"I'm Derek," he said.

"He's recently divorced too," Daphne said to KC. "I was telling him that there's light at the end of the tunnel."

KC nodded and slipped her arm around Daphne's waist. "There definitely is. My pal Daphne here is living proof of that."

"Your name's Daphne?" Derek said to her. "That's unusual. And very pretty."

She smiled brightly. "Thank you." *I think so too.*

"Suits her, doesn't it?" KC said to the men. "Makes me think of a bright bouquet of daffodils."

"You ladies ready to rock these rocks?" Skylar said from behind them.

Daphne looked up at Derek and Phil. "You two want to climb with us?"

"We'd love to," Derek said.

She introduced them to Skylar, then pointed toward the bottom of the stone staircase. "Meet us at the entrance?"

Phil gave the thumbs-up sign again. "Sounds good."

The three women turned and walked away, and as soon as they were out of earshot, KC pinched Daphne's waist. "Did you hear what just happened back there?"

"What do you mean?"

"That entire conversation! You were totally your old self again. Charming, witty, not insecure in the least. It was great!"

"I was?"

KC laughed. "You didn't notice?"

"I guess not."

"Well it was fun to watch, that's for sure. It's good to have you back."

Daphne gave her a warm smile that said, *Thanks for bringing me back.*

"That Derek guy's kind of sexy." Skylar glanced back toward the ticket booth. "What's his deal? I didn't see a wedding ring."

"Recently divorced," Daphne said. "They're here on a guys' trip to, shall we say, *commemorate* it, if you will."

"Talk about a euphemism," KC said, then quickly looked at Daphne. "Did I use *euphemism* right?"

Daphne nodded and patted the top of KC's baseball hat. "Well done."

"Hmm . . . recently divorced." Skylar raised an eyebrow at Daphne. "Maybe you could soothe those wounds a little bit this evening? What man doesn't enjoy the company of an empathetic woman?"

Daphne rolled her eyes. "Yeah, right."

Skylar shrugged. "I'm just saying, there's nothing wrong with a little TLC. And as we've already witnessed this week, it's not like you're averse to a little roll in the hay with an attractive stranger. Why stop at one when you could double your pleasure, double your fun?" She elbowed Daphne.

"Stop it." Daphne laughed and elbowed Skylar back as they reached the base of the stone steps.

"Speaking of attractive strangers, two are rapidly approaching at six o'clock, so you might want to shut your traps," KC whispered.

Daphne craned her neck back at the towering rock formation. "Wow, that is *steep*."

"Wow, that is *steep*," Phil said from behind them.

KC turned around. "Is there a parrot out here?"

Daphne made a sheepish face. "Is anyone else having second thoughts about this?"

"Too late to back out now," Skylar said as she handed their tickets to the uniformed man standing by the roped-off entrance. "Everyone ready?" There were a handful of people on the observation deck at the very top, but the zigzagging path to reach it was clear.

Daphne walked over to Derek and put her hand on his arm again. "This can't be any harder than what we've already been through, right?" She was speaking to comfort herself now, not him.

He looked at her for a moment, then smiled just slightly. "That sounds like something only club members can understand."

She smiled back. "*Exactly*."

The five of them began ascending the steps, which were framed by a rope attached to the rocky walkway with spikes set at intervals all the way to the top. The path snaked left and right, and as they climbed, Daphne kept her eyes focused on the step directly in front of her, too afraid to look anywhere else. Her breathing and heart rate began to increase, and she willed herself to remain calm. *Keep moving. You're going to be fine. You can do this.*

"Damn, this is high!" Skylar called from the front of the group. "Whose idea was this, anyway?"

"Do you think anyone has ever fallen into the ocean from here?" Phil called from the very back.

"Don't be an asshole, Phil," Derek said with a laugh. He was a few steps ahead of Phil. The easy banter between them reminded Daphne of the chatter she'd heard during the flag football game on the beach.

"Humor is a good tool for diffusing tension," Phil yelled. "I learned that at some boondoggle sales training in Vegas."

"I wish I were in Vegas right now," Skylar yelled back. "I should have an enormous guitar-shaped margarita in my hand instead of a rope that looks older than dirt and may snap at any moment, after which I will plummet to my death and probably drag all of you down with me."

Now Daphne laughed too. Apparently Phil had a point. *This isn't nearly as bad as I'd feared.*

They were about two-thirds of the way to the top when KC, who was directly in front of Daphne and had been uncharacteristically quiet the entire climb, stopped moving.

"Did you drop something?" Daphne said.

KC didn't respond.

Daphne gently reached for KC's lower back. "Hey, are you okay?"

"I can't do it," KC whispered.

Daphne climbed up next to her and saw that KC's face was ashen. She was shaking.

"KC, honey, what's wrong?" Daphne asked.

KC shook her head. "I can't . . . move."

Daphne was puzzled. "Are you scared?" KC was never scared.

Slowly the shake turned into a nod, and KC shut her eyes tight. "I've never been up this high. I think I'm going to pass out."

"Is everything okay up there?" Derek was now just two steps behind them.

Daphne nodded. "Yes, we're fine." She put her hand on KC's head and smoothed her hair, then lowered her voice. "You're a strong woman, and you're going to do this, okay? We're going to do this together."

KC's speech was stuttered, her breath short. "I've . . . never . . . felt . . . anything . . . like . . . this." She briefly opened her eyes, then squeezed them shut again.

Daphne kept the tone of her voice soft. "I'm not going anywhere, okay? You're fine. We're almost to the top. You just need to take a deep breath, hold on to the railing, and move one foot, then the other. Can you do that for me?"

KC shook her head. "I can't move."

Daphne put a hand on KC's shoulder. "KC, listen to me. You can do this. You *know* you can do this. Just open your eyes for me, okay?"

Slowly, very slowly, KC opened her eyes. She looked terrified.

Daphne squeezed KC's shoulder. "Good, good. Now keep your gaze on the step directly in front of you. You don't need to look anywhere else. Can you do that?"

KC nodded and stared at the step in front of her.

Daphne spoke calmly. "Good, good. Now just move one foot to the next step. Just like this, okay? There's plenty of room for both of us on this step, so just do as I do."

Daphne took a step up, and KC slowly followed.

"That's perfect. Now do the same with the other foot, can you do that?"

"I'm so embarrassed," KC whispered.

"Don't be. You're doing great. Just keep moving like this, okay?" Daphne took another step up the cliff, then waited for KC to do the same. Derek and Phil followed behind in a respectful silence. Everyone knew this was no time for heckling. After several minutes Daphne glanced up to the top of the rock formation and saw Skylar peering down at them from the observation deck.

Her voice still gentle and relaxed, Daphne coaxed KC to the top. "That's it, that's it . . . See KC? You're doing great . . . We're almost there . . . Just keep your eyes in front of you . . . That's it, keep going . . . just a few more steps. See? You did it!"

Daphne took a final step to the fenced-in platform at the top of the steps, then reached for KC's hand and pulled her up alongside her. KC immediately wrapped her in a hug and squeezed her tight.

"Thank you, Daphne," she said. "Thank you so much."

Daphne stroked her friend's ponytail. "Oh honey, you don't have to thank me."

Skylar approached them as they finished their embrace, her hands on her hips. "You okay there, babe?"

KC nodded and pressed a palm against her forehead. "I am now. I had no idea I was so afraid of heights. I think that was the most scared I've been in my entire life."

"Looks like Superwoman found her kryptonite," Skylar said.

KC smiled weakly. "I guess I did."

"Look on the bright side: if you can do that, you can *definitely* be a grandmother," Skylar said. "Am I right?"

KC laughed, the tension visibly disappearing from her face. "I think you're probably right."

Skylar pointed to the suspension bridge leading to the second rock formation. "You ready for that, or you want to stop here? It's totally up to you."

KC looked at Daphne. "Will you help me get across?"

Daphne put an arm around her. "It would be my pleasure. How about we take a little break first?"

KC smiled. "Sounds good; thanks, Daphne."

Skylar, KC, and Phil wandered to the other side of the platform to take some photos before crossing the bridge. Daphne sat down on a bench and reached into her tote bag for a bottle of water. After a moment Derek walked over and sat down next to her.

"This is quite a view," he said, turning his head in a panoramic sweep.

She sipped her water. "Isn't it? I can't believe I'm up here right now, to be honest."

"Why not?"

She laughed. "Because I'm terrified of heights."

"Is that a joke I'm not getting?" He looked perplexed.

She smiled and shook her head. "Not joking. *Terrified.*"

"Well, you sure fooled me. You didn't look afraid of anything back there. You were really great with your friend. She was having a rough time of it."

Daphne took another sip of water. "I guess my motherly instinct kicked in. It has a tendency to do that."

"Then you're clearly a very good mother, despite your marital status. I heard from a wise woman once that being divorced and being a good parent aren't mutually exclusive."

She laughed, then looked him in the eye. "Thank you. I'm not sure what grade my daughter would give me, but I think I'm doing a decent job." *A fine job, actually.*

"I have a feeling she knows she's got it pretty good. We'll see if my boys figure that out about me at some point."

Daphne glanced in the direction of her friends, then back at Derek. "Skylar likes to say that despite their parents' best efforts to shape them, kids pretty much come with their bags packed. But she doesn't have kids of her own. Do you agree with that theory? Sometimes I wonder about the whole nature/nurture thing."

Derek pointed to the sky. "When my boys are *angels*, I like to believe it's due to nurture." Then he pointed downward. "But when they're *devils*, I cast the blame squarely on nature."

Daphne held up her water bottle. "Cheers to that strategy."

A soft wind began to blow, and she pushed a loose strand of hair behind her ears. "My ex is getting remarried soon," she said softly.

Derek hesitated a moment before responding. "Did he . . . leave you for her?"

Daphne shook her head. "Thankfully, no. Is that what happened to you?"

He nodded slowly. "I never even saw it coming, but the more I think about it, the more I realize that was part of the problem, if that makes any sense."

She leaned over and gave him a friendly nudge with her shoulder. "Believe me, I understand more than you can possibly imagine. I know I sound like a broken record, but things will get better for you. And for your boys too."

"You really think so?"

"I know so. Of course it hurts, but at some point you just have to let go of it. If I've learned anything about getting divorced, it's that it has defined me for too long because I've let it define me for too long. Feeling like a failure, feeling like I should have done things differently, feeling like it's my fault that life didn't turn out the way I thought it would—buying into the idea that being divorced is like having a disease. But I've finally begun to realize that none of that is true, and the only thing obsessing about it has done is keep me mired in the past—and miserable. So if I have any advice to offer to you or anyone else whose marriage has ended, for whatever reason, it's to learn from my mistake and have a shorter mourning period so that you can move on with your life."

"I think that's easier said than done."

She pushed another strand of hair out of her eyes. "Maybe, but it's worth thinking about. And being on this magical island will certainly help, it's nourishing for the soul. When did you get here?"

"Late last night. This is the first thing we've seen."

She smiled and looked up at the sky. "Give it a few days. And wait for the rain."

. . .

"I never thought I'd hear the following words come out of my mouth, but I need a stiff drink," KC said once they were safely back at the bottom of the cliff.

Skylar laughed and gestured to the dusty parking lot. "I can help with that. Ladies, shall we proceed to the car?"

"Another phrase I never expected to say to *you*, but yes, please drive me away now," KC said.

KC and Skylar bade good-bye to Derek and Phil, then made their way across the lot, arm in arm. Daphne hung back for a minute.

"Thanks again for your insight on the whole divorce thing," Derek said to Daphne as Phil went to retrieve their rental car. "You've really helped me see my situation from a different perspective."

Daphne adjusted her bag over her shoulder. "Oh gosh, it was my pleasure. Not that I've got it all figured out by any stretch of the imagination, but I'm definitely in a much better place than I used to be, so if my experience can help others in the least, I'm all for it."

"Well, as one of the *others*, I appreciate your wisdom. Maybe you should start an actual club for divorced parents, although it might be hard for me to make many meetings, given that I live in Chicago."

She laughed. "Now that's an idea. It might be the blind leading the blind, but at least we'd all be jumping off the cliff together, right? But maybe you're onto something. In college I had all these grandiose plans of being a journalist that never materialized, so maybe I could write a blog for divorcées? The first post would, of course, be about the magical healing properties of St. Mirika." *As well as the magical healing properties of a good old-fashioned fling.*

She was joking, but then a thought struck her. *Maybe I shouldn't be joking?*

He pointed to himself. "I'd subscribe to that blog in a heartbeat, so if you get something together, let me know."

"Will do." She glanced again at the parking lot. Skylar and KC were in the idling car.

It was time to say good-bye, and they both knew it.

Instead, Derek changed the subject.

"Where are you staying?" he asked. He stood just a hair closer to Daphne than was necessary. Something was different now.

"In a beach house on the other side of the island. What about you?"

"We're at the Four Seasons."

She felt her eyes brighten. "We went there yesterday for spa treatments! It's beautiful. Nothing like a massage to melt away the tension." She maintained eye contact as she spoke. *This man is attracted to me. And I'm going to enjoy it.*

Derek swallowed. "So, are there any other things you suggest Phil and I do while we're here?"

She patted her stomach. "Be sure to check out Bananarama on the beach if you like smoothies. Delicious."

"Bananarama. Like the band?"

She nodded. "I just adored them back in the day. Oh and speaking of music, you might want to check out the Castaway if you like to dance. The crowd skews a little young, but it's fun nonetheless, at least for a night." *Yes, I'm forty and I'm not afraid to go out dancing. Just not every night.*

She glanced again in the direction of the car, and Derek cleared his throat. "Do you have plans tonight? I'd love to buy you a drink, if you're up for it, that is," he said. He was clearly flustered, which she found endearing.

She smiled at him. "It makes perfect sense. And I'd love to, but we leave tomorrow, so I think we're going to make it a girls' night."

He reached for his wallet and pulled out a business card, then handed it to her. "Does life ever bring you to Chicago?"

She studied the card, then slipped it into her tote bag. "A week ago I would have said no to that question."

He chuckled. "Is that a yes then?"

She gave him a quick kiss on the cheek, then turned to go. "To be perfectly honest, I'm not sure what it is, but I'm looking forward to finding out."

# Chapter Fourteen

"Well aren't *you* the picture of rest and relaxation. You look absolutely revitalized!" Carol greeted Daphne with a smile at the curb outside baggage claim. She moved her enormous umbrella to one side and gave Daphne a quick hug before reaching for her suitcase. "Can you believe this downpour? It's been coming down in buckets nonstop for days!"

"It rained in St. Mirika too, but only in little bursts," Daphne said, already missing the feel of the warm drops on her skin.

Once they were safely buckled inside the SUV, Carol pulled away from the curb, then glanced at Daphne. "Looks like you got a little color on that fair complexion of yours, it suits you. So, how did it go? Was it everything you hoped it would be?"

Daphne sighed and leaned back into the leather seat. "I don't even know how to answer that question."

Carol laughed. "I hope that's a good thing."

Daphne smiled. "It is. I missed Emma, of course, but it was so nice to get away. I had no idea how much I needed that."

"Let me guess. Being with your old pals brought out another side of you?"

Daphne nodded. "I hadn't realized how much I'd changed until I was with people who reminded me of what I was like *before* I got married. I used to be afraid to even think about peeling those layers back, but now that I've started to do it, I'm finally beginning to feel like my old self again, and it feels good."

Carol reached over and gave Daphne's knee a squeeze. "Sounds like you watered those plants with some of that island rain."

Daphne stared ahead for a moment, her eyes picturing the first downpour she experienced on St. Mirika, before remembering what Carol had said just a few days earlier—although it seemed like much longer than that. "I guess I did. We promised to get together at least once a year, even if it's just for a weekend. We already decided that our next trip is going to be to Vegas."

"Good for you." Carol held the steering wheel with one hand and increased the speed of the windshield wipers. "Holy moly, it is *really* coming down today."

Daphne turned her head to the right and gazed out into the storm. Then she smiled. *I used to hate the rain.*

. . .

"Still up for Jeni's?" Carol asked as she pulled to a stop in front of Daphne's house. "I'd still love to treat you to a belated birthday scoop, despite this awful weather."

"It's not *so* bad. Emma's not due home for a few hours, so let me unpack and take care of a few things, and then I'll come over. Would that work?" She opened the door and stepped onto the wet sidewalk.

Carol shifted the gear into park and held up her palms. "I'm all yours."

"Great. See you soon." Daphne was just about to shut the passenger-side door when a thought occurred to her. She turned and poked her head back inside the car. "Hey, Carol? Where's a place to get a good smoothie around here?"

"A smoothie? I have no idea."

Daphne pursed her lips. "That's what I thought. Okay, see you in a bit." She shut the door and hurried up the manicured walkway into the house. The rain was coming down even harder now, and she was already feeling the chilly air creep underneath her coat. Once inside she turned on the lights and rolled her suitcase into the foyer. The house was quiet and still and clean, but it didn't feel so empty anymore. She glanced around and saw it the way Skylar and KC would. Tastefully decorated. Charming. Welcoming and warm.

Daphne hadn't thought of her house that way in a long time, but she was seeing it with different eyes now. It wasn't just a house. It was a home. It was *her* home. And Emma's. *My life isn't empty.*

She stood there for a few moments, the memories of her time on St. Mirika floating around in her head; then she turned and walked into the kitchen to get some water. She reached into the cabinet and pulled down a glass, the clatter of the rain against the windowsill nearly drowning out the sound of the faucet. She took a long sip, then set the glass on the counter and reached into the drying rack for her favorite pink mug. She held it for a moment, then kissed it and gently placed it back inside the cupboard. Then she turned and looked at the refrigerator, scanning Emma's activity schedule.

This weekend was a volleyball tournament. Brian and Alyssa would most likely be there.

Daphne braced herself, expecting to feel a pang somewhere deep inside at the thought of seeing them together. But it didn't happen. She felt no pang. No heartache. No regret. Instead, she felt calm . . . hopeful . . . free. She closed her eyes and sighed. *I'm free.*

She'd finally stopped focusing on the past. She was only just beginning to figure out the future, but that was okay with her. It was more than okay.

She finished the water and set the empty glass in the sink, then reached into her tote bag and pulled out the business card Clay had set on her dresser yesterday morning before dashing out the door to pack. She flipped it over and smiled at the note he'd scrawled on the back: *My door's always open for you, Daphne White. For Fred too.*

She skipped into her bedroom, gave the card a quick kiss, then carefully tucked it into the top drawer of her dresser. She gently closed the drawer, then left her bedroom and strolled into the kitchen. She knew she'd probably never see Clay again, but that didn't matter. It didn't matter at all.

When she reached the refrigerator, she pulled out another business card from her bag, this one from Derek Donovan, strategic consultant, in Chicago. She smiled at the name for a moment, then slid Emma's schedule a few inches to one side before securing the card with a magnet. She probably wouldn't see Derek again either, but then again, maybe she would. *Maybe I will.*

Her future was wide open, and it was all up to her. She smiled. It was time to get ice cream with Carol and celebrate.

She wouldn't be ordering vanilla.

# Acknowledgments

People often ask me if I have the plot figured out before I begin writing a novel. It's a great question, but one to which I don't have a stock answer. The truth is, sometimes I do, and sometimes I don't. Actually, that's not quite accurate. I've never had an *entire* plot figured out ahead of time, but for some of my books I wrote from a general outline without straying too far outside the lines, and with others I began with a vision of the first and last scenes, then figured out the rest as I went. When I started writing *Wait for the Rain*, however, I didn't have an outline. I didn't have a beginning. Or an end. I didn't have anything! All I had was the general idea of three friends reuniting to celebrate a milestone birthday. How that evolved into *Wait for the Rain*, I'm still not sure, but now that I think about it, maybe that's the whole point of the story.

For this book I had the pleasure of working with Danielle Marshall and Charlotte Herscher for the first time, and it was indeed a pleasure. I once read somewhere that editors are part business manager/part therapist, and as the KC character would say, "I'm not gonna lie"—it's pretty true. Ladies, thank you both for your insight, guidance, patience, and passion! I also would like to thank my longtime editor Christina Henry de Tessan, whom I simply adore. I hope you know how much you've helped me grow as a writer.

My high school pal Tami May McMillan gets yet another shout-out for her support and input throughout the entire gestation of this book, as does my mommy dearest, the master proofreader. I'm lucky you two haven't figured out that I should be paying you for all your help . . .

I'd also like to acknowledge a handful of friends who unwittingly contributed to this story just by being themselves. When readers tell me they enjoy how realistic my books are, I always say it's because I like to include funny or interesting things the people in my own life say and do. This time around I have the following to thank for the inspiration/material: Debbie Bolzan, Kat and Mike Burn, Kristi Candau, Amy Clarfeld Lavin, Chris Conroy (who also took the headshot on my bio page—thanks, Conroy!), Deb Custodio, Lynette Ecklund, Annie Flaig, Natalie Gonzalez, Siobhan Jones, Lea (Eaglette) Knop, Anna Krause, Jen Livingstone, Peggy (Turtle!) Prendergast, Lea Redmond, Jen Moscow Rittmaster, Carrie Jean Schmidt, Brett Sharkey, Michele Murnane Sharkey, Trudi Sharpsteen, Gene Sky, Jamie Strait, Steve Summer, Hilary Teper, and Ithti Toy Ulit. If any of you read this book and your contribution doesn't jump out at you, let me know, and I'll refresh your memory. I bet some of you don't even realize how witty you are, but I certainly do.

And to the team at Lake Union Publishing: In addition to Danielle Marshall, it's been a joy working with Terry Goodman, Thom Kephart, Jessica Poore, Susan Stockman, and Gabriella (Gabe) Van den Heuvel. Writing can be a lonely profession sometimes, so thanks for making me feel like part of the gang!